Snowmen

by
Al Browning

Five Points South Productions
Sterrett, Alabama
(205) 678-9486

Cover Photography By

Barry Fikes
Tuscaloosa, Alabama

Cover Design By

Vaughan Printing
Nashville, Tennessee

Copyright (c) 2000 by Al Browning

Published in Sterrett, Alabama by Five Points South Productions, 7460 Highway 51 South, Sterrett, Alabama 35147.

Library of Congress Cataloging-in-Production Data

Browning, Al
        Snowmen/by Al
Browning — 1st edition
                p. cm

        ISBN 1-881590-44-5 $25.00
        1. Crime — Novel

Manufactured in the United States of America

INTRODUCTION

Diana and Carl McGraw and Midge and Mark Cates were watching television inside a spacious house in an upper-middle class neighborhood in Louisville, Kentucky. Their five children, ages five through nine, were upstairs playing in a loft-like room full of toys and books, as they often did on Saturday nights when the business partners and their wives got together for a few drinks, a hearty dinner and more or less trivial conversation.

The laughter and chatter produced by the children were being drowned by the voice of a weather person coming from the television set the adults were watching with varying degrees of interest:

"It's the second week in January and the Deep South is bracing for heavy snow. Between six inches and a foot are expected in Texas, North Carolina, Kentucky and most states in between," said Karen McDowell while providing a weather forecast on the *Cable News Network*. "That's the result of a low pressure system moving in from the west. The heavier blankets are expected in Jackson, Birmingham, Chattanooga and Atlanta, cities that aren't equipped to handle such conditions.

"In Birmingham, for instance, residents remember how a snowstorm a few years ago left many houses and businesses without electric power for more than a week. As you can see by this video tape, the Magic City was more or less devastated after that bout with Mother Nature. Law enforcement representatives recall ..."

Carl was particularly interested in the weather related to an uncommon snow storm. A man with a passion for writing, he had been contemplating the development of a short story based on tempestuous conditions. The more he thought about it, the more his imagination started meshing with reality.

"Would anyone care for another slice of coconut pie?" Diana said as she walked from the den toward the kitchen.

"Not me," Mark said as he poked a few large logs in the fireplace. "A whole barbecued chicken and a pint of cole slaw should hold me until breakfast."

"I'll take a small piece — maybe with a scoop of ice cream on the side," Carl said.

"Why don't you try a couple of celery sticks stuffed with cheese?" Diana said.

"Are you trying to make a point?" Carl said, abruptly, providing his wife with a wrathful look.

"What she's saying is you better watch your weight," Mark said. "We've got summer approaching and those construction sites are going to get hot."

Carl was a trace on the pudgy side after a dramatic weight gain during the most recent five months. He smiled unconvincingly as he glanced toward the lean and slender Mark, his business partner at C&M Construction Company and his best friend since their introduction twelve years earlier as University of Kentucky juniors.

"Maybe you should get into some weight training," Carl said, attempting a counter punch. "You can't hold a two-by-four still enough for anybody to drive a nail in it."

"I can still handle your fat ass," Mark said. "In fact, if you doubt that let's step outside and ..."

Diana sauntered back into the den in time to stop the playful banter that was getting loud and sounding sincere. "I wish you kids would cool it before the real children in the house hear you talking like that," she said while carrying a cup of coffee for Midge and a glass of water for herself.

The women had been college chums, too, Delta-Delta-Delta Sorority sisters at Ole Miss who met their husbands on a spring break trip to Orange Beach, Alabama. They were almost inseparable, conversing by telephone at least once each morning and once each evening and, at every chance, competing as rivals on the tennis court at Triple Pines Country Club. Weight problems were of no concern to them because each had a shapely figure and an attractive face.

Also, the wives had something else in common, an appetite for soap operas. So when they started chatting about an entire week of *As The World Turns, The Guiding Light* and a couple more programs among the multitude, their husbands had to make a decision. They had to get out of the room or, as was the case on this frosty night, muffle the prattle about cheap love gone bad by turning up the volume on weather reports that were dominating the television screen:

"While it's apparent authorities in Birmingham and other cities in Alabama learned something from the snowstorm they experienced during March of 1996, there's no way that state can fully prepare for such an onslaught," McDowell said as she continued a lengthy report on *CNN*. "In the words of Colonel Ed Fullington of the Alabama State Troopers Office, 'When you've got education problems, you don't sink money into snowplows and storm relief centers.'

"So it's a wait and see proposition in the frigid Deep South as a wicked storm system develops in Central Texas. Meanwhile, in normally blustery New York City, the forecast calls for ..."

Carl put aside a celery stick stuffed with cheese, took a couple of robust swallows from a Budweiser can and reached into a shirt pocket. He turned toward Mark and said, "Get your coat and let's go outside and have a smoke."

"No, let's watch a movie," Mark said. "We've got *Casablanca* on Channel 23 and *The Graduate* on Channel 14 — with both coming on in five minutes."

"As much as I'd like to get another look at the youthful and dynamic Katherine Ross, I don't have much interest in hopeless love and a freaked out mother," Carl said.

"You're being pretty difficult tonight," Mark said.

"Maybe you'll like me better after we go outside and I tell you how we can make a lot of money and have fun doing it," Carl said as he pulled on his overcoat and started walking toward the kitchen that led to a spacious wooden deck.

"You just rang my bell," Mark said.

"Mine, too," Midge said with a smile as she and Diana watched the men disappear from their view.

While outside on the deck partially covered with frozen snow left over from the previous day, Carl smoked several cigarettes as he explained a fearless adventure that could be successful if Mother Nature cooperated.

"It's the big hit we've yearned for since college days, an exciting way to pocket some extra cash," Carl said after talking without interruption for several minutes.

"Thank you, but no thank you," Mark said. "Just put it down on paper and see if a magazine will buy it."

"Hey, we can make it work."

"Let's go mix some whiskey and water and talk about building shopping malls, basketball or something we know a lot about," Mark said.

After going back into the house, the husbands heard their wives giggling while scrutinizing a concocted lovemaking scene on a soap opera video tape. The men shook their heads in disbelief as they poured Wild Turkey over two glasses filled with ice. They returned to the deck.

After idle gab about college basketball and who might be Final Four bound, with a few bets made in the process, Carl returned the conversation to his plan.

"Don't bring that scatterbrained idea up at our next Rotary Club meeting," Mark said.

"I'm telling you, it can be a financial boon and it'll definitely be fun," Carl said, becoming more persistent.

"Wait a minute. You're starting to sound serious."

"I'm totally into it," Carl said. "I've been planning this for four years and, by golly, you heard what the weather lady said."

For a second time, Mark suggested the men go back inside the house, where the fire was raging and the warmth felt good. Obviously, he had voiced a strong objection to what Carl had suggested. But, in reality, he was less reluctant than his friend thought and wanted time to think about it. He excused himself and strolled to an upstairs bathroom.

When Mark reappeared after a suspiciously lengthy stay, Midge suggested they begin preparing for a drive home. More snow was predicted overnight and she feared some of the roads would become impassable.

"Let's have one more drink," Mark said. "To my surprise, I'm enjoying helping Carl with a short story."

Armed with fresh glasses of bourbon, the men looked over the deck at the surroundings. There were dense woods in the back, as well as a smartly manicured lawn leading to them. There were houses of equal distinction to their left and right, somewhere in the $300,000 price range.

"This is wonderful and a little boring," Mark said. "Basically, it's the same way along our street."

"Now you're talking like the Mark Cates I love," Carl said. "I knew it wouldn't take long for you to come around."

"It's still a huge gamble, one that could get us sent away for twenty or thirty years," Mark said.

"That's why we need some bankers as partners — and Ed Bass and Sam Mills are ideal."

"Wait a second, Carl. All we know about Ed and Sam are they like to play racquetball, like to bet on the golf course and like to watch nude reviews from time to time."

"Also, we know they're young bankers who know the business and are trying to climb up a crowded ladder at First Commercial," Carl said. "I don't think either man is against taking a shortcut."

"Well, they do cheat on the golf course," Mark said with a smile.

Suddenly, a conversation about foul play surfaced in the den as Midge jumped from a rocking chair and reached for the television set remote control. She punched a button, which caused the screen to become fuzzy, then switched the channel to a network program.

"That damn witch," Midge said, reacting to one of the harlots on the soap opera she and Diana had been watching.

"What's that all about?" Diana said after being startled by the sudden outburst.

Midge did not respond, at least not initially. Instead, she glanced at her friend and then looked away. She was biting her upper lip, without success, and Diana could see tears forming.

"I've got a wretch trying to ruin my marriage just like that redhead on *All My Children*," Midge said.

"Oh no, it's trouble in paradise," Diana said in a low tone. Then she wanted to kick herself because her best friend heard the remark.

There were several hushed seconds.

"Midge, I'm sorry if you've got a problem," Diana said. "I'll listen if you want to talk about it."

"Mark says we don't have a problem, that I'm letting my imagination run wild. But, Diana, a woman knows when her husband is interested in somebody else."

"If there isn't any evidence, there usually isn't a crime," Diana said.

"But there's a definite indication the bitch has the hots for my husband," Midge said.

Midge began telling Diana how she had observed Mark kissing another woman during a neighborhood party on the previous Labor Day. She said her husband told her he was as shocked as she was, that the woman simply walked past him in a hallway, threw her arms over his shoulders and pressed her lips against his.

"Too much alcohol can make people do strange things," Diana said.

"Sure," Midge said. "But this woman is an old friend of his from high school and she's living less than two blocks from us."

"Mmmm."

Silence prevailed again.

"What does Mark have to say about her?" Diana said.

"He said that party was the first time he had seen the wretch, that he didn't have any idea she was living in the neighborhood. He said they talked for about fifteen minutes about old times while sitting in a crowd beside the pool. He said he was walking through the house looking for me when she ambushed him."

"What does her husband do?"

"She doesn't have one," Midge said. "She's a divorced lawyer who moved to Louisville from Frankfort after her marriage turned rotten."

Diana did not respond.

"Don't you think this is a little strange?" Midge said.

"Let's just say it's interesting," Diana said. "But, Midge, thunder doesn't mean the world is about to crumble."

"Well, let me tell you about this redheaded bitch," Midge said, her voice rising with her emotion. "Then I bet you'll agree your husband would be interested in her, too."

"I don't have a problem and I'm not buying one," Diana said.

"She has green eyes that look like they were cut out of a cat." Midge said, ignoring the objection her friend had voiced. "She has shapely and firm legs that look like they stretch for a mile. I don't have a problem with flatness up top, not by a long shot, but this wretch has breasts that look like spotlights and she delights in turning them on."

"Damn, you sound like her talent agent instead of her adversary," Diana said.

"Also, when she dresses she's more interested in what she leaves uncovered than what she covers. Damn it, Diana, I'm in a war for my husband with a tramp."

"Calm down and listen," Diana said as she got out of her chair and stood looking down at her friend. "Let me remind you of all the handsome men at the country club and in shopping malls who have made innocent and not so innocent overtures toward you. You've got everything it takes to turn on a man and you've got everything it takes to hang on to your husband."

"Thank you," Midge said.

"So focus on you and Mark, not the tart redhead."

As Diana attempted to encourage Midge, Carl and Mark tended their drinks for several minutes without talking. One smoked a couple of Marlboro 100s back to back. Not a word was spoken until a dog barked to suspend the silence.

"You know, houses like ours would go for $750,000 or more in New

York City," Mark said.

"A lot more than that," Carl said.

"So why would two contractors on the rise want to risk the security we've got now?" Mark said.

"To get the bigger house on the hill — and to recapture some excitement getting married early cost us."

"What the hell, let's go for it," Mark said. "But don't call Ed Bass and Sam Mills until we've talked some more."

"That's fair enough."

"So what's our next step?"

"Let's meet at the office tomorrow afternoon and spend quality time on a foolproof plan," Carl said. "Then we'll get The Snowmen Project moving at a fast pace."

CHAPTER ONE

Carl McGraw and Mark Cates were moderately nervous as they parallel parked an immaculately kept 1998 Volvo DL station wagon in front of a seamstress shop at the corner of Twelfth Street and Vine Avenue in downtown Louisville, Kentucky. While they were confident they had a strategy that would perform, a blueprint to lead them through a definitely dauntless and potentially lucrative scheme, it was time to expose themselves to an outsider.

They knew the master design they had developed over the most recent week indicated only five other people would be directly involved in The Snowmen Project, or would be able to attach their faces to it, and they were about to meet one of them.

"You know, we started searching for something like this when we were in college," McGraw said as they stepped from the automobile and stopped to chat on the sidewalk.

"Let me guess," Cates said. "Now that we've found the ultimate thrill, you're not sure we have enough intestinal fortitude to complete it."

"Exactly."

"Well, it was your idea if you want to turn back."

"Bull shit."

McGraw adjusted his eyeglasses, plopped a quarter in the parking meter and started walking toward the entrance to the seamstress shop. He was displaying a restored gait. Cates was on his heels, tugging at a pair of sunglasses.

"Wait," Cates said.

"What?"

"I'm wondering about a meltdown," Cates said. "I don't want to spend a bunch of money and see Alabama and Mississippi looking like Florida in late March or early April."

"I don't either," McGraw said. "But either way we'll have the most fashionable Pathfinders in the history of transportation if these people can do what we want."

After going over what they planned to request a couple more times, McGraw and Cates walked through the front door at Passionately Pink and Pleasingly Purple. A jingling bell signaled their arrival. They were greeted by an attendant they surmised to be about forty years old, a pretty lady with dark hair shaped into a Meg Ryan style.

"Welcome to PPPP," the woman said with a pleasant smile. "I'm Paula Peterson, two more p words for you to consider."

"Good afternoon," Cates said.

"I assume you guys need a couple of elegant gowns for your wives to wear on the party circuit during The Derby," Peterson said.

"Not exactly," McGraw said. "We're deer hunters who want to purchase several dresses for a sports utility vehicle."

"Excuse me?"

"We're into the basic colors," Cates said.

"A lot of them," McGraw said.

"Hold on for a second while I catch my breath," Peterson said. "I'm starting to believe you guys are on the up and up."

"We'll need something that can be stripped off quickly," McGraw said. "It'll need to be durable. It'll need to fit snug on a Pathfinder."

"Like my husband's truck," Peterson said.

"That's progress," McGraw said.

"It's still unusual."

"Yes, ma'am," McGraw said. "But we think there's a market for something like this among outdoors enthusiasts who want to protect the bodies of their trucks while driving through the woods."

"Does your husband hunt deer or turkey?" Cates said before Peterson could respond.

"No. He's into golfing and reading, not much more."

"We like golf, too."

"Fine. Let me go to the back and get a notebook. Can I get you some coffee or a soft drink?"

McGraw and Cates declined the offer and sat nervously waiting for Peterson to return. They were men who had done nothing wrong, at least not yet, but they were acting as if they had been charged with a serious crime. They shuffled their feet when the lady walked back their way with a notebook and a couple of financial forms.

"I'm sorry about the delay," she said. "But I've got to do a routine financial inquiry."

"Fire away," Cates said.

After about five minutes, Cates and McGraw had exposed themselves to Peterson, as well as to the entire world, they surmised, and they were ready to place an order.

"Mrs. Peterson, before we talk specifically about what we're interested in, we'd like a confidentiality agreement with you," McGraw said.

"Fine — I think."

"We're businessmen who believe we're onto something big," Cates said. "We don't want a Kentucky Derby gown to show off at the Galt House. We don't want a debutante ball gown. What we want, ma'am, is attire for outdoor vehicles that could earn best of show honors and become a lucrative business venture."

After instructing her associates to deal with other customers who had more normal requests, Peterson listened patiently as McGraw and Cates told her what they wanted. She heard them describe a singular piece of garment that would cover a Pathfinder. She heard them compare it to something a car collector might utilize, only with a secure fit that would not unravel while the vehicle is mobile. She heard them talk about the desire for something that would be easy to slip on and off, even if it took clamps to hold it in place.

"You're talking about paint made from cloth — or some type fabric," Peterson said. "You want something that won't tear when snagged by thorns or put under the weight of tree limbs. You're talking about something that might become tattered in the woods but will protect the factory paint job underneath."

"That's why we're here," Cates said.

"Also, as we might have said, we want something that can be yanked off like a negligee in the heat of a moment — when the sudden urge is there," McGraw said.

"Deer hunters have a way with words," Peterson said, privately acknowledging a twitch somewhere within.

Cates and McGraw smiled.

"Can we give you a few more specifications?" Cates said.

"Please do," Peterson said.

They told her the fit should be tight. They told her the lights, bumpers, tires, windshields, windows, door handles, grill and other parts of the basic frame should be visible when the cover is in place. They told her they wanted a factory body that was not the real factory body.

"I'll need some advice," Peterson said.

"Maybe a body shop will help," Cates said.

"Excuse me, but the only body shop I'm familiar with is the strip joint on Muhammad Ali Boulevard," Peterson said.

She chuckled, finding humor in what she had said.

They were unamused.

"But Tokyo Toyota is a few blocks away," Peterson said.

"Maybe you should check with Moultrie Nissan on Cliff Road," McGraw said. "It's their vehicle. Ask them about a SE-V6 model."

The seamstress nodded as she made a notation.

Peterson started drawing sketches on a notes pad, none that resembled a Pathfinder SE-V6 model to Cates and McGraw. They saw a woman stabbing in the dark.

"It looks like it'll take three pieces that'll blend into one," she said.

"I'm sorry, but that looks like a strange automobile or a boiled egg to me," McGraw said.

"I'll overlook that criticism," Peterson said. "But this is going to cost you gentlemen a chunk of money."

"Shoot me in the heart," Cates said. "But remember, ma'am, we really want this to work."

"$30,000."

"Figure an estimate."

"I'll need ten grand down, ten grand in the middle of the project and ten grand upon delivery."

"Figure this job as a rush order. But we want it completed efficiently and cheaply. We'll shop around if we need to."

"How many dresses do you want?"

"Twelve, with an assortment of colors."

"You want twelve colors?"

"Hey, a person with your experience shouldn't have trouble with colors," McGraw said. "Just think how many shades you can get from red, blue and green."

"I'll say it's a deal contingent on what I find out at Moultrie Nissan. If the people there are encouraging, I'll feel that way."

Cates and McGraw nodded and smiled, pleased with what they had negotiated and heard.

"Mrs. Peterson, remember we'd like for this to remain quiet," Cates said. "We're in business, if you know what we mean."

Peterson nodded, excused herself and went to a back room. She lingered, maybe for eight minutes, and Cates and McGraw started getting anxious, again for no reason. She was carrying a portable telephone and a notes pad when she returned.

"I've changed the deal," Peterson said. "I'll need ten grand in a couple of days, provided I can guarantee delivery. I'll need the rest of the money half way through the project."

McGraw flinched a bit, then said, "What do we get if your dresses don't fit?"

"Crying girls," Peterson said with a smile.

"I can't accept that silly explanation," Cates said.

"I'll give you back half of your money," Peterson said. "Also, you can have the dresses that don't fit so you can get them altered by a seamstress somewhere else."

"In other words, you don't stand by your work."

"You'll like what you get," Peterson said. "If a metallic body suit can be made and the underwear fits right, I'll be able to deliver."

Confident they had cleared one hurdle, perhaps the most important in their scheme, Cates and McGraw left Passionately Pink and Pleasingly Purple and focused on more macho matters, one being the securing of a couple of partners with grit.

CHAPTER TWO

Ed Bass and Sam Mills were no match for Mark Cates and Carl McGraw on the racquetball court at the plush RacquetWorld Sports Center. Although they were five years younger, the bankers from First Commercial in Louisville were not as physically fit as the contractors from C&M Construction.

"Thank God it's almost golfing season," Bass said as the four men dressed in a locker room after taking refreshing showers.

"You'll be too broke to pay green fees if you keep messing with us," McGraw said with a grin. "Come on, guys, you can do better than 21-10, 21-8 and 21-4 in three racquetball games."

"By the way, Sam, you still owe me five bucks from the drubbing we put on you last week," Cates said as he pulled on a shoe and tugged on the laces.

"I thought I paid you."

"Don't give me that bunk, not again this week."

"Well, would believe I'm a little short in the wallet today?"

"Yeah, that I can believe."

The good-natured ribbing continued for several minutes until Mills reminded Cates and McGraw they had been invited to play racquetball with the idea they would be told how to make easy money after the match was completed.

Cates held an index finger to his lips, as if to tell his buddies to keep quiet until they found an appropriate place to discuss business. Then he and McGraw left the locker room while the bankers finished dressing and styling their hair.

"I guess we've been suckers all our lives," Bass said as he and Mills brushed their locks.

"We might be dumb, but I do enjoy being around Carl and Mark, even when they kick us in the butt," Mills said.

Actually, Bass and Mills were smarter than they let on. They had finished in the top ten percent at both Elmwood High School in Charlotte, North Carolina and UNC- Chapel Hill. They had excelled in football and baseball, too, and the athletics scholarships they had enabled them to save money while they got their educations. They were competitors who had fought hard for the same girl, the former Cindy McNamara, who Bass eventually married. Not to be outdone, Mills courted and married the college homecoming queen from their senior year, the former Mamie Simpson, who Bass adored.

That twisted case of romance seemed to add to their friendship, despite the fact their competitive ways had continued as they attempted to work their way up and through the rank and file at First Commercial. Both had achieved officer status, Bass in commercial loans and Mills in corporate marketing, which led to them meeting McGraw and Cates.

"I wonder what the roof builders have in mind," Bass said as he and Mills walked from the locker room to the health center bar and grille.

"I don't know," Mills said. "But those guys are making strides in the construction business, so it'll be in our best interest to listen."

McGraw and Cates were wrapping up a Miller Lite and a Budweiser when the bankers got to their table. They were motioning for a waitress in an effort to order another round.

"As I recall, you like kills shots," the young woman said to Bass.

"What a memory," Bass said. "We'll take two, with an extra slice of banana in mine."

"That'll buzz you after more than an hour of racquetball and fifteen minutes in the steam room," Cates said.

"They'll want a couple more after we're finished talking," McGraw said with a smile.

"Well, let's get a move on it," Mills said. "I told Mamie I'd be a little late, but I don't need to stumble into my house drunk at midnight."

The four men hustled down their drinks and adjourned to a small bar called Five Stars East in the downtown party district of Louisville.

Once there, they ate four large orders of chicken wings, drank two pitchers of beer and talked about a little of everything except how to make money.

After an hour of such small talk, it was apparent Bass and Mills were getting restless, if not downright testy.

"Okay, we've talked about starlets, deerslaying, old loves and golf," Mills said. "Let's talk about high finance."

"Let's hope it isn't with Amway," Bass said.

Cates and McGraw looked at each other with raised eyebrows. They both took deep breaths. One reached for a cigarette and lit it. They were nervous and it showed.

"You're bankers and we're contractors," Cates said. "But that doesn't mean you're not tough as nails and we don't know anything about stocks and bonds."

"Get on with it, Mark," McGraw said after noticing his partner was attempting to move into the proposal too slowly.

Cates accepted the command. For twenty minutes he talked without pause. He detailed what he and McGraw had in mind. He explained that two more partners would be needed, along with enough money to purchase numerous supplies. He pointed out the tight time frame and the need for all parties to be able to move in and out of town quickly.

"That's a deal for lunatics," Bass said.

Mills glanced toward the fellow banker and said, "So I'd say we're suitable candidates."

"I didn't say I'm not interested," Bass said. "I just want to think about it, take a few sober hours to decide if it's worth the risk." "I don't need to see a spread sheet," Mills said. "I know what happens when snow and ice turn the banking world upside down. I know this could be a bonanza if the right markets are tapped."

"Well, spring is just around the corner," Cates said. "There won't be a market when the sun starts getting hot."

"Let me call Cindy and tell her I'll be a while," Bass said.

By the time Bass returned to the table and announced he had bought half of an hour, Cates was preparing a checklist of items the group would need to make The Snowmen Project a success. He was writing on the back of a paper place mat. On the table beside it was an oversized red bandanna he used to wipe away spilled beer. The inventory register was long, as well as expensive.

The equipment needed included, among other items: three Pathfinders, deer hunting equipment, three blasting pads, several boxes of blasting caps, three detonators, camping gear, three walkie-talkies, three police band radios, a portable television set, a portable radio, three torches and an assortment of other tools, a dozen and a half duffle bags and six snow suits with gloves and masks.

"We might as well buy a department store," Mills said.

"It isn't that expensive," McGraw said. "If you'll think about it, we've already got most of that stuff."

"How much will it cost?" Bass said.

"I'd say twenty grand each, max, provided we split the cost of the Pathfinders," Cates said. "We'll probably get in under that."

"I don't like your math," Mills said. "Four guys could barely buy the trucks for that much."

"I'll explain that after we get a commitment from you," said Cates, who realized Mills had forgotten about two other partners being solicited for the scheme.

"Let's go for a walk," Mills said as he looked toward Bass.

The bankers returned in about fifteen minutes. They were smiling, which made McGraw and Cates feel good. Their moods escalated when they saw Bass check his pocket for change as he walked toward a pay telephone in the rear of the room.

When Bass returned to the table, Cates continued his spiel, pointing out the need for two more partners, men with courage and good sense.

"I've got the men for you," Bass said.

"If you've got a pair that can bring something to the table, fine, let's hear about them," McGraw said.

Bass looked toward Mills and smiled.

"Fred Long and Ben Bobo," Mills said, knowing his guess was good.

"You got it," Bass said. "They're two good friends who can be trusted, both insurance professionals, and one is well-connected."

"What does that mean?" Cates said.

"Let's just say Fred Long is connected to the right people in such a manner I don't care to know how connected," Bass said.

"That didn't answer the question," McGraw said.

"We call him the China Man because he knows how to wash dirty laundry," Mills said.

"I like that," Cates said. "But let's hear how you got hooked up with those guys."

Bass explained how he and Mills enjoyed betting on college football and that a couple of seasons previous they ran up an excessive tab with bookmakers. He said the heat was turned up, with all manner of threats included, and it was suggested Bobo might be able to help them alleviate the problem.

"He loaned you money at a high rate of interest," McGraw said.

"Exactly."

"The syndicate got cash going and coming," Cates said.

"You got it."

"How much did you guys lose betting that season?" McGraw said.

"More than thirty grand," Bass said.

"Damn."

"Yeah, and that's one reason we're sitting with you now," Mills said.

Mills explained how he and Bass were sometimes made aware of smart stock options through their dealings with other bank employees. He said they passed along such inside the trade information to Bobo, just to show their appreciation for him helping them when Southern Miss upset Notre Dame in football and Florida upset Kentucky in basketball.

"Bobo and Long made a smash hit on the stock market because you got info straight from Wall Street," McGraw said.

"You better believe they did," Mills said. "But we really have no way of knowing how much they made. All we know is they gave us a nice gratuity after the deed was done."

"It seems to me you guys should make that your primary business," Cates said.

"No," Mills said. "We get info like that three or four times a year. Not all of the tips pan out."

"I think I see your logic," McGraw said.

"Let me put it this way," Bass said. "We've been told Bobo and Long don't like business deals that turn sour, that they've got the resources to make bad tipsters pay a price."

A silence settled around the table, lingering for at least a minute.

"Even with that type risk involved, I really like Bobo and Long," Bass said after concluding he was getting a negative reaction.

"Set up a meeting," Cates said.

CHAPTER THREE

As the assistant golf pro at Sahara Dunes Public links made out a credit card receipt for Mark Cates and prepared to give him a golf cart key, the contractor appeared preoccupied. His mind and his eyes were on two men chatting outside, his business partner Carl McGraw and his associate in crime Ed Bass.

"Thank you, Mr. Cates, and I hope you have a nice round today," said the assistant golf pro.

There was no response.

"Mr. Cates, excuse me, but here is your receipt."

"Oh, I'm sorry," Cates said. "My partner is talking to an old friend of ours and ..."

Cates suspended the explanation for his inattentiveness, knowing it was not needed.

"Well, I hope they aren't rigging the match."

Cates accepted his receipt and the golf cart key and started walking toward the door.

"Hey, Mark, wait up," Sam Mills said as he emerged from the pro shop bathroom. "I want you to be the first to see my new driver, Booming Betty, the best blaster to ever hit the blue grass of The Commonwealth."

"Gee whiz," Cates said. "Get a grip."

"It already has a great one," Mills said as he placed his hands around the golf club.

It was a beautiful March afternoon, with the ides approaching, and the newest golf course in the Louisville area looked magnificent to its first-time visitors.

"We've got a few minutes to hit some practice balls on the range,"

Cates said. "Monster Mash Mills has a Booming Betsy driver he's dying to show off."

"Booming Betty," Mills said as they crawled into golf carts and hurried toward the practice tee.

When they got there, before a swing could be taken, McGraw summoned the group to his golf cart and gave the other three a progress report related to The Snowmen Project. He told them they had two Pathfinders, with another on order, four specially made, diversely colored covers for each, two willing insurance agents and a hot and humid afternoon in Kentucky that indicated spring had arrived.

"We're about $80,000 in debt and badly in need of a snow and ice storm," McGraw said.

"Thank goodness Bass and Mills are on the firing line for approving the truck loans," Cates said. "Now let's talk about how to deal with Fred Long and Ben Bobo."

"We're scheduled to meet them tonight at about seven," McGraw said. "The more I hear about them, the more they sound like ideal partners who'll add something to our plan."

"That can wait," Mills said as he stuck a golf tee into the ground, placed a ball on it and got ready to take a swing. He made a good pass.

"Boom, look at ol' Betty work, straight down the middle and farther than Fred Couples and Tiger Woods," Mills said, obviously pleased with his shot.

"Don't get carried away," Cates said.

Bass was more interested in the debt the group had accumulated. He wanted to know how the bank loans would be repaid if Mother Nature did not cooperate. Cates reminded him that he and McGraw had made a large down payment out of the C&M Construction equipment account.

"You guys need to relax," McGraw said after hearing all he desired about money woes. "I've been studying weather patterns on the internet. We've got a lot of bad stuff swirling around in the Pacific Ocean."

The golfers were summoned to the first tee.

"You know, Mother Nature can be fickle," Bass said after driving his first shot of the season down the middle of the fairway.

"She can be brutal, too, which would be good in this case," Mills said. He hit the golf ball a long way with Booming Betty, but it landed in trees to the right of the airway.

"I don't see why you're cursing the weather," Cates said. "You should let dear ol' Betsy have an earful."

"Screw you, Mark," Mills said. "And, damn it, for the last time her name is Booming Betty, not dear ol' Betsy."

As the golf carts moved along a path, playing partners McGraw and Cates conversed about the insurance agents who had joined the team. They agreed they sounded like perfect fits, especially Long, who had experience in the underworld. They looked forward to learning more about him and Bobo over dinner.

By the time the foursome reached the ninth hole, a blustery storm was approaching. The howling wind and lightning seen in the distance made it a unanimous decision to cut short the match.

"All bets are off," McGraw said as he made a quick glance at their opponents.

"To hell you say," Mills said. "The scorecard says you're down four dimes to me, Ed and Booming Betty. You're going to pay if I have to take her and beat the shit out of you."

"You already have," Bass said, adding salt to the wound.

Cates suggested the two teams play the tenth hole, with double or nothing hanging in the balance.

"I'll pass on that," Mills said. "But I'll bet you we're in for some icy weather by next weekend."

"That's wishful thinking," McGraw said.

"I don't think so," Mills said. "In fact, I won't be surprised if Miss Priss on Channel 12 tells us to start bundling up as early as tonight."

"I believe you crave that weather girl," McGraw said.

Mills did not reply, at least not for a few seconds. Then he said, "Forget the sexy one and let's go to Buster's Grill and let you guys buy the drinks for a change."

Miss Priss came through for the four business partners and golfing foes after they arrived at Buster's Grill, a nightspot that featured cold drinks, loud rock and roll music and busty women dressed in tight, somewhat transparent blouses. As they watched the television set intently, the weather forecaster said, "The weather outlook for the latter part of the week calls for snow and ice throughout Kentucky and a chance of rain mixed with snow in Tennessee and the upper portions of Alabama and Mississippi. That front has another one coming behind it, so it's far too early to say spring has sprung."

The men smiled.

"Bingo," Mills said. "If she's on the money, we might be about to go on a classic deer hunt in Alabama or Mississippi."

"South Georgia, not Alabama or Mississippi," Cates said, offering a quick reminder of something important included in their master plan.

"Ooops, my bad," Mills said.

"Leave your dumb ass mistakes in Kentucky," Cates said.

At seven o'clock on the button, after all hints of agitation between Mills and Cates had been washed away by beer and whiskey, Long and Bobo arrived. When Bass introduced the newcomers to the others, McGraw requested the six men be moved to an out-of-the-mainstream table so they could talk in a quieter environment.

After they were seated in a corner far removed from the jukebox, it became apparent to Long the two men he had just met were sizing him up. He was accustomed to such scrutiny, as his reputation as a smart business man who sometimes operated in shadows might indicate, but that did not make him less uncomfortable.

Feeling more uneasy as a round of drinks was served, Long made an effort to take an edge off of the situation. He said, "Gentlemen, please allow me to tell you a little about my friend Ben Bobo."

"Great," Bobo said. "Then I'll tell you about Fred Long."

Actually, there was not that much to divulge unless the two men were keeping hole cards hidden.

Long began his introduction:

"Ben is a good insurance agent with expertise in risk management. You would think he would be a good poker player, given his abilities when it comes to probability, but he's terrible, pure and simple. He grew up in Chicago, city tough, and married a wonderful lady, Frances, who is too damn nice for him. They have one child, Samantha, age nine, and two dogs, Bo and Mo. Ben does okay handling pressure, perhaps because he has survived in a tough world forty- four years, but he's a better planner than a doer. I'd advise you to get to know him better because he'll become an invaluable friend."

The smoothness Long exhibited impressed the others. Bass was moved to hoist a drink overhead. That led to a clanging toast over the middle of the table.

Bobo began his introduction:

"If you have not heard, Fred couldn't care less about the insurance business. He's into real estate, stocks and bonds, the gold and silver markets and a lot more. He thinks he's a bigtime player, when in reality he's a middle-level worker who knows people in high places. His wife, Barb, is nice enough, but she's quiet and she's hard to get to know. There aren't any children, by choice, and there aren't any pets. It's too late for kids now because he's forty-eight years old. There are a few things about Fred that anybody dealing with him should remember. He's honest, a good guy reared in Philadelphia, so be honest with him. Listen to him. Debate with him if you see a need. But don't screw over him because if that happens the people he's used to dealing with will screw over anybody who screws over him."

Cates and McGraw were shocked by those remarks, particularly the tail portion. Bass and Mills seemed less surprised. Regardless, a silence abounded for several seconds and nobody offered a toast.

Finally, Long said, "Ben, the reason you haven't been able to get to know my wife very well is because I don't want her associating with somebody like you."

When Long smiled, so did the other men.

"Let's order a round of fine champagne, toast the formation of a successful business partnership, make some plans and have some dinner," Cates said.

McGraw took the lead going over the plan he and Cates had designed and Bass and Mills had approved. He pointed out that Birmingham,

Huntsville, Meridian and Jackson were the cities targeted for their scheme.

Bobo asked if Nashville had ever been considered, pointing out the influx of money from pro football and ice hockey, as well as country music fans traveling in and out of the city for special events.

"We need hills and trees, a lot of both," McGraw said. "Besides, the folks in Nashville handle snow and ice pretty good."

"Does anybody at this table know anybody in any of those other cities?" Long said.

He looked at each man and saw only shoulder shrugs and shaking heads.

"All I know is what I've seen on television," Cates said. "It gets back to a lot of twists and turns in the landscape, particularly in Birmingham, which looks like a city built in the middle of woods. As for people who live there, I don't guess I know a soul."

"Then I guess you bankers need to hop a plane tomorrow or the next day and find out what we've got to work with down there," Long said. "Hills and trees are one thing. Banks located in clusters are the key."

McGraw did not seem to mind that he was no longer in charge of the proceedings.

"Can you guys make a quick trip like that?" Bobo said.

"We can if we've got a remote chance to develop a loan with a major government supplier that deals with NASA," Mills said.

"I like that attitude," Long said. "But more than anything I like the idea of bankers studying banks."

"We've been doing our homework," Mills said.

"So what do you know about security systems?" Long said. "I mean, hell, that's a long way to go to get caught in the parking lot."

"Most of them are similar," Bass said. "Most of the time it depends on the size of the building and the layout."

"That doesn't tell me a damn thing," Long said. "Maybe I need to call some folks and get a better description of what we'll be dealing with wherever in hell we're going."

"With all due respect, Fred, I don't think anybody else needs to know what we're attempting," McGraw said.

"I know that," Long said. "Your point is understood."

"Maybe you'd like to go with us on the scouting mission," Bass said.

"Hell no," Long said. "I've got bigger fish to fry."

"No matter who makes the trek to the south, it needs to be done quickly," Cates said. "Miss Priss said we might have a storm front in Mississippi as early as Friday afternoon. I've studied this enough to know the snow falls hard in Alabama and Mississippi when it originates in Texas. I've lived long enough to know there are few opportunities like this during spring."

"Damn, you guys are scientific," Long said.

"I don't know any other way to make money," Cates said.

"Well, I do," Long said. "I know darker, warmer and dryer ways."

"I'm not sure I want to know more about that," McGraw said.

"Yes you do," Bobo said. "Fred knows where, who and how when it comes to turning a few bucks into a pile."

"Did you hear what Ben just said? Mills said.

Nobody answered the question.

"Bucks — like deer running through snow in South Georgia."

"I think we better call it a night and get to work," Long said. "I don't have time to sit around and listen to a bunch of frivolous bull shit."

After the six men were in the parking lot at Buster's Grill, with the wind blowing harder and feeling colder, McGraw asked Long and Bobo if they were interested in knowing when they could pick up a Pathfinder.

"I don't need the truck," Long said. "I've got a M-Class Mercedes that works nicely, thank you."

"But you're paying for half of it, even if you don't drive it," Bobo said, his remark followed by a grin.

"Yeah, yeah, yeah," Long said.

"It'll be waiting for you at Moultrie Nissan at nine o'clock tomorrow morning."

As Long and Bobo started walking toward their cars, one took a couple of steps and turned around.

"Hey, guys," Long said. "Do you know where my M-Class Mercedes was put together?"

"Germany, I guess," Cates said.

"Damn, do you think every foreign car is built overseas?" Long said. "If you do believe that, how in hell do you think that damn Pathfinder I'm getting tomorrow got here so fast?"

"Come on, Fred, just tell them where the M-Class was built so we can go home," Bobo said. "It's getting late and the alcohol is kicking in."

"Right down I-59 from good ol' Birmingham," Long said. "The way money turns over in a hurry, that might be worth something to us down the line."

CHAPTER FOUR

After dealing with suspicious wives who wondered why their husbands had been summoned out of town on banking business on the spur of the moment, Sam Mills and Ed Bass caught a pre-dawn flight from Louisville, Kentucky to Huntsville, Alabama that made a brief stop in Atlanta, Georgia. Once there, they rented a dark blue Lincoln Town Car, made a quick pass through the Rocket City and hurried along Interstate 65 to Birmingham.

Now they were on U.S. Highway 280 moving toward Childersburg, thanks to a suggestion from a service station attendant who had been asked about fledgling corporate business developments in the Birmingham Metropolitan Area. They knew the rapidly growing Inverness Corners area across the Cahaba River in Shelby County would probably have numerous office buildings and large shopping centers. They concluded that would mean several banks would be in the area, too.

"I've heard of this place, Cahaba Heights," Mills said as the automobile moved past a water treatment plant about six miles from the south side of downtown Birmingham. "It backs up to Mountain Brook, one of the more affluent cities in the nation."

"I see what you mean," Bass said as he pointed at mansions on a nearby hill, estate houses barely in view because leaves were starting to cover hardwood trees. "If that's Cahaba Heights and not Mountain Brook, I'd like to see where the rich people live."

They traveled across the Cahaba River and Interstate 459, a connecting thoroughfare between Interstate 59 west of the city, Interstate 65 south of the city and Interstate 20 east of the city.

"Let's make a note about this highway," Mills said. "It might come in handy because the sign said Atlanta one way and Montgomery and

Tuscaloosa one way."

Mills and Bass were not disappointed as they approached the Inverness Corners area about a dozen miles from downtown Birmingham. After driving around the district, they were more excited. In the immediate vicinity of two large shopping centers they found Central, American, Patriot and North Star, bank branches within a stone throw of each other. Just down the street they found Sector, the biggest building among them, and First Columbus.

"American and North Star are the power brokers," Bass said. "But Sector isn't a slouch."

"If I'm not wrong, Patriot has been robbed several times," Mills said. "I'm thinking that branch has been hit at least twice."

"I can see why," Bass said. "That building and the one across the street, American, look like they're in a picnic area the way they're tucked in the woods."

"Hills and trees, that's our ticket," Mills said.

"Unless those folks have learned something about security," Bass said.

Across the street from those two branches, Mills and Bass noticed a massive shopping center. A Winn-Dixie supermarket was featured on the left, a Books-A- Million was featured in the middle and a Wal-Mart was featured on the right. It was the fourth they had encountered within two miles of each other, with each adjacent to several upper tier eating establishments.

It was just after one o'clock and the visitors from Louisville were delighted to see lunch traffic lighten. Mills steered the Lincoln Town Car further down Highway 280, still going east, taking it about four miles before the tract became too steep to consider.

"We wouldn't be able to get up and down this mountain in snow and ice," Bass said.

"With a Pathfinder, we probably could," Mills said. "But it's lean from a business and bank standpoint."

"Go back to Highway 119 and take a left," Bass said. "It looks a little secluded down that way."

The men found more than they had hoped for, a sign directing them to

Oak Mountain State Park. They followed the instructions and were awestruck when they found a paved road leading them up a treacherous hill into the woods.

"How far do you guess we are from those banks?" Mills said after paying a park ranger two dollars so two adults could pass through a security gate leading to the park.

"I've already written it down — less than ten minutes," Bass said as the driver steered the automobile around a lake that was being visited by numerous fishermen.

Rather than make a quick exit from the park, Mills and Bass found a quiet place to park the car. With their legs stiff after a morning of flying and driving, they decided to take a walk. Then they drove back to the security gate to see what they could learn from the park ranger.

Mills and Bass told him they were on their first visit to Birmingham, a short business trip, and they complimented the area. He asked where they were from.

"We're with Florida Power and Light, one of the Southern Company affiliates, like Alabama Power," Mills said. "We thought we had all the beauty in the world in our state."

"You should've seen this area five years ago," said the park ranger. "It's getting too crowded now."

Bass mentioned he had noticed a lot of construction in the area. He inquired about residential versus commercial.

"It's a mixture, really," said the park ranger, a man who appeared to be about sixty and seemed to be enjoying the attention. "You've got businesses all along Highway 280. You've got houses going up everywhere else. Hell, they're cutting a path right down the hill."

"I saw that, a nasty construction road built within a few hundred yards of this magnificent park," Mills said.

"There isn't any honor in the world," said the park ranger. "God gave us this beautiful land and the rich tycoons are trying to develop a residential area in it. They're taking heaven and turning it into hell, as far as I'm concerned."

"We're not going to let them take our beaches and destroy them,"

Mills said as he and Bass said farewell.

"You guys be careful," said the park ranger. "Also, you better get out of town on schedule. We've got some bad weather on the horizon, maybe even snow by the weekend."

On the way out of the park, part of the way down the hill, the bankers saw more than a construction road. They saw a place for mice to hide if cats started chasing them.

Mills and Bass spent another hour riding through the Inverness Corners area of Birmingham. They found something else they favored on Valleydale Road, just below Hickory Ridge, and they carefully surveyed the bank buildings and made meticulous notes.

"We'll have a fine report to offer," Bass said. "I don't see any reason to mess with Meridian and Jackson."

"But let's give Birmingham a little more of our time," Mills said. "It's almost perfect now. We might be able to improve on that."

After driving through the Wildwood area, another quickly developing tract, and the Eastwood area, one already bustling, they stopped at a Hampton Inn Hotel to use the telephone. They made airline reservations. Then they called their associates in crime to suggest a lengthy lunch meeting the next day.

At eight o'clock Mills and Bass were boarding a direct flight to Louisville at Huntsville International Airport adjacent to the Marshall Space Flight Center.

"At least we didn't lie when we told our wives we were about to brush sleeves with NASA," Bass said.

"Nor will we have to lie when we tell McGraw, Cates, Long and Bobo that we've found an almost ideal place to do business," Mills said.

On the flight home, the bankers sat in the rear of the airplane, basically alone, and talked about the prime targets they had found.

First Columbus:

The branch is constructed far short of state of the art. It is a small player. The building sits just off of Highway 280, with a road running beside it, and there are woods in the back.

Sector:

The branch is modernistic, with a lot of glass. That is for show. At its back is a teller window hidden from view. The building is about two blocks east of First Columbus. There are woods in the back.

North Star:

This could be a tough one. The building sits across the street from Sector and First Columbus, in the heart of a relatively small shopping center. The view from Highway 280 is full and clear.

Central:

This could be tougher than North Star. The view from Highway 280 is somewhat full and clear. Adjacent to the building is a relatively small shopping center anchored around a Food World. Across the street, Valleydale Road, is a larger shopping center anchored around another supermarket, Bruno's. If anything helps, the bank branch sits in a tiny valley protected by bushes and other buildings.

Patriot:

This bank branch is easy prey. It sits in the woods, sort of, and it features a lot of glass. A rock and roll concert could be staged there without motorists noticing.

American:

Ditto, the report on Patriot, only it is more secluded.

"The others will like to see this report, all the way down to hills and trees," Bass said.

"Do you think The Snowmen Project will work?" Mills said.

"It will if Pathfinders are all they're hyped to be," Bass said.

"You forgot the key player," Mills said.

"Okay."

"Mother Nature."

The lunch meeting at Triple Pines Country Club was lively and so lengthy Mills, Bass, Mark Cates, Carl McGraw, Fred Long and Ben Bobo were moved into the 19th Hole to continue their discussion. Part of their collective enthusiasm stemmed from the cold mist falling on the golf course, a mixture of gentle rain and feathery sleet, and the weather forecast all of them had seen that morning. The wintry storm was approaching swiftly, with Texas under attack, and it was supposed to arrive in Alabama by no later than sunset on Friday.

The group concurred they had a game if Birmingham got at least six inches of snow. It was heightened by reports that a foot might be on the ground, with ice mixed with it.

"We've read what happened down there a few year ago," McGraw said. "If history repeats, we've got a wonderland."

"But we've got to be on the move by no later than noon on Friday if we're going to enjoy it,"

Cates said. Cates looked at his partners and did not sense an objection.

"Thank God for Eastern Standard Time," McGraw said. "It's a long haul between Louisville and Birmingham."

"Yeah, and I've got to go down there in a damn orange Pathfinder," Long said. "If there's one color I hate, it's orange."

"But it won't be orange most of the time you're riding in it," Cates said with a smile.

The meeting was interrupted when the daytime bartender approached the table. Excuse me, Mr. Cates and Mr. McGraw, but your wives are at the door leading to the golf course."

Cates apologized for forgetting this was a day for tennis at the indoor facility at the club. He and McGraw hurried to the entrance and greeted Midge and Diana with kisses that were more obligatory than heartfelt. They asked the women about the tennis match, which Midge had won in straight sets, and then asked if their wives had a problem.

"Not really," Midge said. "We just noticed your cars parked in the lot and thought we'd come by and say hello."

"I'm glad you did," Cates said. "But we're trying to wrap up a business meeting in there and ..."

"Who's with you?" Diana said, looking a bit mischievous. "I thought I saw Ed Bass through a crack when they opened the door."

"He's in there, yeah, and so is Sam Mills and couple of other people you don't know," McGraw said.

Midge and Diana had a lot of time on their hands, which meant they sometimes liked to create headaches for their husbands, all in the name of fun. They were so conniving they once staged a telephone call from a bank asking the contractors to pay a loan in full because it had been learned the tract on which they were building a strip shopping center was in a sink hole area. Now they had something else on their minds.

"This might be an ideal time for two women to break down the barrier that separates the rest of the world from the 19th Hole," Diana said.

"I don't think so," Carl said. "Maybe you should play another set of tennis and go home."

"Abe Lincoln didn't have us in mind, but we've been emancipated, too," Midge said.

Mark looked at Carl and in a light tone said, "Damn, our wives are on a crusade."

"Well, let's just beat the hell out of them," Carl said with a smile.

After more gentle coaxing, the men said goodbye to the women and returned to the meeting.

"I'm sorry about that," McGraw said. "Our wives never have understood that rule that bans females from the 19th Hole."

"I've got a suggestion if it happens again," Long said.

Long told the group how he handled a similar situation at the Top Hat Club downtown, a swank establishment. He said his wife and a friend attempted to enter the sacred doors every week for a month. He said on their fifth try, the door was opened and they were exposed to an extremely crude male stripper in the raw.

"Barb and Susan almost fainted, screamed and hauled ass," Long said with a chuckle.

"That's an idea," Cates said.

"Well, maybe not," Long said. "My wife and her friend never came back. But for six damn weeks in a row we had most of their pals in the lobby at noon on the button."

For the next several minutes the men talked about deceiving their wives in another way, the development of a contrived deer hunting trip to South Georgia. They decided the departure should be at ten o'clock Friday morning, to make sure they got to Birmingham with time to spare. Also, they agreed to meet the next day at C&M Construction to load the Pathfinders and take an inventory of items they might be overlooking.

"Let's have breakfast every morning and review our plan," McGraw said. "We can't be wrong, not once."

"That's a good point because we're bound to have something go sour down there," Bobo said.

"That's a sublime attitude," Long said, his voice rising and the tone sarcastic. "Hell, Ben, you're talking like a chicken shit person who expects to fail."

"I'm being realistic," Bobo said. "We'll be in the dark. One bad move and we'll be lost in an unfamiliar jungle."

"Bull shit, bull shit, bull shit," Long said. "We don't need any more of this melodramatic bull shit."

"What we need is perfect preparation," Cates said. "Spend time checking the plan for flaws. Don't forget anything, even something as insignificant as a toothpick or a pouch of instant coffee."

CHAPTER FIVE

Carl McGraw cast skeptical eyes toward the overcast gray sky as the meticulously packed and conspicuously crowded 2000 Super V-6 Pathfinder he was driving past a sign on Interstate 65 that said he and Fred Long were sixteen miles north of Birmingham. Already, flakes of snow blended with soft rain and moist discharges from the rear of transfer trucks were making the windshield wipers earn their keep.

It was a quarter past three on Friday afternoon and there was reason to believe the weather forecast they had digested that morning was not going to pan out. They had hoped to see snow on the ground instead of simply trickling from overhead.

"Don't fret the small stuff, not yet," Long said as he scribbled notes on a pad. "In Philadelphia we called this the mildness before the madness."

McGraw looked at Long and chuckled. He turned down the volume on the compact disc player, an effort to take a break from the heavy metal pounding of AC-DC. He wondered how the oldest man in the group could favor such penetrating music.

"If you're wrong, that song we're listening to is prophetic," McGraw said. "We'll be on a *Highway To Hell* for sure."

"Then if it makes you feel better, change over to *Stairway To Heaven* and let me get some work done," Long said. "Honest to God, I'm not sure I've ever seen so many pessimistic people in my life."

"Okay, let me give you something else troubling to consider," McGraw said.

"Shoot."

"Let's say you're right. Let's say we're about to get a heavy dumping of snow, as planned."

"Okay."

"That's reason to worry about the other guys getting to that campground at Oak Mountain State Park before the roads get too bad to negotiate."

Long shook his head, as if he was tired of such chatter. Privately, he was wondering the same thing because the other four men were lagging behind after encountering problems at work and testy wives at home.

"That's just part of rolling dice," Long said, attempting to settle McGraw. "If the Pathfinders can't get to the lake this afternoon, they sure as hell won't be able to get out of there later tonight."

Long paused as a brainstorm hit him.

"By the way," he said. "You need to make sure the gas tank is full before we go camping."

McGraw nodded and wondered if the other men would think about doing the same. He looked toward Long and said, "Fred, you're one weird but delightfully brilliant man — mafia connected as you are."

"I'm not in the mafia," Long said. "I'm in the brotherhood. The mafia whacks people. I crunch numbers — and that's what I'm thinking about now if you don't mind."

About forty minutes later, McGraw and Long were approaching Inverness Corners on Highway 280. With snow forming a thin white blanket on the roadside grass, they noticed First Columbus as they passed the small building on their right. Sitting near it, as outlined, was larger and more modernistic Sector. Across the six-lane thoroughfare with a median splitting it were several strip shopping centers dominated by fast food restaurants, novelty shops and real estate offices. They saw North Star sitting among them and understood why the scouting report said that might be a tough nut to crack.

They were not enamored when they saw a Brinks Truck a few vehicles ahead of them. They felt better when they saw it roll past Central at the intersection of Highway 280 and Valleydale Road, sitting in a valley across the street from the Bruno's supermarket.

"Let's don't overstay in this area," Long said. "Kentucky license plates will stick out like sore thumbs."

"It's unbelievable how good Mills and Bass are when it comes to painting pictures," McGraw said. "They said BP station on the right. They said Captain D's on the left. They said ..."

"What they failed to mention is that fire station we passed a short ways back," Long said. "I don't like that being so close to the action."

"I'm more troubled by that Central location," McGraw said. "That damn bank might as well be a part of the meat market at Food World."

The parking lots at Bruno's and Food World were filled with cars. Shoppers were moving to and fro at rapid paces, trying to secure generous supplies of food and beverages and get home before the storm.

Long looked at the snow falling harder and thought the shoppers better get a move on it. He was pleased when the Pathfinder passed Patriot and American and he saw only a few cars in the parking lot at each location and saw a few customers carrying money bags while walking toward the front doors. He was not as happy when he looked across the street at a large shopping center and saw several cars in front of a Winn-Dixie supermarket.

"I'm encouraged," McGraw said.

"Don't get impatient," Long said.

"I just need some air," McGraw said.

"You aren't going to get any until we take a spin through the Sunny Meadows and Hickory Ridge areas off Highway 119, the secondary route to that golf practice facility on Valleydale Road."

"Give me the directions," McGraw said.

McGraw turned right on Highway 119, just short of a Texaco Food Mart and drove the Pathfinder about four miles before he saw a sign that said Oak Mountain State Park was on the left. He continued past that road until he got to a traffic light leading to Sunny Meadows, which led to Hickory Ridge. The terrain started getting hilly and he contemplated going to four-wheel drive. After about ten minutes, they reached Valleydale Road and saw the golf practice facility across the street.

As they rode, they listened to good reports on two types of radios, commercial and police band. McGraw heard radio news people present a weather forecast that sounded like Birmingham was about to reach the end of the world, or at least its existence in it. Long heard police officers talk about the trouble they expected attempting to drive on soon to be treacherous roads and he heard reports that men with higher rank were instructing their troops to stay close to their precincts unless an emergency situation forced them to battle the elements.

"I like that," Long said as he surveyed the golf practice facility and realized it would be difficult for anybody to see it from Valleydale Road in the dark of night.

"I'm ready to construct a campsite," McGraw said as he turned around the Pathfinder to start a backtrack.

"As long as there isn't anybody hanging around that park," Long said. McGraw put the Pathfinder in four-wheel drive before he started up the steep hill leading from Highway 119 to Oak Mountain State Park. He was pleased with the traction and realized it would probably be better when more snow was on the pavement.

"There's our construction road," Long said.

McGraw drove the Pathfinder along the road and into a large clearing. He cowered when he saw a dump truck, then relaxed when he realized nobody was in it. He stopped the vehicle behind some bushes.

"I'll take a hard hike and see what's going on in the park," Long said.

"Be careful," McGraw said. "A hill can become a mountain when covered in snow and ice."

Long was gone about fifteen minutes. When he returned he looked at an inquisitive McGraw and said, "C-L-O-S-E-D — and quiet and desolate."

"We just got over a big obstacle," McGraw said.

"Then let's put up a tarp to keep us dry," Long said.

"If you think we're deep enough in the woods, I'd like to gather a big load of fire wood before it gets too wet," McGraw said.

"Fine. But let's build it in a hole just to be on the safe side."

CHAPTER SIX

Almost an hour elapsed before Carl McGraw and Fred Long heard the sound of truck engines and were joined at a hastily developed campsite by Mark Cates and Ben Bobo and Ed Bass and Sam Mills. The two Pathfinders arrived simultaneously after the four men met by chance at the Winn-Dixie supermarket on Highway 280, where both sets of partners in The Snowman Project stopped to purchase food that would help them get through much of the night.

"Did you guys go brain-dead or what?" Long said as he watched charcoal in a new Weber grill turning white and saw Bobo and Bass putting garlic powder, salt and pepper on six large New York strips.

"What do you mean?" Bobo said.

"Damn, that was dumb stopping at a shopping center with six million people in the parking lot, especially with out of state license plates on the back of the trucks."

"You mean Alabama license plates," Cates said. "We picked up three sets at no charge at a closed junk yard in Cullman — and you or McGraw need to get yours on before it gets too sloppy to move up here."

"Basically, we looked like everybody else in Birmingham, frantic and in need of food and drink," Bobo said.

Long felt better, even more so after hearing the other teams in the caper had filled their Pathfinders with gas.

So the men sat and chatted as they ate steaks complemented by sauce, potato chips, a loaf of bread and soft drinks. They conversed about the beautiful setting they were in and wondered how wonderful Oak Mountain State Park must be on a placid spring afternoon with the temperature mild and fish jumping in the water. They felt warm beside an entrenched fire as they listened to a battery operated radio that kept providing grandiose news:

"The national weather service is predicting a minimum of six inches of snow between now and tomorrow morning and said the Birmingham Metropolitan Area could get as much as ten inches. The Jefferson County Sheriff's Department is cautioning everyone to stay at home unless an emergency exists. That same warning has been issued by the Shelby County Sheriff's Department and other law enforcement agencies.

"There have not been serious traffic accidents thus far. But representatives from the Alabama Department of Public Safety have predicted numerous state highways and county roads will be closed during the next several hours. At present, it appears interstate highways and federal highways will remain open, although drivers are asked not to attempt traveling on them unless there is an emergency.

"Alabama Power remains optimistic that electrical service will remain intact in most areas. However, officials there want to remind people to make sure they have plenty of warm clothing and blankets at their disposal. Also, people should have flashlights with strong batteries ready for use.

"Anyone needing food, clothing or shelter should call emergency relief centers as soon as possible. The telephone number is 1-800-223-7669 or 1-800-BAD-SNOW. The representatives from emergency relief centers want to caution people that they might not be able to meet such requests later in the night. That number again is 1-800- 223-7669.

"With temperatures dropping quickly, people are being advised to store as much water as possible, even if it means filling a bathtub. Most of the Birmingham Metropolitan Area can expect to be without water tomorrow and, possibly, for few days after the snow and ice pass through.

"Stay tuned to WERC Radio for up to the minute ..."

"We couldn't have drawn it any better," Cates said. "It's a quarter past eight. This place will be a disaster area by midnight."

"But we might freeze to death before we spring into action," Bass said.

"In fact, I think I'll slip into my snowsuit and try to nap for a while.

Bass heard objections around the campfire. He was told the group should change the colors on three Pathfinders and go over the master plan once more.

"Let's have a drink while we work," Bobo said.

"No way," Cates said. "When we go into war I want my trench mate to be as fit as he can be."

After about half of an hour, plus some well-rehearsed, methodical labor, the three Pathfinders had changed colors and the equipment inside them had been arranged to better fit the needs of the six men as they neared the next stage in a daring adventure.

The trucks looked like a Space Shuttle, with each part of the cargo packed in a place that would provide good access. At the top were flashlights, drills and other tools that would be used first, as well as blasting pads, blasting caps and detonators. Each man knew how to reorganize the equipment as the night unfolded hour by hour and precarious step by precarious step.

"I'm wondering if these blasting pads are strong enough," Long said to nobody in particular.

"They worked in a Western Kentucky rock quarry that was like an echo chamber," Cates said. "I don't see a reason to doubt they'll do better down here."

"Did everybody remember to get those walkie-talkies out of the boxes and loaded with batteries?" McGraw said.

He did not hear a negative answer.

"Fine," McGraw said. "Then let's remember to keep our babbling to a minimum. As we've agreed, Fred and I will go out first and scope the area. Then we'll be the team in charge as far as communication is concerned."

"What he's saying is we don't want to hear from you unless you're responding to a course of action or you've got something important we all need to know," Long said. "Also, we don't want to hear names, just team colors, unit numbers and the like."

After hearing another weather report, this one stating temperatures could drop into single digits, Mills and Bass were asked to explain bank alarm systems. They told the others what they should look for in an effort to determine if the main system or the backup system was operable.

"If I remember correctly, the first thing we want to do at each location is clip the telephone line," Long said.

"Precisely," Mills said.

"Then get the power lines that fuel the main alarm system," Bass said.

"If a backup alarm system is triggered, it might ring inside the bank," Mills said. "But it won't work without the telephone line."

"That's the way it works at First Commercial," Bass said.

"Is that state of the art?" Bobo said.

"It's the industry norm, pretty much," Mills said.

"Again, the bottom line is this," Bass said. "Cut the telephone line. Then cut the main power line. If a backup alarm system sounds inside the bank just knock the shit out of it with a hammer to turn it off."

Silence prevailed for a several seconds. Then Bass said, "But that won't be a worry until later. Remember, we're hauling ass to cool our heels after busting down the exterior walls."

The thought of hitting and running like that seemed to bring the entire strategy home. The men became pensive as flames dance in front of them. The moment was so tranquil nobody noticed when Long walked to one of the Pathfinders, reached under a seat, grabbed a bottle of vodka and took three hard swallows. Nor did anybody think it was unusual when McGraw went to the rear of another truck and prayed.

"What are we forgetting?" Long said.

"The Fargo Security Systems signs for the side of the Pathfinders and the yellow lights for the top," Cates said.

"Those don't need to go on until we get ready to go back to the banks the second time," Long said. "Until then, we just want to look like wayward nuts out riding around."

"But all the while we want to look like snowmen with jumpsuits pulled snug, masks over our faces and, by all means, gloves on at all times," Mills said.

"It's getting colder and I'm getting dressed," Bass said.

CHAPTER SEVEN

The snow was deep enough for the oversized tires to leave noticeable tracks as Carl McGraw and Fred Long moved their yellow Pathfinder along the curving downhill road leading from the entrance to Oak Mountain State Park to Highway 119. The flakes continued to fall and they appeared to be getting larger.

When they cleared the first half mile or so and prepared to turn right on Highway 119, they looked to the left to give the houses in a large subdivision their utmost attention. They saw little to cause discomfort, discounting a man and two boys building a snowman in the front portion of a lawn. The trio did not seem to notice them as they moved carefully along the right lane.

"This looks like a Christmas card," McGraw said. "Dust on the ground and smoke bellowing from fireplaces."

The view became prettier, at least from their point of view, when they rounded a curve and were provided a clear look at the intersection of Highway 280 and Highway 119. Two automobiles were in a ditch on the right side, their images reflecting in the yellow glow of an emergency light blinking beside them. The Texaco Food Mart was closed. They passed the wreckage, saw nobody, and made a left turn, their last maneuver leading to a straight path to Patriot, American, Central, Sector, First Columbus and North Star.

McGraw and Long continued past Inverness Corners, which was barren except for shoppers at Bruno's supermarket, and they did not stop until every bank had been passed. They pulled into the shopping center in which North Star was located, stopped the Pathfinder and reached for a walkie-talkie.

The radio inside the truck said it was a few minutes past midnight.

"Gentlemen, start your engines," Long said.

At the campsite, Mark Cates and Ben Bobo and Sam Mills and Ed Bass were seated in their white and red Pathfinders, respectively. The engines were already running, with the smoke from the exhausts mixing with that being exhaled by a perishing fire. The trucks had already been turned toward the exit from the state park.

"10-4," Cates said. "Come again."

"The world looks empty," Long said as McGraw turned the yellow Pathfinder back toward Highway 280.

"10-4," Cates said. "Team White and Team Red are ready to roll."

"Watch yourselves coming out," Long said. "Follow the tree lines. Be easy on the turns."

"10-4," Cates said. "I'd guess you left some tracks."

"Good idea," Long said. "Just get in the trenches."

"10-4."

"10-4."

"Team Yellow will take Unit One and Unit Two. Team White will take Unit Three and Unit Four. Team Red will take Unit Five and Unit Six. Do all of you copy?" Long said.

"10-4."

"10-4."

"Team Yellow will try Unit Two first," Long said, referring to Sector. "It looks more sophisticated than Unit One."

As McGraw started the yellow Pathfinder rolling toward Sector about a block and a half away, the white and red sports utility vehicles started their perilous treks down the entrance road to Oak Mountain State Park. By design, they departed three minutes apart. They found the incline much easier to negotiate because of the tracks they had to follow.

McGraw and Long rode past Sector on a boulevard that ran between it and First Columbus. The road led to Valleydale Road and on past Inverness Country Club less than a mile from the golf practice facility. When they were confident there were no other vehicles in sight, they turned around and went back to the bank. The driver parked the Pathfinder about six feet from the auto teller window, where it was shielded from view by trees and bushes.

"Team Yellow has parked at Unit Two ... Team White has clear sailing into Unit Three," Long said.

McGraw and Long moved quickly, appearing a little uneasy. They got out of their Pathfinder and pressed their noses against the tinted auto teller window.

"I don't like those tiny red lights on the wall," McGraw said.

"Like Bass said, it's part of the backup security system," Long said. "So let's snip some telephone lines."

The two men walked to the side of the building, with flashlights showing the way, discovered a power box hidden by a bush and noticed three black wires running from it to inside the building. A closer look allowed them to read three words: South Central Bell.

"Let's cut them all and keep our ears open," Long said.

Nothing was heard. Also, most of the tiny red lights inside the bank building went black. The exception was one blinking under a surveillance camera mounted on a wall.

McGraw and Long went back to the Pathfinder to send an important message to the other men. They assumed Team White was across the street at Unit Three, North Star, and Team Red was a couple of miles up Highway 280 at Unit Five, Patriot.

"Team Yellow to Team White and Team Red," Long said. "Telephone lines are dead at Unit Two."

"10-4, the same at Unit Three."

"10-4, the same at Unit Five."

"Team White can back out and sit tight until we make a pass at a boom," Long said. "Do you copy?"

Team White, Cates and Bobo, drove their Pathfinder to a position behind a state beverage control store at the far end of the shopping center. If something went wrong at Sector, they had two ways out, one an alley running behind three stores. But they were more concerned about the position of the North Star branch.

While the auto teller window was at the rear of the building and pretty much out of sight, the other sides were easily visible to anybody driving along Highway 280, as well as anybody driving along a road that ran past a Wendy's hamburger restaurant and into a residential area. Adding to their consternation was a Hardee's hamburger restaurant at the front of the shopping center, a place they thought might open for breakfast early the following morning.

"I sure as hell don't like the location we've drawn in this deal," Cates said to Bobo after about half of an hour. "That damn North Star branch could just as easily be a Burger King with neon lights glowing."

"Yeah, those lucky bastards are in closets and we're sitting on the front porch," Bobo said.

"We might make a move to get out of this predicament, especially since we've also drawn that damn Central across the street from Bruno's," Cates said. "There aren't any trees and bushes to help us at this location."

As their anxiety was growing, Cates and Bobo heard something encouraging on the police band radio, word that two cruisers were in a ditch and the Shelby County Sheriff's Department was suggesting other mobile units return to station houses as soon as possible. There was four inches of snow on the ground and ice was forming on top of it. The driving conditions were getting worse by the minute.

McGraw and Long discovered the auto teller window at Sector to their liking, exactly like it had been described by Bass and Mills, and they were busy unloading blasting materials from their Pathfinder. It was taking them a long time, too much in their estimation, and they decided to let Team White get started placing blasting caps at Unit Three.

The order was placed by walkie-talkie.

"10-4," said Cates, who was not excited about getting started again at North Star.

Bass and Mills were making good progress at Patriot.

As soon as Cates and Bobo parked their Pathfinder against the rear wall at North Star and got out of it, they heard laughter in the distance behind them. It was obvious a hearty group of individuals was playing in the snow a few blocks away, probably at a large apartment complex they had been told about.

"Shit," Cates said. "I don't know how much money is inside this joint, but I don't think it's worth the risk."

"I'm with you," Bobo said as they walked back to the Pathfinder and got inside without unloading anything.

"Let me go look to be sure," Cates said.

Cates walked about a block and a half along the road running from Highway 280 beside North Star. He stood on one hill and looked at the top of another. He saw what appeared to be two dozen people having a sledding party. He hurried back to his partner and hastily grabbed a walkie-talkie.

While he was away, Bobo took a swallow of vodka.

"Team White to Team Yellow and Team Red," Cates said.

"10-4, this is Red," Bass said.

McGraw dropped the drill he was using at Sector and picked up the walkie-talkie on the ground beside him. "10-4, this is Yellow."

"Be advised that Unit Three is rowdy tonight," Cates said. "There are people partying about three blocks away. This is not a good place to be on an evening like this."

McGraw was quick with his response: "We've noticed some chatter, so maybe golf would be a better game for you to play for a while." He hoped the inference hit home with Cates.

"10-4," Cates said. "We'll go practice."

Bass and Mills saw no reason to respond.

It did not take long for Cates and Bobo to evacuate the area. Nor did it take more than a minute for them to feel heavy pounding inside their chests. They peered out of the white Pathfinder as it moved along the side street leading from the shopping center to Highway 280 and saw two Shelby Country Sheriff's Department cruisers turning right as if they were answering a call at Sector Bank.

"Damn, it's over and we've barely begun," Cates said as he reached for the walkie- talkie on the seat between him and Bobo. He was ready to sound an alarm. But to his relief the cruisers continued along the boulevard the visitors to town remembered as leading to Inverness Country Club.

"The good news is they're gone," Bobo said. "The bad news is we've got to follow them."

"Not necessarily," Cates said.

"We'll go up Highway 280 to Valleydale Road and turn right. That'll get us to our private golf course."

Team White followed that route and chose not to tell Team Yellow and Team Red about the two law enforcement cruisers in the area.

"This isn't going like I thought it would," Bobo said. "We've got cops on patrol."

"Think on the bright side," Cates said. "Not long ago we heard the Shelby County Sheriff's Department calling in the troops. I'd like to think the deputies in those cruisers are following orders."

CHAPTER EIGHT

Team Yellow moved like ants beside the auto teller window at Sector Bank. They had drilled six small holes at the base of the bullet-proof glass, then had expanded and cleaned them with a pointed screwdriver. They had placed blasting caps inside and had applied packing, like a doctor would to a gaping wound.

They were wrestling with a blasting pad and stringing wire to a detonator when they realized something more shocking.

"Son of a bitch, it's single-digits cold, or thereabouts, and I'm sweating like a whore in church," Fred Long said.

"Don't fret over the small stuff," Carl McGraw said. "This baby is the industry standard, Emerald Coast, which means we'll be pleased if we can get this blasting pad in place."

"I thought Bass said this window is as good as they make," Long said.

"He did," McGraw said. "But he also told us we'd have clear sailing if we found four small holes at the bottom of the right corner and four small holes at the bottom of the left corner. I counted eight when I took my first look."

"I love you," Long said.

At Patriot, Unit Five, Ed Bass and Sam Mills were moving more fastidiously than their partners could have imagined. The bankers knew the territory better than the contractors and the insurance agents and that showed. They had blasting caps in place and were in the process of getting the blasting pad ready.

But they had spotted a peculiar green light that had them troubled. It was above the front entrance to the building. They surmised it might be some kind of extra security put in place after the branch had been robbed in the past.

"I'm at a loss," Bass said as he pulled up the mask covering his face to his chin to let in some cool air. "I guess it could be motion-sensitive."

"Maybe we should crawl around the perimeter of the building and see if we can find some other wires," Mills said.

Bass and Mills did that, to no avail, and resumed their drilling, packing and covering procedure.

"If the cops don't show up when we blow open this place, I'm going to beat the hell out of that green light when we go inside," Bass said.

"What have we got left?" Mills said.

"That's it, as soon as the detonator is in place," Bass said.

At Sector, McGraw and Long were tidying up after setting explosives in place. They stretched the detonator, letting it come to rest in bushes. They picked up trash. They rearranged their Pathfinder. They were killing time they did not have to waste because Bass and Mills were working at an equal pace.

"Team Red to Team Yellow," Bass said into the walkie-talkie.

"Yellow copies," Long said after being surprised by the greeting he had received.

"We need a status report."

"Come again."

"We need to know how you guys are coming."

"We can boom at your discretion," Long said.

"Then give us a countdown," Bass said.

"Hold the phone."

McGraw and Long were amazed by the speed with which Team Red had completed its work. Now, it was concerned about Team White, which had been in retreat.

"Team Yellow to Team White," Long said.

"10-4, we copy you," Cates said.

"Yellow and Red have steak on the grill."

"White has a golf ball on the tee."

"We'll be with you soon," Long said.

Then he said, "Do you copy, Team Red?"

"10-4."

"Is three minutes until a boom okay?"

"Three is fine."

"Then let's go three from this countdown — seven, six, five, four, three, two, one and three minutes."

"10-4."

The normally unflappable Long was getting jittery. He wondered what would happen when the detonator was ignited. He feared the entire building would come down and every person within six miles would be awakened or alarmed.

McGraw attempted to console him. "It'll be about like a hungry giant with a growling stomach," he said. "At the worst, it'll be thunder with shattered glass."

"I can handle that," Long said. "I've heard enough thunder already tonight."

"I know," McGraw said. "Alabama snowstorms seem to have it all, lightning and thunder included."

"Don't add too much to it when you flip that switch," Long said.

"Well, just consider this blasting exercise a tuneup," McGraw said. "It'll take more firepower to open that vault."

The detonator at Sector was activated — boom.

The detonator at Patriot was activated — boom.

The sounds were muffled, indeed, to the extent McGraw and Long and Mills and Bass could barely hear the blasts. Both teams moved quickly to unhook the detonators from their wiring and to get into the Pathfinders. Then, with headlights off, they started drives from the bank branches.

McGraw and Long, drove along the boulevard leading to Inverness Country Club and Valleydale Road. Near the end of it they noticed a small fire station hidden by trees and, more importantly, six Hoover City Police Department cruisers in the parking lot.

"Damn," Long said. "Nobody said anything about a police department being in this area."

The fire station and police department were less than a mile from the golf practice facility, with a townhouse development and some hardwood trees in between.

Mills and Bass drove through Sunny Meadows and Hickory Ridge en route to Valleydale Road. They found the going tricky in some spots because of the steep hills in the second neighborhood.

"Team Yellow to Team White," Long said as the Pathfinder in which he and McGraw were riding inched closer to the golf practice facility.

"10-4."

"We're blinking headlights and coming in on top of you."

"10-4," Cates said. "We're tucked in the woods at the far end of the parking lot."

"Do you copy, Team Red?"

"We're coming down this mountain of a street and will be there in three minutes," Bass said.

The stay at the golf practice facility was brief, by design, because the six men only wanted to listen to a police band radio to make sure the two blasts had not prompted suspicion. For less than a quarter of an hour they drank coffee and reevaluated a plan that had already been altered because of a sledding party near North Star. Mills and Bass were thoroughly chastised for not including a nearby police department in their scouting report on the area.

A new order of business was finalized:

Team White, Cates and Bobo, would go out first, drive past Unit Four, survey the area in and around the Bruno's supermarket and the Food World supermarket and, if it was unobstructed, establish its position at Central.

"We'll let you know if it's clear enough for you to move," Cates said.

Team Yellow, McGraw and Long, would go to Sector and see how the blasting went at the auto teller window. Then they would go inside the building and place explosives in the area of the vault. After that task was completed, they would move down the street to Unit One, First Columbus, and place blasting caps in the area of the auto teller window or the best location available.

Team Red, Bass and Mills, would follow a similar procedure near the vault at Unit Five, Patriot, and near the auto teller window at Unit Six, American.

"What in hell are Mark and I going to do after getting explosives in place at Central while you guys change locations and keep working?" Bobo said.

"Find a quiet spot to hide," Long said.

"This place looks good to me," Bobo said.

"Hell no," McGraw said, his voice firm. "Don't you come out of that area unless you know you won't be noticed."

"Damn," Bobo said. "Here we go again, the most unlucky bastards known to mankind."

"How much longer before we go?" Mills said.

"Let's just sit and listen for a while," McGraw said. "By my calculation we're running ahead of schedule."

On the police band radios they heard that cruisers were having problems on the slick streets, even with tire chains in place. The hilly terrain was taking a toll on anybody who did not have a sports utility vehicle with four-wheel drive.

"Hooray for the Japs," Bass said.

"Shit," Long said, shaking his head.

On commercial radios they heard music interrupted by a lot of weather bulletins. The temperature was headed to a position below ten degrees. The news report they listened to said power outages were already occurring, with most in remote areas. Listeners were told to stay at home.

"Those damn people we saw at Bruno's supermarket must not have gotten the news," Cates said. "There must have been a dozen cars in that parking lot when we came past there en route to here."

"Were most of them trucks and jeeps?" McGraw said.

"I'd say it was a mixture," Bobo said.

"Well, these folks driving regular cars are going to learn something about snow and ice," McGraw said. "If anybody at that store drove in there in a Taurus or a Century, they'll be there for a while."

They heard more encouraging news as it related to law enforcement agencies. The Birmingham Police Department was having difficulty getting over Red Mountain on the south and east sides of the city. The Pelham Police Department and the Hoover Police Department were citing a shortage of tire chains as the reason they could not answer numerous calls from frantic citizens. The Shelby County Sheriff's Department was having to focus on rural areas like Wilsonville, Chelsea, Westover, Four Mile and Columbiana, where narrow and curving roads were extremely hazardous. The Homewood Police Department and the Vestavia Police Department were stymied, dead in their tracks.

"It's starting to sound like a good night to rob banks," McGraw said.

"Good or bad, we're too far into it to turn back," Long said.

CHAPTER NINE

The nervousness and agitation Ben Bobo felt at the golf practice facility escalated when he and Mark Cates reached the intersection of Valleydale Road and Highway 280. To the left, at the Food World shopping center, they saw a parking lot with six or eight cars covered with snow that had been abandoned by their owners. But to the right, at the Bruno's supermarket, they saw more activity.

"Shit, we've got a ton of people moving in and out of that place," Bobo said as Cates drove the white Pathfinder through the intersection and turned left. "I don't want to work across the street from that."

Actually, there were a couple dozen cars in the parking lot and about that many people moving around inside the dimly lit food store.

"It isn't that bad, Ben," Cates said. "Remember, Central sits in a valley. Those people won't see us."

"But we can't work at that auto teller window," Bobo said as he pointed toward an area of the bank they could see with ease from Highway 280.

"We'll work the side door," Cates said.

Cates and Long rode past Sector and First Columbus and saw nothing. Then they turned around, moved along Highway 280 and drove past Patriot and American and saw nothing.

"Team White to Team Yellow and Team Red," Bobo said.

"10-4," Carl McGraw said at the golf practice facility.

"I guess you can come out now," Bobo said.

"What do you mean guess?"

Cates was skillfully maneuvering the Pathfinder along a service road beside Highway 280, an effort to get to Central while staying out of the view of anybody who might enter the Bruno's supermarket parking lot. He quickly looked toward Bobo, with an angry scowl hidden by the mask he was wearing. He was starting to question his partner.

"Do you copy me, Team White?" McGraw said after he did not get a reply to his question.

Cates grabbed the walkie-talkie from Bobo and said, "10-4, we copy you. All is clear. We're at Unit Four and ready to go to work."

"10-4," McGraw said. "We're on our way."

When Cates refocused on Bobo, he saw his partner taking a couple of swallows of vodka from a bottle he had pulled from under the seat.

"I can't do this alone," Cates said.

"I don't like having my ass in a sling," Bobo said.

"Ben, take a look at that Bruno's supermarket," Cates said, trying to reason with his upset partner.

When Bobo looked that way, he could see only a small portion of the roof because he and Cates were in a hole of sorts while parked beside the bank building. Several large bushes provided more protection.

"Okay, you win," Bobo said. "Let's give it a whirl."

Utilizing the knowledge they learned from Team Yellow and Team Red during the break at the golf practice facility, Cates and Bobo had an easy time getting blasting caps and a blasting pad in place in the area of an employee entrance at Central. They decided the door was less secure than the auto teller window because it did not seem to have extra fortification.

At Sector and Patriot, respectively, McGraw and Fred Long and Sam Mills and Ed Bass had similar good luck working on vaults. They entered the buildings through large holes the previous blasts had created at the base of auto teller windows, spaces big enough for them to get through after crouching only slightly. They sprayed black paint over the lenses of surveillance cameras. One put a menacing green light to rest with a hammer.

"It's so damn quiet in here it's eerie," Bass said as he and Mills put a heavy dose of explosives along the bottom and left side of the vault.

"It's better than bells ringing and sirens roaring," Mills said. "Remember, the song said silence is golden."

About a two miles away, McGraw and Long were loading their Pathfinder to start a trip down the street to Unit One. They were satisfied with their work at Sector and wanted to begin at First Columbus. As they toiled they wondered out loud about how much money was in each vault and concluded the amount they gathered would be worth the effort.

The minutes passed quickly. The wind was whipping. The snow on the ground, fluffy when it arrived, was getting harder.

"Team Yellow to Team White and Team Red," Long said into the walkie-talkie.

"Team White copies," Bobo said.

"Team Red copies," Bass said.

"Team Yellow has changed locations," Long said. "What are your locations?"

"Team White is finished and sitting," Bobo said.

"Team Red is moving to Unit Six," Bass said.

"Be advised that Team White will be changing colors in the near future," Bobo said.

"Good," McGraw said.

Cates and Long had to work in unpleasant surroundings as they changed the cover on their Pathfinder. They were parked behind Food World next to several dumpsters and the smell of rotten vegetables and spoiled meat was nauseating. After completing that task and waiting for the others to place explosives at First Columbus and American, they turned on the police band radio to hear what was going on in the Birmingham Metropolitan Area. Everything they heard was encouraging, as they expected after slipping and sliding as they changed the color of their sports utility vehicle:

"Roger, Unit 52," said a police dispatcher. "The woman said her mother is in the house and there isn't any heat. She's an older woman who could be in serious danger."

"What's the location?"

There was a lot of static.

"Did you copy, dispatcher?"

"Yes. 424 Mistletoe in Mountain Brook."

"We'll do our best. But police cruisers aren't performing well in this mess. Maybe the Mountain Brook Fire Department can get an engine to that location."

"I'll check with the MBFD."

"All units in the vicinity of Eagle Point, there's a reported intruder at 3459 Castaway Circle," said a dispatcher with the Shelby County Sheriff's Department.

"Roger, Unit 132 will answer. Is the intruder inside the house at that location?"

"Negative. The caller said there's a mysterious noise outside the house."

"Then get verification of an intruder on the property. I've already been in and out of one ditch tonight."

"Roger, Unit 132. We'll seek verification."

Throughout the Shelby County Sheriff's Department new shifts were reporting for duty and they were skeletons at best. A similar situation was developing at the Birmingham Police Department and the Hoover Police Department, where men and women on duty were being asked to spend the night at precincts.

"I don't know what good that's going to do," a police officer said to his watch commander at the precinct just off Valleydale Road. "We can't move as it is and there isn't anybody out there to watch over."

"Then maybe staying here will keep you alive," said the watch commander. "If you can't drive a specially equipped police cruiser on a night like this, you won't have a chance in hell of getting home."

The moments passed slowly for Cates and Bobo as they sat behind the Food World and waited for the other four men to make contact.

"I'm going to look across the street," Bobo said.

"Sit tight," Cates said.

"Hell no, I'm out of here."

Cates pounded the steering wheel as he saw Bobo bounding across the parking lot and turning right at the corner of the Food World building. His patience was wearing thin. He reached under the seat and grabbed the vodka bottle, a quart, and noticed it was almost half empty.

Six minutes later, Cates saw Bobo running toward the truck. He shook his head when saw his partner hit the ground after slipping.

"There are six or eight people in front of that Bruno's and there's a big truck out there, too," Bobo said.

"What kind of truck?"

"Hell, I don't know," Bobo said. "It looks like they're unloading stuff from it, something like big air conditioning units on pallets."

Cates knew what was happening. Bruno's was equipping itself with power generators in the event electrical service was interrupted. He had surmised it was a matter of time before the lights went out when he and Bobo passed the supermarket the first time and noticed how shadowy it was inside.

"Team Yellow to Team White and Team Red."

"10-4."

"10-4."

"We are ready to open another location," Long said as he and McGraw finished their work at First Columbus.

"Team Red has been waiting for you," Bass said as he and Mills stood beside the auto teller window at American.

"We're on go at Unit Four," Cates said. "But we'll have to walk to that location because there are people unloading a truck across the street."

"Food or gas?" Long said, his way of trying to find out what street Cates was talking about.

"Food," Cates said.

"Does Team White want to leave now?" Long said.

"Negative," Cates said. "But give us time to put on a sign and a light before we have fireworks."

"Come again," Long said.

"We'll go boom at Unit Four, then wait before leaving this location," Cates said. "We want to put on a sign and light before we go boom."

"Time is running short," Long said.

"We can have fireworks in six minutes — five, four, three, two, one and six minutes and counting," Cates said.

"10-4."

"10-4."

Cates and Bobo quickly put Fargo Security Systems signs on the front doors of their Pathfinder and a yellow light on top. They walked toward Central, briskly while taking an out of the way path through foliage so they would not leave easy to discover footprints in the snow. They checked the detonator connection. They had one minute.

"I'm going back to the truck now," Bobo said.

"Please do," Cates said.

The countdown continued.

Boom.

Boom.

Boom — and the latter one, at Central, was louder than the others and caused the ground to shake.

"Son of a bitch," Cates said as he hurried back to the Pathfinder. He arrived in time to see Bobo chugging vodka.

The rumble captured the attention of the men and women inside Bruno's supermarket, a dozen and a half shoppers, and the four men unloading the powergenerators. It was not long before everybody except the store manager and three checkout clerks were in the parking lot looking toward the sky or in all directions on the ground.

Suddenly, the weather became more furious. Lightning flashed and thunder roared.

"That wasn't thunder we heard a few seconds ago," said Martin Shaw, one of the men unloading the generator truck.

"Then what in hell was it?" said Susan Arenberg, a 26-year-old woman who had been in the food store most of the evening because she did not want to stay alone in her apartment.

"Maybe it was thunder," said Tim Dubose, a 34-year-old man who had rushed outside when he heard the noise.

"Believe me, it wasn't thunder because there wasn't any lightning in front of it," Shaw said.

"I'm calling the fucking police," said Arenberg, who was more frightened in public than she would have been at home.

The conversation on the walkie-talkies was about as brisk as the banter at Bruno's supermarket.

"Team Yellow wants to know if everybody is safe," Long said.

"Team Red is fine," Bass said.

"Team White is fine, but a little nervous," Cates said. "We had an interesting fireworks show."

"So we heard," Long said.

Long paused, then said, "Hold your positions and let us confer."

McGraw and Long attempted to decide the best course of action. They knew it would be dangerous attempting to travel back to the golf practice facility. Ultimately, they concluded Team White should stay put, behind the Food World supermarket, and Team Yellow and Team Red should find out of the way places until excitement subsided.

That plan was advanced.

"Team Yellow to Team Red and Team White."

"10-4."

"10-4."

"Team Yellow will find an out of the way place for rest, then continue with the next project."

"10-4."

"10-4."

"Team Red copies and likes the idea," Bass said. "We're anxious to change colors. We have a place to work nearby."

"Team White agrees," Cates said. "We can keep an eye on the folks across the street and let you know."

"10-4," Long said. "The hour is late. We'll attempt to get some more inside work done at Unit One."

"10-4," Bass said. "We can work inside at Unit Six."

"Good luck, Team White," Long said.

"We might need some."

McGraw and Long pulled onto Highway 280 and moved west, toward Birmingham. The were pleased to have the only vehicle on the road. They went about two miles and pulled into an almost full parking lot at a massive Marriott Hotel.

"I don't like this crowd," Long said. "I'm voting we move back toward our work sites if we don't see traffic developing."

Bass and Mills drove around the corner to an expansive corporate complex. They found refuge between two clean dumpters used by an engineering company to discard shredded paper and cardboard.

"You know, ol' buddy, we're mighty fortunate to have a quiet area all to ourselves," Bass said.

Cates and Long sat beside several nasty dumpsters while knowing they had nowhere to run if a law enforcement agency cruiser came around the corner of the Food World.

CHAPTER TEN

Susan Arenberg followed up on her vow to contact the police department. She hurried to a pay telephone at Bruno's supermarket, fumbled frantically through the directory and placed a call.

"Birmingham Police Department," said the woman.

"There's something strange going on and I want you to do something about it," Arenberg said.

"Yes ma'am. But attempt to calm down and tell me about it."

"I'm at Bruno's in Inverness Corners and there has been an explosion. We don't know what it was but it sounded like ..."

"Ma'am, is anybody hurt?"

"No, but it was like thunder, except it wasn't thunder."

"Ma'am, is there a fire?"

"No, not yet. It's just spooky up here and I'm concerned."

"Don't leave the building, ma'am and we'll get somebody on it as soon as possible."

The woman at BPD talked to a supervisor, Sergeant Ted Farley, who immediately placed a call to the Shelby County Sheriff's Office.

"We've had more than a few calls about that," said Sheriff's Deputy Dan Alexander. "Right now, it looks like those people heard a hard clap of thunder. We've got a lot of that rolling through this area."

"That's your jurisdiction," Farley said.

"We've called the manager at Bruno's," Alexander said. "He said there's no reason to be concerned. The woman is a bit on edge."

As every law enforcement agency in the area experienced a telephone blitz that was growing longer and more dense by the moment, Team Green, Carl McGraw and Fred Long, sat behind the Logan's Road House

Restaurant on Highway 280. They had moved from the congested Marriott Hotel parking lot and had stripped the yellow cover from their Pathfinder, sliced it and disposed it in a dumpster.

Team Cream, Ed Bass and Sam Mills, had retreated to the road leading to Oak Mountain State Park. They wanted to walk around a bit to loosen up tense muscles and to keep their blood circulating in the cold. They backed about a hundred yards off of Highway 119, changed the cover on their Pathfinder and worried about Mark Cates and Ben Bobo.

Team Brown was still stuck behind the Food World supermarket and one of the men was taking pills with his vodka, some form of prescription sedatives.

"If you're going to kill yourself with that shit, I'm going to take a look across the street," Cates said to Bobo.

"You aren't leaving me alone down here," Bobo said as he opened the door and, with a staggered step, got out of the Pathfinder.

Cates had wanted to get away from Bobo because his temper was reaching a dangerous level. Instead, he had to use a slow pace while walking to the high bank that kept people in the Bruno's parking lot from having a good view of them. He crawled up the embankment and liked most of what he observed.

The lights inside the food store were much brighter, with power generators working. The truck was gone. Nobody was in the parking lot except a man who had just arrived and was walking toward the entrance.

As Cates turned to start back down the embankment, a barking dog made him jump. He lost his balance and rolled down the bank, coming to rest at Bobo's feet. They both turned their heads fast enough to see three deer running from the mongrel in pursuit of them.

"Shit, what a night," Cates said.

"Yeah, and look who's stumbling now," Bobo said.

"Let's go to work," Cates said, his faced flushed.

After returning to their Pathfinder, Cates and Bobo made contact with the other men and told them things were quieter in the Bruno's parking lot. It was three o'clock and lot of labor remained in front of them because they had five vaults to blow open and clean out.

"This is the tricky part," McGraw said by walkie-talkie. "We've still got to unleash our fireworks simultaneously, but I don't think we need to have a vehicle trapped near Unit Four when that happens."

"Team Brown is for that," Cates said. "But I'm not sure we've got two people who can drive a vehicle out if one of us stays behind on foot and lights the fireworks."

"What does that mean?" McGraw said.

"One of us is a little unsteady," Cates said.

"Can you guys drive out, walk in and run out?" McGraw said.

"That's a plan," Cates said.

"Do you copy, Team Cream?"

"10-4 — and we have an idea," Bass said.

"Go for it."

"We've got backup firepower, two Remington JML packs. Let's try for five booms at once instead of three. Let's go for it all in one pop."

"I like it," McGraw said. "Then we can stay a little longer on the golf course and catch our breath."

Inside Bruno's supermarket, the store manager, Harvey Bolton, had restored some sense of order among frantic customers who had not heard any unusual noise for quite a while, other than thunder during a snowstorm. He attempted to make his position stronger by talking to them on the public address system, in the process assuring them the food store was a safe place to be at that hour.

Thirty minutes came and went. Team Green and Team Brown were finished and waiting.

McGraw and Long had two detonators in place, one at Sector and one at First Columbus.

Cates and Bobo had already driven from the back of the Food World supermarket, with a yellow light flashing, had turned left on Valleydale Road, had turned left on Highway 280 and had parked their Pathfinder at a SportPlex fitness center less than two hundred yards from Central.

"I'll go back to the bank alone," Cates said as he stood beside their Pathfinder. "You can get some rest."

Bobo objected, loudly. "Screw you," he said. "I'm not going to let you leave me alone to die."

Cates had seen and heard enough. He opened the passenger door, pulled Bobo out and beat him to a pulp — landing at least six hard punches to the face before regaining control. He shoved his partner back inside and started walking through underbrush toward Unit Four.

Ten minutes passed as Bass and Mills struggled with the vault at American. It was different than the others they had seen, with larger and thicker hinges on the door. They had to drill twice as many holes as had been the case at Patriot and it was more difficult packing them with blasting caps.

Finally, they were ready.

"Team Cream to Team Green and Team Brown," Bass said.

"10-4."

"10-4."

"At last, we are in place at Unit Five and Unit Six."

"Is Team Brown ready?" McGraw said.

"On foot and on go," Cates said.

"Team Green is ready at Unit One and Unit Two," McGraw said. "Two minutes from the countdown — five, four, three, two, one and two minutes from now."

Thirty seconds later, security lights in parking lots and street lights in the area went black, the result of a power failure, and the bank robbers and everybody else were more in the dark than they had been. The only apparent glow came from inside Bruno's supermarket. Lightning flashed, seemingly close by, and thunder roared.

Then ...

Boom ... Boom.

Boom.

Boom ... Boom.

McGraw and Long could hear glass shattering.

Cates could feel the ground trembling.

Mills and Bass could hear wood splintering.

Customers inside the food store screamed.

In the parking lot, Ed Ivory, a 31-year-old man who had come out on a dreary night to get milk for his young daughter, dived to the ground beside his Jeep Wrangler.

Cates ran as hard as he could toward the SportPlex fitness center parking lot. He could not see well enough to avoid bushes and other forms of underbrush. He fell down four times before he got back to the safety of the truck. When he got inside, he saw Bobo sound asleep with a vodka bottle at his feet.

"I hope I didn't kill the bastard," Cates said as he turned the ignition key and started rolling. "But I hope I got his attention," he said as he stopped the Pathfinder, got out and turned on the yellow flashing light on its top.

Cates decided it was time for Team Brown to fish or cut bait. He turned right on Highway 280, then right on Valleydale Road. He drove in front of Bruno's supermarket and continued along the winding road until he was near the golf practice facility. He gulped hard when he saw the lights of a vehicle approaching on the boulevard that ran beside the fire department and police station.

As he passed it, he glanced to his right and through a foggy window saw what he perceived to be a Pathfinder like the one he was driving. He could not be sure, but he had no choice. He turned into the entrance to the golf practice facility and was delighted when he realized it was Team Green trailing in his tracks.

The Hoover Police Department and the Shelby County Sheriff's Department were being bombarded with telephone calls, with many coming from frantic patrons at the food store.

Using local knowledge obtained on a scouting trip about a week earlier, Team Cream took a flat route to the golf practice facility, choosing to bypass Sunny Meadows and Hickory Ridge. Mills drove the Pathfinder onto Highway 280, turning left, and then turned left again beside a Movie Gallery video tape rental store that was a part of a familiar shopping center. He steered the truck down a modest hill, along a service road that ran behind Bruno's supermarket and Kmart and, ultimately, turned left onto Valleydale Road.

"Team Cream to Team Green and Team Brown," Bass said.

"We read you," McGraw said.

"Be advised we're a minute or two away and we're coming in on Valleydale Road."

"Get a move on it," McGraw said. "This radio is telling us all hell is about to break loose."

CHAPTER ELEVEN

The weather turned more unmerciful, the lower teens according to a local television station they were watching on a portable set, but Team Green, Team Cream and Team Brown found reason to believe the heat was about to rise as they sat at the golf practice facility. They did not dare start a fire as they listened to a police band radio that featured lively conversation between the Hoover Police Department just off Valleydale Road, which was shockingly near to them, and its two cruisers on perilous patrol and the Shelby County Sheriff's Department and its six cruisers that were attempting to cover a broad area.

"Can you answer the call at Bruno's?" a male dispatcher said to Hoover PD Unit 145.

"I'm in Greystone at a sledding accident," the officer said.

"What's your time of departure?"

"I'm trying to get an ambulance up here. There might be a broken neck involved."

"Dispatcher to Unit 115."

"Go ahead."

"What is your location?"

"I'm ditched at Blue Bell Lane and I'm about to hike back to the precinct."

"I'll call Shelby County for assistance ... Hoover PD to SCSD dispatcher."

"Roger, HPD."

"Do you have a car that can get to Inverness Corners? We have what sounded like a series of explosions. We don't have a unit capable of getting to that location."

"Unit 39 is at Highway 119 and Highway 280. I'll check and see if those officers can answer the call."

"Unit 39 will take it. But be advised the road conditions are treacherous."

"Roger — and thank you."

Shelby County Sheriff's Department Deputies Emmanuel Ruiz and Tim Barber rolled toward Bruno's supermarket in the Inverness Corners Shopping Center. When they arrived they saw faces pressed against the glass in the front of the building. Once inside, they were rushed by frightened men and women.

"Hey, let's get a grip here," Ruiz said. "We aren't the enemy. We're your friends."

"This is the end of the fucking world, my friend," said John Noel, who had just entered the food store when the most recent round of blasts occurred.

"Pardon me," Barber said.

"It's written in *The Bible* that there will be strange sights and sounds in the sky before the rapture starts," Noel said. "By God, that's what we've seen and heard."

"Okay, well ..."

"Listen to the bastard," Susan Arenberg said, her voice animated. She had been there for several hours, eating complimentary ice cream and afraid to go home. "That dumb son of a bitch has this figured out."

The telephone at Alabama Power Company in the heart of Birmingham was ringing incessantly. There were emergency calls that needed attention as soon as possible. Also, there were delirious calls that needed to be treated for what they were.

At the golf practice facility, Carl McGraw, Mark Cates, Sam Mills, Ed Bass, Ben Bobo and Fred Long ate honey buns and drank coffee as they kept wary eyes on Valleydale Road. They dusted ice from their snowsuits. A couple took a few shots of Wild Turkey 101.

"I don't want anything to drink," Bobo said. "I've learned my lesson."

The other four men looked at Cates, who said nothing.

Law enforcement agencies were trying to deal with active

switchboards, with most calls coming after the five blasts were heard in the Inverness Corners area. Lieutenant Bill Grimme of the Shelby County Fire Department on Valleydale Road received one from Captain Simon Williams of the Shelby County Sheriff's Department in Pelham that he did not want to handle.

"Alabama Power called to see if you would be willing to dispatch a fire engine to Inverness Corners," Williams said to the man in charge of the station house about two miles down Valleydale Road from where the bank robbers were in hiding.

"Do you want to give me that shit again?" Grimme said.

"Can you take a fire engine to Inverness Corners?"

"Do you have a point?"

"We think there have been some unusual sounds in that area. With bank branches so prevalent, well, you know there could ..."

"I know where the bank branches are," Grimme said. "What I'm interested in is smoke."

"Pardon me."

"If you've got smoke, you've got a fire. If you don't have smoke, you've got a bunch of crazy yokels with wild thoughts in their heads."

"Bill, this is an Alabama Power request."

"Well, grab my nuts and hang on," Grimme said. "It's moving toward five o'clock on the most miserable morning we've had in several years and I'm supposed to jump like I've got dynamite stuck up my butt."

Grimme paused for a few seconds.

Then he continued: "Fine, I'll send both engines up there, Six and Eight, and they can drive around that Bruno's food store and entertain all of those maniacal people. Maybe we can make this a damn Christmas Day parade that got under way a little late. Do any of you know where we can find Santa Claus and Rudolph?"

"Bill, I really appreciate this," Williams said.

"Oh, Simon, you're all wet," Grimme said. "I'm delighted to send out eight men on a night like this. Hell, maybe they can bring some doughnuts back to the fire station and we can have a feast."

The men who designed The Snowmen Project perked up when they heard sirens in the distance. They were at full attention as they watched Fire Engine Six and Fire Engine Eight roll past the golf practice facility.

"Exactly what did we leave at those bank branches?" McGraw said.

"A lot of rubble and some wires," Cates said.

"Plus a lot of effort," Bass said.

One of the men, Bobo, was out of the norm quiet. The sedatives and vodka were at work, but not as much as a dose of humility.

When the firemen arrived at Bruno's they were greeted with cheers from the customers inside the supermarket. They talked a few minutes with the manager, Harvey Bolton, who told them he had been spooked by the blasts but did not think there was much to them. He offered them coffee, which they gladly accepted and drank as they took a stroll around the rear of the shopping center.

"Make a mental note that there are some relatively fresh car tracks on this road," said Fireman Tim Whacker. "We'll see where they stop after visiting with the nuts inside."

The customers were skittish, led by Noel and Arenberg, so those two were taken aside by Fireman Richard Swartz, who interrogated them for about fifteen minutes.

They told Swartz they had been in the store for several hours. They said the blasts sounded like cannons being fired, not thunder. They said they could not pinpoint exactly where the noise originated, that it was like surround sound in a movie theater. They said they had seen a few vehicles in the area, other than those that parked at the supermarket, and most of those were jeeps and recreational trucks.

Fire Engine Six went to the back of the shopping center and attempted to follow the relatively fresh tracks the firemen had noticed. The men on board concluded the markings had been left by a customer who simply preferred to exit the supermarket on a back route.

After conferring by telephone with Grimme, Fire Engine Eight made a longer trip through the area, mostly for show. The big red machine stayed away from hilly areas, as commanded. It turned right on Highway 280, traveled to Highway 119, turned around, traveled to the shopping center across from Sector, turned around and returned to Valleydale

Road. The darkness created by the power outage made it almost impossible for anybody on board to see the tire tracks in the SportPlex fitness center parking lot and the mostly covered tire tracks in the Food World parking lot.

The firemen went back inside Bruno's and, as commanded, picked up several bags of tasty pastries and a few other items before making the cold trek back to the fire station.

At the golf practice facility, three police band radios were being used, all set on different channels.

On Channel 11 they heard:

"I'm going to transport this injured man in my patrol car, if possible."

"Roger, Unit 145. Do you have chains in place?"

"That's an affirmative, although they aren't helping much on inclines."

"Be aware of the liability involved in transporting an injured citizen."

"Roger."

"What's your destination?"

"Brookwood Medical Center."

"Give me a minute, Unit 145."

There was static.

"Do you copy, Unit 145?"

"Roger."

"Stop at Fire Station 44 on Highway 280. Paramedics are inside and will attempt to assist you."

"Roger."

"Where's that fire station," Long said.

"That's the one on Highway 280 toward downtown," Bass said. "It's near the river."

On Channel 36 they heard:

"Unit 178 to SCSD."

"Go ahead, 178."

"I'm in the Pelham area, at 119 and 31. Be advised the snow is turning to hard ice. I'm requesting permission to take a long break at the Holiday Inn Express."

"That's a 10-4. Keep your portable radio with you."

"Roger."

"All SCSD units should be advised that driving is becoming more dangerous by the minute."

"Let's start getting ready to roll," McGraw said. "We don't have long before daylight."

"Let's go over our departure plans one more time," Cates said. On Channel 23 they heard a conversation that featured Williams of the Shelby County Sheriff's Department and Grimme of the Shelby County Fire Department:

"Again, Bill, I appreciate you letting your guys take a look at Inverness Corners," Williams said. "I realize the request was ..."

"Let's see smoke before we go back up there," Grimme said.

"That's fair enough.

"Like I said, all we've got are a set of tire tracks in the snow and some crazed people."

"What's your best guess on the racket they heard?" Williams said.

"Power pole transformers exploding in the cold," Grimme said. "It went dark at about the same time the blasts were heard."

"We'll stay in touch," Williams said.

"I'll be taking a needed nap."

Noel thought he needed to do the same thing, so he decided to leave Bruno's supermarket and attempt to make a drive to his house six blocks away on Inverness Point Drive. He stood in the checkout line and became impatient as Carla Wilbanks tried to repair a faulty cash register.

"Get a move on it," Noel said. "I'm ready to get out of here."

"I'm trying, sir," Wilbanks said. "I'm afraid the power generators are running low."

After five minutes, with the store manger standing beside him, Noel said, "Take a fucking screwdriver and open that damn thing. I'm ready to get out of here and I want the change coming to me."

"Please calm down," Bolton said.

"Where did you find this incompetent bitch?" Noel said.

"That's enough of that," Bolton said. "Take your money and your bread and milk and go home."

Noel did that. He walked to his car in the parking lot, scraped snow and ice off of the windshield and drove away.

Bolton faced another crisis inside the store. Wilbanks was crying at the end of a long night of tension. The cursing she had heard finally put her over the edge.

"You can take this store and shove it up your ass," Wilbanks said, causing Bolton to flinch. "I'm out of here, too."

"Just go to my office and take a long break," Bolton said. "We'll talk about your outburst next week."

Wilbanks ran toward the back of the food store.

At the golf practice facility, the bank robbers were preparing for the final stage of their heist, at least as it pertained to Inverness Corners. Their first order of business involved deciding whether Team Brown should park its Pathfinder at the SportPlex fitness center adjacent to Central or behind the food store.

"I'm not going to haul duffle bags full of money from the bank to the workout place," Cates said.

"I don't know another way to soften your risk," McGraw said.

"It'd help if my damn partner could walk straight," Cates said.

"Maybe we need to change the lineup," McGraw said.

"Hell no," Long said. "We're doing fine like we are. All we've got to do is hold it together."

"I'm okay," Bobo said as he looked toward Cates. "Mark, I might be a little on edge, but I won't let you down."

Cates ignored the statement. Then, after a period of silence, he said,

"I'll drive into the Food World shopping center at the entrance most distant from Bruno's. We'll park beside that damn dumpster and do our work at Central on foot."

"That's a load to haul," McGraw said.

"Let's hope so," Cates said. "If not, at least that'll allow us to shuffle our feet in the muck and take the boot prints out of play."

"I forgot we're supposed to be doing that," Bass said. "We'll do some backtracking at Patriot and American."

"Thanks for the reminder, partner," McGraw said to Cates, who needed to hear a compliment.

"We're on a hot seat, but we'll be okay," Cates said. "Ben and I will go in without any money and come out with a load."

"Don't use lights when you go in," Long said. "But be sure they're on when you come out."

CHAPTER TWELVE

Carl McGraw used a powerful flashlight to read his watch and said, "Gentlemen, it's a quarter until five."

"My, how time can fly when you're having the time of your life," Mark Cates said.

"So let's go over a few things," McGraw said.

McGraw reviewed the plans they had made.

Team Green, McGraw and Fred Long, and Team Cream, Ed Bass and Sam Mills, would leave the golf practice facility before Team Brown, Cates and Ben Bobo. The first group would travel down the boulevard that ran beside Inverness Country Club en route to Sector and First Columbus, where vaults full of money were waiting. The second group would travel down Valleydale Road to Highway 280, turn right and continue to Patriot and American.

If the coast looked clear, so to speak, both in the area of the Hoover Police Department around the block and the area of the Bruno's supermarket up the road, Team Brown would be notified and start its trip to the Food World shopping center in which Central was located.

"Snow is beautiful is what you'll hear," Bass said.

After looting the vault at Central, Team Brown would attempt to make it back to the golf practice facility to wait until Team Green and Team Cream completed their work.

"We've heard Alabama Power say it'll start dispatching service trucks just after dawn," McGraw said.

"That means we've got to get a move on it at those bank branches."

"What Carl is saying is don't get greedy," Mills said. "Remember, most vaults have small areas near the front for teller cash. Don't be fooled by that. Go for the big stuff in the second room."

"That second room should be open, given the blasts we had," Cates said. "If not, a little work with a torch will do the trick."

"Beware of surveillance cameras inside the vaults," Bass said. "You can spray them if you want. But the most important thing is the masks stay on. Obviously, the gloves do, too."

"What about bills that have dye on them?" Bobo said. "That's no problem," Long said. "We'll be dumping these damn suits as soon as possible."

"Let's talk about our exit from town," Long said.

They agreed they should leave at intervals not far apart so they could stay in contact by walkie-talkie.

Team Green would depart by way of Valleydale Road, after going through Inverness Estates, until it reached Interstate 65. Then McGraw and Long would go north until they reached Nashville.

"You've got I-459 as a backup route in case something goes wrong," Bass said. "You can take it to I-65 by turning left."

McGraw nodded.

Team Cream would depart by way of Highway 280, going east until it reached Highway 119. Bass and Mills would turn right and go south until they reached Interstate 65.

"That's our only way out without coming back by that damn Bruno's," Mills said.

Team Brown would depart by way of Valleydale Road. Cates and Bobo would use Interstate 65, too, despite some misgivings about going through downtown Birmingham.

"Can't we go up I-20 to Atlanta? Cates said.

"No way, not with this storm traveling that route," Long said. "They'll have a foot of snow in Atlanta. The forecast is for six inches max in Nashville."

They discussed the trash they would have until depositing it in an out of the way place.

"We've got to make sure we don't leave anything incriminating inside those banks," McGraw said.

"Basically, the junk should go where it can't be found," Cates said as he used an oversized red bandanna to wipe sweat from his face.

"Under water, under bushes and under ground, that's where the garbage should go," Long said.

"Or in the bottom of a garbage bin," Mills said. The men grew pensive. Nobody said anything for a couple of minutes.

"Let's go for it," McGraw said.

"Yeah," Long said. "It's every man for himself until we meet at the Maxwell House Hotel."

The six men attempting to complete the most trying phase of The Snowman Project were moving toward their recreational vehicles when an interesting radio transmission took place between the Shelby County Fire Department on Valleydale Road and the Hoover Police Department precinct near Bruno's supermarket:

"HPD should be advised a resident in Inverness Estates has called the Birmingham Police Department to report a steady stream of traffic along the boulevard connecting Valleydale Road and Highway 280," said the SCFD dispatcher.

"Thank you, SCFD. We've noticed some of that, mainly customers trying to get to and from the supermarket."

"Roger, HPD. This was an insomnia case, no doubt, who said there has been a four-wheel drive vehicle of some type on the road with an emergency flashing light on top."

"Why would that person call BPD when we're right down the road from the residence?"

"You got me, HPD. Nor do I know why BPD would call the fire department."

"Roger, SCFD. Well, we've got a few cruisers who have been in and out of the precinct on false alarms. They haven't reported anything like what you just described."

"Roger, HPD."

"Do you have a name and a telephone number for the resident who telephoned BPD? Maybe we can get some more information."

"That's a negative, HPD. I would guess BPD would have the name and could give it to you."

"Roger. What's your best guess on this, given the fury of activity we've had at Bruno's?"

"My guess is more of the same, a panic attack."

"Roger, SCFD. We'll see what we can turn up to the contrary."

CHAPTER THIRTEEN

Sam Mills and Ed Bass wanted to laugh when they observed the green Pathfinder being driven by Carl McGraw slide out of control as he attempted to make a left turn off Valleydale Road onto the boulevard he and Fred Long planned to follow on their way to Sector Bank. But when the vehicle came to rest with its front wheels in a ditch, they thought the better of it. Also, they recalled, a Hoover Police Department precinct was within two blocks.

"Damn, I don't remember discussing anything like this," Long said he attempted to calm down McGraw, who was pounding the steering wheel.

"I'm experienced driving in snow," McGraw said. "I should have known better."

"Obviously," Long said. "But at least we've got help."

Mills and Bass had made a cautious stop on Valleydale Road. They backed up the cream Pathfinder, grabbed a flashlight and hurried to help Team Green.

"Team Cream to Team Brown," Bass said after surveying the damage to the vehicle and finding none.

"Team Brown," Bobo said.

"We've had a delay, a truck in a ditch. But stay put and don't worry. We'll get back to you."

"10-4."

Bass, Mills and Long pushed the Pathfinder out of the ditch, at one point literally shoving it sideways on the slick snow topped by ice.

"Let's get rolling," McGraw said after he took another look at the truck and did not see anything broken.

At the golf practice facility, Cates attempted to make peace with Bobo after almost knocking him unconscious a little earlier.

"That's fine," Bobo said after hearing an apology. "I had it coming."

"How bad is it?"

"Well, chances are better than not that I've got a nose broken in a couple of places."

"How do you feel otherwise?" Cates said.

"Totally sober and ready to work."

"Good. It won't be long before you can drink all the vodka you want — and I might join you."

Mills and Bass watched Team Green until it vanished from sight, then moved along Valleydale Road to Highway 280. They were pleasantly surprised to find there was not anybody outside Bruno's supermarket.

"What a wonderful sight," Bass said.

"Yeah, for now," Mills said. "When daylight arrives and people call and find out that food store is open, well, we better look out."

Bass had a walkie-talking in hand.

"Team Cream to Team Brown."

"10-4."

"Snow is beautiful — absolutely beautiful."

Team Brown moved into action. The Pathfinder rolled out of the golf practice facility, turned left on Valleydale Road and continued toward the heart of Inverness Corners. As Cates and Bobo reached the bottom of a small hill, with an elementary school on the right, they were stunned when they saw another vehicle topping the large hill in front of them.

The headlights made it difficult to see, so Cates stopped the Pathfinder and let the other vehicle come past. He rolled down the left window so he could get a better a view and exhaled powerfully when he realized it was a pickup truck and not a police cruiser.

A couple of minutes later, Cates drove the Pathfinder through the first entrance into the Food World shopping center. He steered it carefully along what he perceived to be a road covered with thick snow until, at last, he and Long were behind Mayfield's Cleaners.

"Well, our favorite dumpster is up ahead," Cates said.

"Don't remind me," Bobo said. "Let's just grab a few duffle bags and go see what we've got."

"I'll get the police band radio, too," Cates said. "See if you can carry the torch."

"I'm with you, step for step.

At Sector, McGraw and Long were as excited as children in a toy shop. Not only had the explosives blown open the doors to both sections of the vault, it had wiped outa motion-powered surveillance camera, which they found on the floor.

The glow of two flashlights brought even better news.

"This place is loaded with cash," Long said as he and McGraw began filling duffle bags.

About two miles away, Bass and Mills were using torches to gain access to the rear section of the vault at Patriot. They had looked inside and were delighted by the large stacks of bills they saw. They had overcome the urge to check out the contents of safety deposit boxes that had been blown open, although the temptation was strong because they were stepping on gold necklaces, old watches and diamond rings.

"Don't mess with those bags of rolled coins," Mills said. "They'll be too heavy for us and the truck."

Cates and McGraw had put two duffle bags of cash in the Pathfinder sitting beside the dumpster near Central. When they went back into the bank to get more, they heard interesting chatter on the police band radio that made them slow down for a couple of minutes:

"Are the suspects still on the premises," a police officer said to a dispatcher at the Homewood Police Department.

"We think they fled because there isn't a vehicle there," said the dispatcher.

"You're sure somebody saw a truck in the area?"

"That's an affirmative," said the dispatcher. "A driver in one truck met another truck on the road."

"Give me that address again."

"It's 742 Live Oak Road."

"Wow, I'm sweating and my ass is as tight as a drum," Cates said as he struggled to find something to use while wiping his face.

"Let's finish up, clean up and get moving," Bobo said.

Although it was overcast, to say the least, the sky was starting to lighten a bit. The sun was not ready to improve visibility for a metropolitan area that had survived a dark and dreary night, but daybreak was not far away.

At Bruno's supermarket, Susan Arenberg was getting on the nerves of everybody in building, including store manager Harvey Bolton. She was more composed than she had been during most of the night, but every time a shopper walked through the entrance she felt compelled to ask them about the thunderous blasts she and several other people had heard about an hour earlier.

"I'm still not sure it wasn't aliens," Arenberg said to David Craig, a married man who was flirting with Sandy Edwards, a single woman, as they stood near a checkout line.

"Well, they're gone now," Craig said in an effort to get rid of the pesky woman.

"It's still dark outside," Arenberg said.

"You'll see the light soon enough," Craig said.

Across the street, Cates and Bobo were carrying and dragging debris from the bank building to the brown Pathfinder parked behind Food World. They were satisfied they had not left evidence behind and were getting ready to stash what they could in a dumpster.

"Well, partner, if you've got a hangover you're about to throw up," Cates said.

"I already feel like doing that," Bobo said.

The two men reached inside the dumpster and rearranged all manner of trash. They had to pull some of the garbage out so they could bury their rubbish under it. The odor was sickening, for sure, and the bin was full when they finished.

"Damn, we didn't leave room for this brown cover we've got on the Pathfinder," Bobo said.

"We'll find some place else for that and the rest of the stuff we need to discard," Cates said.

A major disappointment surfaced at Unit Two, First Columbus, where McGraw and Long found only a smattering of cash in the vault.

"Damn, we blew apart this building for peanuts," Long said.

"That's a good way of putting it," McGraw said. "The money in here could be carried out in a paper sack."

"Well, let's start cleaning up both joints," Long said.

A bigger problem had developed at Patriot. When Bass and Mills started their trek across the street to American, they discovered a large tree limb had fallen across the entrance to the bank branch they had looted and left relatively spotless.

"It's too big to move by hand and I don't think the Pathfinder can get over it," Mills said.

They walked across the parking lot and studied the terrain leading to Highway 280. It had a significant slope. Obviously, it was slick.

"That's the best way out," Bass said.

"We better get it done before daylight," Mills said. "If somebody sees us tearing up the landscape, it'll be impossible to explain."

Team Black, the former Team Brown, was attempting to get out of the Food World shopping center without being seen. The Pathfinder was behind the Mayfield's Cleaners when Cates and Bobo contemplated walking to the edge of Valleydale Road and taking a look.

"I don't think that'll help our chances," Bobo said. "Let's just turn on the flashing yellow light and look like we're supposed to be here."

Craig had been successful flirting with Edwards inside the Bruno's supermarket. He had told her he would be more than happy to go to her apartment and show her how to start a fire. They were standing in the parking lot when Team Black emerged from the shopping center across the street.

"Well, it looks like somebody finally got an emergency crew on the road," Craig said as he pointed toward the Pathfinder as it was turning right onto Valleydale Road.

"So why didn't it come through here, too?" Edwards said as they watched Cates and Bobo disappear from their sight.

"That's a good question, but one for another day," Craig said. "Let's go to your place and let me teach you how to use a fireplace."

Craig and Edwards began cleaning the snow and ice off of their windshields.

A few blocks away, at Patriot, Mills was attempting to get the Pathfinder out of a parking lot the hard way. He and Bass had tried the slope leading to Highway 280, but could not get enough traction to top it. So in the interest of saving time his partner had taken three duffle bags across the street, to American, which left him trying to drive the truck through a wide flower bed with bushes and trees that separated the bank branch from a side street.

Mills had little room to spare and the falling snow made it difficult for him to see. He was annoyed when he had to stop trying and respond to a walkie-talkie transmission.

"Team Green to Team Brown and Team Cream."

"10-4. Team Brown is Team Black."

"10-4, this is Team Cream."

"Team Green is en route to a golf game on a cold morning."

"Team Black is playing golf."

"Team Cream is trying to get a damn Pathfinder out of a parking lot blocked by a tree limb."

"Come again, Team Cream."

"Part of Team Cream is working at Unit Six and I'm trying to get this truck blocked by a tree limb out of here."

"10-4 — and call for help if nothing happens soon."

"10-4."

As Bass filled three duffle bags with cash at American and started piling up debris and dancing across the floor in an effort to distort boot prints, Mills struggled with the Pathfinder. He was wedged between two bushes and had a tree limb precariously close to the top of the truck. The traction was somewhat better because of pine straw in the flower bed, but he was unable to get enough speed to drive out. Then, to his alarm, he saw a vehicle coming toward him on the side street.

"Shit," Mills said, quickly thinking about the duffle bags full of money behind him and wondering if he had covered them.

Mills got out of the Pathfinder as the other vehicle, a Ford Bronco, stopped on the street. He saw a man who appeared to be in his early fifties. He turned on the yellow flashing light so it would illuminate the Fargo Security System signs stuck on the doors of the truck.

"Hello, sir," Mills said.

"Good morning. It looks like you've got a mess."

"Yes sir, a tree limb at the entrance."

The man looked that way, saw the limb and shook his head.

"So what brings you out on such a miserable morning?" Mills said.

"Breakfast," the man said. "The wife thinks we need some pancakes, sausage and eggs."

"Bruno's is open," Mills said.

"That's where I'm going after I yank you out of here," the man said.

Mills was hoping he would not hear the sound of the walkie-talkie, at least until after the man departed.

"I think I've about got it," Mills said. "If not, I'll call ..."

"What are you doing up here?" the man said, suddenly acting a little skeptical and forceful.

"Our security company has been making rounds all night," Mills said. "It has been a rough shift, to say the least, and I'm about to call it quits and go home."

"I'll be glad to help you get out if you have a ..."

"Team Green to Team Cream."

"Excuse me," Mills said as he walked to the door of the Pathfinder and opened it. He grabbed the walkie-talkie as quickly as he could.

"Roger, Team Cream."

"Do you need assistance?"

"Let me get back to you. I've got a nice man trying to help. But I think I can make it without him."

"Roger, Team Cream. Call if you need us."

"10-4."

"I appreciate your offer, sir, but you can go do your shopping unless you want to stand around in this snow and ice."

"I think I'll go get groceries." The close call made Mills more concerned and more determined. After contacting Team Green and Team Black and giving them an improved status report, he discovered an innovative way to produce traction. It was not long before he bounced the Pathfinder over a curb and into the street.

"How's my partner doing?" Mills said as he entered the American branch across the street.

Bass jumped, then said, "Damn, you scared the shit out of me."

"Sorry, but you don't know the meaning of the word."

"Let's get loaded and get rid of some of our junk in those dumpsters down the street," Bass said.

As they worked, Mills told Bass what he had experienced.

"I guess that explains the whiskey on your breath," Bass said.

"That's a partial explanation," Mills said.

At Bruno's supermarket, another interesting conversation was developing.

Craig and Edwards had decided not to have a fling, or at least to delay it, and they were back inside the food store talking with the manager and Arenberg. As they discussed the mysterious appearance of the vehicle they had seen leaving the shopping center across the street, the man who had offered to help Mills get his Pathfinder unstuck stood at a distance and eavesdropped. Finally, he walked toward the group.

"You know, I just saw a truck like that up at Patriot Bank," Andrew Carroll said. "In fact, I talked to the man driving it."

"Tell us more," Craig said.

"It seems he worked for a security company, Fargo Security Incorporated, I believe, and it was obvious he was out checking bank branches," the man said.

"Hold that thought and come with me," said Bolton, the store manager, who had suddenly become suspicious.

CHAPTER FOURTEEN

After both had experienced restless evenings because their husbands were on the road and the climate was uncharacteristically nasty, Diana McGraw and Midge Cates were up early in Louisville, Kentucky. Having spent the previous night together, they were drinking coffee at the same table that several weeks earlier had featured barbecued chicken and coconut pie. A television set on a counter in the kitchen told them the weather conditions between The Commonwealth and South Georgia were dismal, with snow mixed with ice on the ground. They worried about the safety of the men they loved.

Upstairs, snuggled in bed were children who had gone to sleep the night previous with thoughts of snowmen dancing through their heads. Their mothers had promised to let them play in the yard all day and they had formulated several hours worth of plans.

The weather channel the women were watching brought bad news, at least eight inches of snow on the ground and ice on top.

"How can you be so concerned about your husband now after being so infuriated with him last night?" Diana said after the women heard South Georgia had been hit hard.

"I slept alone," Midge said.

"Given what you've told me, that'd make me happy," Diana said as she recalled what her best friend had explained about a physical relationship between her husband and a lawyer who had moved to town.

"The son of a bitch might be sorry, but I didn't say I wanted him dead," Midge said.

"Yes you did, or something comparable," Diana said. "You wanted to cut out his nuts. To a man, that's dead."

"I'm taking back the vodka and tonic talk," Midge said.

At Bruno's supermarket in Inverness Corners, store manager Harvey Bolton was thumbing through a telephone book, frantically, and he was not finding a white pages or a yellow pages listing for Fargo Security Incorporated or any other company of that type that started with the letter f.

"I told you there was a skunk in the closet," Susan Arenberg said. "We've got something happening out there that isn't nice and I still think it's aliens."

"Miss Arenberg, why don't you sample our chocolate mint banana nut ice cream?" Bolton said.

"I'm allergic to nuts," Arenberg said.

Rather than argue with his pest, Bolton placed a telephone call to the Hoover Police Department.

Meanwhile ...

"Team Cream to Team Black and Team Green."

"10-4, this is Team Black."

"10-4, this is Team Green."

"I think it's time to leave," Sam Mills said. "I didn't like the way that motorist reacted to me being stuck at Unit Five."

"Be advised Team Green has become Team Gray."

"Okay, and Team Cream is now Team Purple. But you and Team Black should consider starting your departure."

"What's your situation?" Carl McGraw said.

"We've got an eye on a departure down Highway 119 — the sooner the better," Mills said.

Bolton was on the telephone with Carl Stover, a new watch commander at the Hoover Police Department precinct across the street from the Inverness Country Club golf course.

"Captain Stover, I don't want to be an alarmist but ...," Bolton said.

"It's Sergeant Stover, not Captain Stover, and I want to know who I'm talking to," Stover said.

"I'm sorry, sir. I'm a little excited. This is Harvey Bolton, the manager of the Bruno's store up the street."

"Nice to meet you."

"Sir, we've got reason to believe there's something unusual going on at bank branches in the area."

Stover collected his thoughts. He asked Bolton if the situation had anything to do with blasts heard in the middle of the night. He was told that might be the case.

"I've read the reports," Stover said.

"This might be something new," Bolton said as Arenberg, David Craig, Sandy Edwards and Andrew Carroll stood beside him and listened.

"We've seen a vehicle come out of the place across the street, where there's a Central bank branch, and one of our patrons has seen a man at the Patriot bank branch down the street."

"That is a new development," Stover said.

"Sir, can you send a car up here? Bolton said.

"We'll see, Mr. Bolton. I'm afraid we'll need to get assistance from the fire department since there's so much snow and ice."

Immediately, Stover went to work. He checked with his dispatcher and discovered there were two mobile units available. Already, he knew the two fire trucks from the shared precinct were answering a five-alarm call at an apartment complex in Pelham. Then he did what he dreaded the most, placed a telephone call to Lieutenant Bill Grimme at the Shelby County Fire Department on Valleydale Road.

"We really need to get the hell out of this place," Fred Long said as he sat idly with three men at a golf practice facility.

"Let's make sure the cops aren't getting uneasy," Mark Cates said. "We've digested a lot in the last half of an hour."

"We've got to establish a deadline for departure, good or bad," Ben Bobo said. "It won't be long before people can see us down here."

"Team Purple to Team Gray and Team Black," Ed Bass said into the walkie-talkie.

"This is Team Black," Cates said.

"This is Team Gray," Carl McGraw said.

"I'm having bad vibes," Bass said. "You guys need to hit the road and we're ready to go, too."

Grimme was hot at the SCFD.

"You bastards want me to send out another truck when I don't have one to offer," Grimme said to Stover. "I've got one delivering a baby in Sunny Meadows. I've got one at that damn inferno in Pelham."

"We can't check those banks with a police cruiser," Stover said. "In fact, from what I've heard we'll need a truck to get a tree out of the way at Patriot."

"When we get one back in the station, we'll come up your way," Grimme said. "Engine Six said the newly born child is doing good and they might be back within minutes."

"What's your ETA?" Stover said.

"Sergeant Stover, I can't give you an ETA. I'm not a damn obstetrician."

Diana and Midge had put aside talk about a possible affair and were contemplating a call to the Georgia State Highway Department to check on their husbands. The children were coming downstairs, dressed and ready to play. The wives were trying to put off the inevitable.

"I'm afraid they're stuck on the side of the road freezing to death," Midge said.

"Don't get panicky," Diana said. "There are six of them down there. I'm sure one or two are smart enough to determine how they should deal with the elements."

"What's that town they're near?"

"Brunswick."

"Then let's at least call the police department there."

"No, Midge. I can't imagine how our extremely proud men would react if we did that."

The macho men, as well as four other bank robbers, were changing clothes. The bulky snow suits were coming off and conventional deer hunting apparel was going on. The heavy stuff was packed in garbage bags for disposal. The gloves and boots remained intact.

The Pathfinders were rearranged, too, with deer hunting equipment piled on top of duffle bags full of cash and other items the men did not want anybody to see. Shotguns and rifles were placed in racks.

"Team Gray and Team Black to Team Purple," McGraw said.

"10-4," Bass said.

"Let's roll."

"We're going out 119 to I-65," Bass said.

"We're going out 280 to I-459 and on to I-65," McGraw said. "Team Black is going out Valleydale Road to I-65."

"10-4 — and we'll see you in Nashville," Bass said.

Bass and Mills found the going easy as they drove through a corporate park to Highway 280 and turned right to get to Highway 119. They made one stop en route, at two dumpsters, where they carefully disposed of a few unneeded items.

McGraw and Fred Long turned left on the boulevard that ran past Inverness Country Club. They thought they saw two police officers standing in front of the combination fire station and Hoover Police Department. Further along the road they saw a pond at a corporate park. They dumped their snowsuits and rolled toward Highway 280, where they turned left and continued en route to Interstate 459.

A police cruiser with Eddie Mangrum and John Curry in it pulled out of the HPD precinct.

"There are some fresh tire tracks," Mangrum said as he pointed at the ruts left by the gray Pathfinder. "Maybe we should follow them."

"No, let's get to the supermarket," Curry said. "We need to find out exactly what we're looking for."

Cates and Bobo were moving along Valleydale Road, with Interstate 65 their destination, when they noticed something interesting at Fire Station 22. Fire Engine Six was rolling out as they were rolling past. They breathed a sigh of relief when they saw the red truck turning right.

"Team Black to Team Gray and Team Purple," Bobo said.

"10-4."

"10-4."

"They're sending a fire engine in the direction of Inverness Corners," Bobo said.

"Did they see you?" McGraw said.

"They waved as we went by," Bobo said. "We're not hard to miss now that daylight has arrived."

"Do you have the signs and light on your truck?" Bass said.

"Negative."

"That's good — and keep moving."

The police officers were conducting interviews at Bruno's supermarket, focusing on sports utility vehicles.

"I'd say the one I saw at Patriot was light colored," Carroll said. "In fact, I know it was by the way the yellow light reflected on it."

"What color would you guess?" Curry said.

"White or beige," Carroll said. "It could've been yellow."

"The one I saw was darker," Craig said. "In fact, I'd bet it was charcoal or navy."

The police officers thanked the customers for their assistance and told the store manager to tell the firemen to wait for them. They left the shopping center and drove to Patriot Bank, where they found the tree limb in their way.

"Damn," Curry said. "If the snow can knock down a monster like that, I can't imagine how messy the rest of this city is this morning."

The folks at Alabama Power were attempting to find out. They placed a telephone call to the Alabama Air National Guard Unit at Birmingham International Airport. Tom Scarbrough, the emergency maintenance director, was connected to Airman Kurt Willoughby, who had been roused from his bed.

"Are you in charge this morning?" Scarbrough said.

"Yes sir, I am," Willoughby said.

"We're requesting the Air National Guard put a couple of helicopters in the air so we can better tell what type problems we have," Scarbrough said. "That way we can be more efficient taking care of them."

"I'd like for you to repeat that," Willoughby said.

"We'd like to borrow a couple of helicopters so we can ..."

"That's what I thought you said."

"Is that possible?"

"Hell no, that's not possible," Willoughby said. "Do you think I'm a fucking idiot?"

"Well, sir, we've got thousands of people out there ..."

"Listen to me," Willoughby said. "I'm the best damn chopper pilot in this state. But I'm not going to take a bird with frozen rotors up into a dense system with the wind blowing at twenty knots."

"I'm sorry to have bothered you," Scarbrough said.

"Who authorized this call?" Willoughby said.

"Well, it was an Alabama Power decision."

"Get the damn governor to call next time. That's who we work for during situations like this."

Although the conditions were as bad as Willoughby said, particularly in the air, a fair amount of traffic was appearing on streets in Jefferson County, Birmingham and Shelby County. Citizens had awakened to find a rare winter dreamland, only this one during early spring, and those who had four-wheel vehicles were anxious to drive around for looks.

There was a wide assortment of jeeps, trucks and sports utility vehicles to be found, including three with Kentucky license plates that were making good progress in an effort to get out of the area. Team Black was out front, having already moved through downtown Birmingham. Team Gray trailed by five minutes. Team Purple was seven minutes behind.

"Team Black to Team Gray and Team Purple," Bobo said.

"10-4."

"10-4."

"Be advised that a lot of utility trucks and other vehicles are on the streets in the downtown area."

"We just came past two from Alabama Power," Long said.

"When do we change colors?" Bass said.

"Somewhere between Cullman and Huntsville."

"10-4."

"10-4."

"Stay on top of the police band radios," Long said.

Fire Engine Six started its trek around the Food World Shopping Center. On board were Sam Graddy, Richard Getz, Ed Brinkley and Tim Crawford. Following behind it was Hoover Police Department Unit 46. A large crowd had come out of the Bruno's supermarket to observe the parade and some people wanted to follow it on foot.

The big red truck moved around the Mayfield's Cleaners and stopped at every door along the service road in the back of the shopping center. The firemen checked each to make sure it was secure. The tire tracks they saw let them know somebody had traveled that route at some point during the night.

Near the end of the row of businesses, Fire Engine Six approached the dumpster at which Cates and Bobo had spent a multitude of anxious minutes. In fact, it was the numerous tire tracks and footprints they left that prompted two fireman to get a little excited.

"Slow down," Getz said. "This area has been trampled a little."

"I see what you do," Brinkley said. "It looks like somebody had a barn dance out here."

"Or else a couple of teenagers found an extremely out of the way place to park," Graddy said.

"Yeah, I can hear that pitch now," Crawford said. "Baby, let's go sit by a giant garbage can and act like a couple of rabbits in heat."

The other men laughed.

Then one of the firemen noticed something important. "Am I wrong or does this dumpster have a whole lot less snow on top of it than the others?" Getz said.

"Damn, you should have been a cop," Mangrum said.

"I think I'll stop there," Getz said. "I've got a bad feeling about what we're going to do next."

"Open the top and let's take a look," Mangrum said.

The firemen and police officers saw liquor boxes at the top of the trash pile, a common sight since the Midnight Beverage Store was the owner of the dumpster. But as they started pulling out cardboard, they began noticing an assortment of interesting items. They saw wire that appeared to be nondescript. They saw a couple of honey bun wrappers. They saw of couple of throwaway cups, one with a few drops of coffee still in it.

"That hasn't been there long," Curry said.

"Let's keep digging," Mangrum said.

Then they saw a cardboard box with writing on it that indicated it had at one time contained blasting caps.

"Son of a bitch — and be careful with that box," Mangrum said. "We don't need to destroy fingerprints."

"Wire and blasting caps adds up to explosives," Graddy said.

Curry hustled to the police cruiser, grabbed the radio microphone and said, "Unit 46 to HPD, Inverness."

"Go ahead, Unit 46," said the dispatcher.

"Hook me up with Sergeant Stover," Curry said.

"Sergeant Stover."

"Sir, be advised that we've found some wiring and blasting caps in a dumpster in the Food World shopping center. It's behind the Midnight Beverage Store."

"Have you checked those banks?"

"Negative. We wanted to make sure we didn't contaminate this evidence, if it is that."

"Leave it as is and take a look at those banks. Unit 51 will be dispatched to assist you."

Team Purple, Bass and Mills heard that transmission on the police band radio, although there was a lot of static because they were well outside downtown Birmingham.

"Did you get all of that?" Bass said.

"I got enough to know we need to keep moving."

"Team Purple to Team Gray and Team Black."

"10-4, this is Team Gray," Long said.

There was no response from Cates and Bobo.

"They found blasting caps in the dumpster at Food World."

"Damn," Long said. "What else have they found?"

"Nothing. But it's just a matter of minutes."

"10-4."

"Do you copy, Team Black?" Bass said.

"Team Black is out of your range," Long said. "We'll try to relay from this position."

"10-4."

McGraw and Long tried to reach Team Black several more times during the next two minutes.

"For all we know, they could be in the back of a police car," Long said. "Hopefully, they're being quiet if that's the case."

"I wouldn't worry about that," McGraw said. "Mark Cates can be as tough as he is sneaky."

"I'm not sure," Long said as he picked up the walkie-talkie: "Team Gray to Team Black ... We have a problem ... Team Gray to Team Black ... Do you have a problem?"

CHAPTER FIFTEEN

The four firemen and two police officers hurried to an American bank branch adjacent to the Central bank branch in the Food World shopping center. They were electrified because they sensed being the part of a major crime and being able to help solve it.

But they discovered nothing out of order at the brick building that sat nearest to Highway 280. Mystifying them more were the footprints they saw extending from that location in the direction of the SportPlex fitness center.

At the nearby Hoover Police Department precinct, Unit 51 was being dispatched and Sergeant Carl Stover was anticipating what he would have to do next.

"If this pans out like it might, we'll need to contact the FBI as soon as possible," Stover said to an associate. "But I want to find out all we can before we do that."

The crowd at Bruno's supermarket was growing restless because neither Shelby County Fire Engine Six or Hoover Police Department Unit 46 had resurfaced after going into the Food World shopping center.

"It's like the *X-Files*," Susan Arenberg said as she stood on the edge of the parking lot on Valleydale Road and gazed across the street. "If aliens want to swoop down and get you, you're history. I saw one show about a guy who ate human brains, a dude who worked at a hamburger joint."

"Damn you've got a wild thought process roaring in your head," said a male in his early twenties.

The firemen and police officers walked around American twice. They did not find evidence of foul play. Nor did they find footprints or anything else that indicated the bank branch had been visited.

But when they walked several yards to Central, they found that and much more. They rushed through the hole in the wall as soon as they saw it, without the slightest thought of danger lurking inside.

"My God in heaven, look at this mess," Fireman Sam Gaddy said as he and fellow firemen Richard Getz, Ed Brinkley and Tim Crawford and police officers Eddie Mangrum and John Curry surveyed the dismantled bank branch lobby.

There was rubble piled high, from parts of wooden desks to shattered glass to pieces of iron, at least two feet deep in spots. There were papers strewn across the room, checks, deposit slips, loan applications and a lot of other varieties.

"The people who blasted this joint must be dead or badly injured," Curry said.

"But we don't see any bodies," Mangrum said, destroying that theory offered on an impulse.

Getz saw something that interested him more. "Look at that damn vault," he said. "It's ransacked, except for a chunk of money up front."

"Normally, that cash is packed with dye, at least a portion of it," Mangrum said about the money earmarked for bank tellers to use. "These dudes, whomever, knew what they were doing."

Several miles away, Team Black, Mark Cates and Ben Bobo, Team Gray, Carl McGraw and Fred Long, and Team Purple, Ed Bass and Sam Mills, were attempting to communicate by walkie-talkie. At last, they were in sync with what had been discovered, at least the blasting caps in the dumpster, and they were attempting to make sure The Snowman Project did not get off track.

"Team Black to Team Gray and Team Purple," Cates said on the walkie-talkie.

"10-4."

"10-4."

"We're trying to find some friendly voices," Cates said.

"You should be," Long said.

"We understand," Cates said.

"You put those damn boom caps and wire in a garbage can," Long said. "What were you thinking?"

"I'm sorry."

"So, I guess you've heard," Long said.

"By way of truckers," Cates said. "Sometimes they hear news before it becomes news."

"Is there any drinking going on up that way?" Long said, after sensing the obvious.

"One of us is shooting down booze." Cates said.

"It sounds like you might be that one," Long said.

"10-damn-4."

There was a period of silence. Then Long said, "Team Gray wants to know your location — and please be sketchy."

"Fifty miles out."

"10-4 — and we aren't far behind."

"Team Purple is on your heels," Bass said.

"The big orange eye in the sky says it's close to time to change dresses," Long said.

"10-4."

"10-4."

Stover had been told what the four firemen and police officers found at Central. He rerouted Unit 51 to the Sector Bank down the street. He requested that Unit 46 and Fire Engine Six take a look at Patriot.

Then Stover contacted Lieutenant Bill Grimme at the Shelby County Fire Department on Valleydale Road.

"I'll be damned," Grimme said after being told Central had been robbed. He reasoned he would look like a fool for reacting so slowly.

"I assume it's okay for Fire Engine Six to go to Patriot," Stover said.

"Hell yes," Grimme said.

"I'll contact the FBI as soon as we confirm a hit at that location," Stover said.

"Do it by telephone," Grimme said. "Crowd control can become a major problem in that area, as if that hasn't already been the case on a smaller scale."

"We'll need help keeping gawkers out of there," Stover said.

"I'll advise the Shelby County Sheriff's Department," Grimme said.

It took the firemen quite a while to get the tree limb out of the way at Patriot. They had to use a chain saw and a couple of axes to cut it. Their labor drew the attention of four motorists, who stopped to watch them work. So, with observers on the scene the police officers decided to wait before peeking inside the bank building.

With Mangrum and Getz handling crowd control, Curry, Graddy, Brinkley and Crawford drove to the rear of the building and uncovered what they expected. The mess was not as bad as had been observed at Central, but the result was the same — an open vault that appeared pretty much empty.

Hoover Police Department Unit 51 made a similar report after taking a look at Sector Bank.

By that time four Shelby County Sheriff's Department cruisers were at the Food World shopping center, blocking the entrances to the parking lot. One was dispatched to Patriot. One was dispatched to Sector.

"What's in there, a bunch of dead people?" Arenberg said to a deputy sheriff who was experiencing her for the first time.

"No, ma'am," he said. "We've got a security situation because some water mains appear ready to explode."

"What's so bad about that?" Arenberg said.

"Ma'am, if one of those babies rips and you're standing near it, your ass will be in Helena in one minute."

Arenberg was convinced, as well as spooked, this time for another reason. She retreated to Bruno's supermarket.

Every available police officer or deputy sheriff in the area was en route to the three bank branches to help secure the areas. After two other Hoover Police Department cruisers reported breakins at American and First Columbus, some units were rerouted to those locations.

"Those crooks weren't greedy," Graddy said to Getz as the firemen boarded Fire Engine Six for the ride from Patriot to Central, where more security was needed due to an open expanse.

"They were tidy, too, at least as much as people can be while handling sophisticated explosives," Getz said. "I'm not a cop, no matter what the guys from Hoover PD might think, but I have no doubt this was the work of professionals."

"We're professionals, too, only from a more honest sector of society," Graddy said. "Otherwise, I'd have about ten grand stuck in my coat pockets."

"You're telling me you didn't take any money?" Getz said, at first shocking the other firemen with his humor.

CHAPTER SIXTEEN

Sergeant Carl Stover was nervous as he walked into the watch commander's office at the Hoover Police Department just off Valleydale Road. He lit a cigarette, dug through a desk drawer for a telephone number and started dialing. He was convinced his troopers had done all they could to secure the areas near the bank branches, with assistance from the Shelby County Sheriff's Department, and it was time for him to follow protocol he might have already violated.

"Birmingham FBI Office," said the woman on the other end of the telephone line.

"This is Carl Stover of the Hoover Police Department in Inverness. I've got five bank robberies to report."

"We'll call you back," said the woman.

Stover was stunned. He had telephoned the Federal Bureau of Investigation to report a serious crime and had been told a return call would be made.

But it did not take as long as he thought it would. The special agent who answered the telephone in downtown Birmingham quickly called FBI Special Agent in Charge Jim Wilcox at his house in Riverchase. He was asleep, as were most of the men and women from his office. Like everybody else in the area, they found driving too perilous to report to duty on such a frigid morning.

After being told he had an urgent call from the Hoover Police Department, a code red, Wilcox grabbed a notes pad and pen from a drawer beside his bed as one of the two special agents on duty in his office patched him through to Stover.

"Sir, we've got bank robberies to report at five locations near

Inverness Corners," Stover said.

"Not on a morning like this," said Wilcox, a 42-year-old veteran of sixteen years with the FBI who had a reputation of taking his business serious but always finding amusement.

"Well, there are holes in the walls and the vaults are wide open at Central, Sector, First Columbus, Patriot and American," Stover said. "You can draw your own conclusions."

"I assume this is the result of those frantic calls everybody got last night about loud blasts in the area," Wilcox said, suddenly turning more sincere.

"It looks that way, yes," Stover said.

"Are there injuries?"

"No."

"Are there other explosives ready to blow?"

"No, at least none that are apparent."

"Is the area sealed?"

"Totally."

"That's good work, Carl."

"Thank you."

Wilcox found his mind swirling, albeit less than five minutes after he had been awakened. He was trying to find out as much as he could before springing into action.

"Are there suspects?"

"None other than people who were driving a couple of sports utility vehicles last night," Stover said.

"Tell me more."

"We've interviewed customers at Bruno's supermarket who said they saw two vehicles like that, one with a Fargo Security Systems sign on it. Also, both trucks had yellow flashing lights on top."

"Did you say trucks?"

"Actually, sports utility vehicles like a Ford Explorer, a Land Cruiser, a Rodeo, a Chevrolet Blazer or, well, I guess you get the picture."

"Where were they seen?"

"One was coming out of the Food World shopping center on

Valleydale Road. One was stuck at Patriot Bank in the parking lot."

"What color were the vehicles?"

"It was difficult to tell," Stover said. "We've concluded the first one was dark, maybe black, and the second one was light, maybe white."

Wilcox was piecing together a scenario. Already he had concluded there were at least two people involved and he figured there had to be more because of the complexity of the entries into the buildings and vaults. He was more than a little pleased when his wife, Angie, appeared at his side holding a large cup of hot coffee. He acknowledged her nice gesture with a nod and a smile.

"How many explosions were there?"

"Six or eight, maybe more," Stover said.

"Those numbers don't add up," Wilcox said, thinking out loud. "We've got five entries to buildings, then five entries to vaults, unless they were able to torch the latter."

Stover sat quietly and listened. Already, he had thought about simultaneous explosions.

"What's the time frame?" Wilcox said.

"I'm guessing, but probably midnight to six. The roads in that area were passable, at least somewhat, until the clock struck twelve. Then we had daybreak about six hours later."

"Has anybody checked all of those other banks up there, Allied, First National and..."

"That's an affirmative. We've got five that were hit. They hit a Central and left alone an American beside it. They hit a Patriot and hit an American across the street from it. Also, they hit the Sector and First Columbus just down Highway 280."

"Can we get there by car?" Wilcox said.

"Yes," Stover said. "But drive carefully and take the flat routes."

"We'll be there as soon as possible," Wilcox said. "Keep the area secure. Don't touch anything. Get everybody you can spare into that area. By all means, Sergeant Stover, make sure they keep their hands in their pockets, if you know what I mean."

"I understand."

"What have we missed?" Wilcox said.

Stover thought for a few seconds, then said, "Oh, that man who saw the vehicle stuck at Patriot, Andrew Carroll, said he talked to the guy, tried to offer him help."

"And ..."

"Well, he can't make an identification because he said all he could see of the guy was part of his eyes, his nose and his mouth. He said he was dressed like an oversized mummy or a humongous snowman."

"What about the voice?" Wilcox said.

"It was southern without a heavy drawl," Stover said. "He wasn't from up north, for sure."

But the bank robbers were moving in that direction and the Pathfinders were not the same colors as they were when they left Inverness Corners. All of the covers had been changed between Cullman and Huntsville and the old ones, as well as a few other items, were sinking in the quickly flowing Tennessee River near Decatur.

Carl McGraw and Fred Long were riding in an orange vehicle and were near the Tennessee State Line.

Mark Cates and Ben Bobo had already crossed that boundary and were riding in a blue vehicle.

Sam Mills and Ed Bass has just tossed debris over the side of an arching long bridge on Interstate 65 and were riding in a crimson vehicle.

"Team Orange to Team Blue," Long said into a walkie-talkie.

"This is Team Blue," Bobo said.

"How does it look up ahead?"

"The snow and ice are thinning a bit. The commercial trucks have cut us a nice path."

"10-4 — and do you copy Team Crimson?"

"10-4 — and the weather forecast we just heard said there is even less snow on the ground to the north."

"But there's more ice," Bobo said.

Wilcox patched himself into the telephone system and computer network at FBI headquarters. Even with sketchy information in hand, he issued a code red, number three alarm, alerting special agents in the city and instructing them to report to Inverness Corners as soon as possible. He received quick positive responses from three.

Wilcox instructed a fellow special agent to send out a code red, number three alert through a computer system linking Birmingham to FBI headquarters in Tennessee, Georgia, Mississippi and Florida. He telephoned Birmingham International Airport to see if helicopters were available to assist in the combing of the area. He made similar calls to airports in Atlanta, Tuscaloosa, Montgomery, Huntsville, Columbus, Mississippi, Memphis and Nashville.

This time, Airman Kurt Willoughby of the Alabama Air National Guard had somebody on the line with whom he was willing to converse.

"Special Agent Wilcox, we'll do all we can to help you," said Willoughby, who had been awake for a while and had eaten breakfast, which made him feel much better than he did when Alabama Power telephoned him. "But, sir, I'm afraid that'll take a while."

"I was afraid of that," Wilcox said.

"If you'll be patient, I'll see if we can get a couple of choppers in the air in about an hour and a half," Willoughby said. "I know that sounds like a long time to you, but those engines are finicky, to say the least, and ..."

"Do what you can as quickly as possible," Wilcox said, abruptly ending the conversation so he could get on to other matters. He knew it was important to react fastidiously to a bank robbery, that the first hour was the most important and that time had elapsed long ago.

That left Wilcox frustrated and only able to offer a common story while conversing with special agents in other locations: "No, we don't know who we're looking for. No, we don't know the exact hour the banks were hit. No, we don't have positive identifications on the vehicles observed in the area. No, we don't have a feel for whether local people or people from another state were involved. We'll have to digest information as it comes in and get back to you."

The temptation was strong for Wilcox to order the stopping of every sports utility vehicle seen on the road in Alabama, South Tennessee, West Georgia, East Mississippi and North Florida. But he knew that would be an impossible proposition, one his bosses in Washington, D.C. would overrule. He did put out a command for law enforcement officials in the Metropolitan Birmingham Area to conduct raids of sorts on local hotels and motels, most of which were filled to capacity by travelers who did not want to risk driving.

"Special Agent Wilcox said you should be cordial and take your time," a special agent at FBI headquarters in Birmingham said to every law enforcement agency she contacted.

"Ma'am, with all due respect, we don't have the manpower to knock on hotel and motel doors," said Captain Fred Beavers of the Birmingham Police Department.

"That's a common thought," said the special agent. "I think we're more interested in a surveillance of the parking lots and parking decks, with emphasis on sports utility vehicles. After all, Captain Beavers, those people have to put a lot of money somewhere."

"That's better," Beavers said. "But if I had just robbed five banks, I'd either be at home in bed or getting my ass out of town."

Team Blue, Cates and Bobo, were doing something more precarious. They pulled their Pathfinder into a TransAmerica Truck Stop with three things in mind, refueling the gas tank, getting something to eat and learning what they could about their fate from truck drivers. There were numerous commercial carriers in the parking lot, with a couple dozen automobiles sprinkled among them.

It was after ten o'clock when an impetuously assembled FBI team arrived in Inverness Corners, surveyed the wreckage at the bank branches and completed initial interviews with individuals who had heard eccentric noises for several hours the night before. The special agents were not amused by the mass of curious onlookers around which they had to work. Nor were they happy with the conclusion they drew.

"We sure as hell don't have much to work with," Wilcox said. "These damn people either built the banks, worked at the banks or knew more about the banks than anybody who works for FDIC."

The scenes at the bank branches were strikingly similar. There were holes in each structure just large enough for a couple of large individuals to enter, whether at an auto teller window or at a door frame. There was so much glass, concrete and wood scattered throughout each lobby, it was apparent an outward-to-inward power force had done the damage. There were holes about the size of a basketball at the top right corner, the bottom right corner and top left corner of each vault. The caging that separated the entrance to each vault from the money deposited within had been blown from its support frame. There was an indication a torch had been used to gain better access to the cash at a couple of locations.

"Look at these surveillance cameras," Wilcox said as he stood in the mess at Patriot Bank. "The lens were painted black. Then, as if that wasn't enough, those bastards ripped the damn insides out of them."

"I don't want to sound stupid, but what in hell happened to the alarm systems?" said Martin Bell, an officer with the Hoover Police Department. "We're certainly supposed to be notified when somebody enters a bank."

"They clipped the telephone lines, then clipped the power lines leading to the alarm systems," Wilcox said. "They have one hell of a team — people who know explosives, people who know banks and, obviously, people who know how to drive in snow a foot deep."

The FBI special agent in charge became more exasperated when he walked out of Patriot and saw television cameramen and reporters rushing toward him. "Shit," he said. He knew four local stations had been airing reports about the bank robberies for more than an hour, each fueled by at times erroneous information offered by customers at Bruno's supermarket, and now they were closing in on him in an effort to get an official statement.

"Before I give you a brief interview, or summation, tell me what you've aired so far," Wilcox said to a female reporter from WVTM, the NBC affiliate.

"I don't think that's an appropriate thing for me to do," said the reporter. "I can assure you we'll be accurate and fair with our story."

Wilcox bit his lip. Then he said, "Well, lady, what if I decided to place you under arrest for obstruction of justice, specifically refusing to share information with a special agent from the Federal Bureau of Investigation?"

Nervously, the reporter instructed the cameraman to fetch a tape of their latest report. It said: "Law enforcement agencies are searching for phantom bank robbers who apparently took advantage of snow and ice to hit five branches in Shelby County. At this time, citing security reasons, the local FBI, the Hoover Police Department and the Shelby County Sheriff's Department are reluctant to discuss the case. However, a spokesperson for FBI Special Agent in Charge Jim Wilcox told Channel 13 News, 'We think this is a professional job that could involve several local people. Other than that, we don't have any information to report at this time.'"

"Who was my spokesperson?" Wilcox said, obviously angered by the attribution.

"I'm not sure, just somebody at your office downtown," the reporter said, suddenly sounding frazzled.

"There isn't anything to add at this time," Wilcox said.

"Can I get that on the record?" the reporter said.

With the camera rolling, the reporter got her answer in the form of a penetrating glare. Then, as Wilcox was walking briskly toward a car that would carry him to a meeting with other special agents, he heard the woman talking behind him: "Obviously, as you can tell, the FBI is totally at a loss and is more than a little agitated."

"That silly bitch will be working in Demopolis next week," Wilcox said as his gait increased.

At the TransAmerica Truck Stop, Cates and Bobo ate plates of sausage, eggs, grits and biscuits and tried to blend in with the crowd. Also, they listened intently as truck drivers pieced together the sparse information they had received about the action that went down the night previous in Inverness Corners.

Bits and pieces of the stories they heard were wilder than the scene they remembered:

"It's my understanding they blew away the banks, knocked down a couple of walls at each one," said a truck driver wearing a plaid cowboy shirt and a white hat that looked like it was made out of plastic.

"Rambo Sambo said on the radio that two guards were killed in the process," said a truck driver who wore tight jeans and pointed boots.

"I believe I'd try something like that for a couple million bucks, which is what I heard the robbers got," said a truck driver wearing a blue sweatsuit and running shoes.

"A guy who rolled out of Birmingham a couple of hours after me said they've got them in jail down there," said a truck driver. "But another dude said they haven't got a clue what happened."

"That's what they just said on the news out of Nashville," said the truck driver wearing the white hat. "They said the feds are focusing on Alabama, Tennessee, Georgia, Mississippi and Florida, that they'll be combing those states on the ground and in the air."

A waitress stopped by the table to see if Cates and Bobo wanted anything else. She started to warm their coffee, then stopped after being told they would take a couple of cups to go.

"Surely you guys haven't been hunting this morning," the waitress said, obviously after noticing the camouflage suits they were wearing.

"We gave it try," Cates said. "But it's just too dangerous in the woods with this much snow on the ground."

"It looks likes your buddy has already taken a hard spill," the waitress said as she pointed toward Bobo's swollen nose.

"I slid right into the back of the truck," Bobo said.

As Bobo paid the tab at the cash register, Cates went into the parking lot to start the Pathfinder so the heater could work. He paused before he opened the door when he saw a Tennessee State Trooper car being parked in a space near the front entrance. He held his breath when his partner brushed bodies with the men in uniforms as he exited.

"The next stop for us is the Maxwell House Hotel," Cates said.

"You're damn right about that," Bobo said.

Cates was wrong about the Maxwell House being the next stop, as Team Orange had already discovered. While Team Blue ate at the truck stop, McGraw and Long passed by on Interstate 65 and, five miles closer to Nashville, were halted by a long line of backed up traffic. A commercial carrier had overturned and wreckers were attempting to get it upright and out of the way.

"You know, Carl, I've been impressed with the way you've handled yourself on this junket," Long said as they sat on the interstate highway. "I'm not so sure you wouldn't fit in the brotherhood."

"I appreciate the compliment," McGraw said. "But your second job probably isn't for me."

"No, I'm serious," Long said. "You haven't become ruffled in any situation we've faced. You've stayed cool. You've got what it takes. I can't say that about the others."

McGraw chuckled and said, "I'd be interested in your impressions."

"Well, we already know about Bobo. He's an alcoholic and, maybe, a drughead of some type. I'll talk to him about it because he's a friend and because I cautioned him about that type behavior before we departed on this trip."

"I trust you aren't going to have him whacked," McGraw said, hoping his attempt at humor would be taken the right way.

Long laughed loudly, then said, "Carl, I don't think you really realize what I'm into. We've got a narrow circle with a broad range that specializes in questionable finance."

"You mentioned a disdain for my buddy Mark," McGraw said, trying to change the focus as the traffic inched forward.

"He's drinking with my friend Bobo," Long said. "That tells me he's a little careless."

"He was drinking earlier, too," McGraw said.

"I'll rest my case," Long said. "But not until I tell you Mills seems like a risk-taker, for no good reason, and Bass likes to talk too much, a take-charge guy when he should be quiet."

Suddenly, they heard the walkie-talkie.

"Team Crimson to Team Blue and Team Orange," said Bass, who was attempting to find out what the long line of traffic he and Mills had come up on was about.

"See what I mean," Long said. "We're in the midst of a lot of people. It's time to be quiet. But Bass wants to talk."

"I'll brush him off, quickly," McGraw said as he reached for the walkie-talkie.

CHAPTER SEVENTEEN

If ever an important meeting was staged, it was the one FBI Special Agent in Charge Jim Wilcox called to order at the Shelby County Fire Department on Valleydale Road. This was about half an hour after he left Patriot Bank in a huff, thanks to a tart television news reporter, and the man in charge of investigating the bank robberies was only mildly subdued when he arrived.

Already in the room were special agents Paul Conrad, Pat Embry, Joel Deaton and Tim Perkins, his four aces who had been examining the busted opened confines of Central, Sector, First Columbus, Patriot and American. Also present were Shelby County Sheriff Matt Coleman, Hoover Police Chief Andy Westbrooks, Birmingham Police Chief Jimmy Johnson and their host, Lieutenant Bill Grimme of the Shelby County Fire Department, who had been on duty for almost a full day.

"Bill, do you have your super scouts from Fire Engine Six available in case we need them?" Conrad said to Grimme.

"They're in the chow room."

"Andy, what about your police officers?"

"Same place, same food."

The firemen and police officers were not eating. They were listening, like little kids eavesdropping, after calling their wives and children and telling them they were viable good guys in the midst of a serious crime that was sure to make national news.

Conrad, an experienced 58-year-old special agent, a Dallas native who knew he wanted to become a member of the FBI from that day when John Fitzgerald Kennedy was killed by Lee Harvey Oswald, or whomever, hesitated for a few seconds. He took a swallow of hot coffee and collected himself. Then he continued in a slow, methodical manner:

"We're looking for suspects traveling in sports utility vehicles with Alabama license plates. If I was them, I would've changed the license plates, but it's damn impossible to predict how every criminal mind works under pressure."

Wilcox jumped to his feet. "Hold on a minute, Paul, and let's tape this for others to hear." Perkins hurried outside to his car, gathered a large tape recorder and carried it into the room.

Conrad continued:

"We've had individuals who said they saw at least one dark and at least one light vehicle in the area at some point before dawn. The makes and models are not known, which adds to this nightmare. But we think they're relatively new sports utility vehicles. For now, take a choice, Toyota, Nissan, Chevrolet, Ford, Dodge, Mercedes or whatever.

"Frankly, we think the Japs are the best in the business. But the Germans have made an impact with that M-Class truck made down the road in Vance. I'd imagine any crooks as smart as these bastards seem to be know that."

Wilcox wanted the group to brainstorm before Conrad could move to another subject. He pointed out the focus at that time was on dark vehicles, black, green, blue and brown, and light vehicles, white, beige and yellow. He asked if any of them had knowledge of sports utility vehicles, specifically how much storage room each had. He said it was obvious the bank robbers had carried extensive cargo.

"I'll get some specs for you," Grimme said. "I've got a Blazer and an Explorer. There are larger types, for sure."

"You might as well consider two men working out of each truck," Conrad said. "It'd be impossible for one man to handle all of those materials in the dark — blasting pads, detonators and things like that. Given the wide area they tapped, I'd say we've got at least four suspects, maybe more."

"Have we talked to anybody from the banking industry?" Wilcox said.

"Yes, the vice president for operations at American," Conrad said. "I believe his name is Vic Meadows. He's stunned by this. He can't believe it was done so quickly and, apparently, with such ease. He's concerned we're dealing with people who are closely aligned with the profession. He's more troubled by the thought some local people might be involved."

Conrad was joined in front of the group by Embry, a 28-year-old eager beaver, as his fellow FBI special agents called him. He was reared in South Alabama, Conecuch County, and requested an assignment in his home state after being presented his badge. Already, he had been the man on the point during the solving of two bank robberies, one in Montgomery and one in Oneonta. A key to those successes had been his ability to determine a prime geographical area of investigation.

"So we aren't simply focusing on Jefferson County, Shelby County, Blount County, Walker County and Tuscaloosa County?" said Dan Henning of the Alabama State Troopers Office. He had arrived late, having hurried to the meeting from the Alabama Department of Public Safety at the state capital, and had heard Embry talking about zeroing in on multiple states.

"If this had happened an hour or two ago, yeah, we'd be blanketing Metro Birmingham," Embry said. "But they've been on the run for at least three hours, maybe as many as six, so we've got to go a little more to the north, south, east and west.

"Gentlemen, most of us realize we're in deep shit if we don't get a break within the first twelve hours."

"By the way, Dan, I assume the interstate highways and federal highways are still open," Wilcox said.

"All of the interstates are open and fairly clear, although they remain treacherous. Some of the federal highways are passable, with 280, 31 and 78 being the best. It's better to the south than to the north, obviously. The snow isn't as thick in Middle Tennessee, Eastern Kentucky and Western Kentucky. But there's a lot of ice up there, which makes the traveling harder and more dangerous."

It was cold in Louisville, Kentucky, where Midge Cates and Diana McGraw drank hot chocolate as they watched their children build their third snowman of the day. One of the women was giving her best friend a lecture of sorts after hearing more about infidelity.

"Midge, you're really starting to sound paranoid when discussing Mark and that woman," Diana said. "You don't have proof anything has happened since they kissed at that party. Now you're trying to convince yourself, as well as me, that our husbands are off having romantic flings instead of trying to track down deer in the snow."

"I'm telling you, I know my husband and my husband has been extremely distracted during the last week," Midge said. "I've been trying to talk to a wall."

"Okay, and I'll admit Carl has been somewhat out of sorts, too," Diana said. "But goodness, Midge, they have a lot going on at work, some extremely hard deadlines ahead of them. Maybe that's what the preoccupation has been about."

Midge stood silently for a few minutes, watching the children put sticks in the snowmen they had constructed. Diana watched her, carefully, and concluded her pal was not sold on her explanation.

"I wonder whatever happened to Fred Rouzie," Midge said about a former lover from her college years, the last man she dated before meeting her husband.

"Good gosh," Diana said. "You're going over the edge."

"Seriously, Diana, I've been thinking about him a lot since Mark had that affair. I know he never married. I've heard he's living in Chicago, which isn't that far away."

"Damn," Diana said. "Let's go inside, warm ourselves and try to get you back to your senses. First of all, your husband hasn't had an affair, at least that's probably the case, and you're talking like a panicked woman who is about to run the risk of losing everything good in her life."

"If you're wrong, I'll kill him," Midge said. "I'm not going to let him run in the fast lane and make a mockery out of me."

Team Blue, Mark Cates and Ben Bobo, were not moving quickly at all. In fact, they were still stuck just outside Franklin, Tennessee, inching toward Nashville in a traffic jam on Interstate 65. Team Orange, Mark McGraw and Fred Long, were a few minutes ahead of them. Team

Crimson, Ed Bass and Sam Mills, were several miles behind and looking for a way to get off the road for a while.

"Let's make a move at that next exit," Mills said after noticing several food establishments on a sign one mile from their next chance to leave the interstate.

"I think we need to keep rolling," Bass said. "I like the idea of being in this mass of humanity."

"We need gas and we need food," Mills said.

Bass looked at the gas gauge and saw it hovering at less than a quarter of a tank. He thought about the long line of traffic in front of them. He decided his partner was probably right because the last thing they wanted was to be stuck on the side of the road with a Tennessee State Trooper stopping to see if they needed assistance.

The conversation continued at the Shelby County Fire Department, where FBI Special Agent Jim Wilcox and his team were attempting to find some relief for themselves.

"We've got people in Tennessee, Georgia, Mississippi and Florida on red alert," Wilcox said. "Maybe they'll turn up something."

"We've got the manpower to stop every sports utility vehicle in the southeast, if that's our wish," Embry said.

"That's what I want to do," Wilcox said. "But the folks in Washington won't okay that, not yet, because people on the road aren't having the best of times as it is."

"We've got air support," said Joel Deaton, a 46-year-old special agent who had been out of the room checking with the Alabama Air National Guard. "Helicopters are going up in five states. The airmen down here are focusing on back roads."

Deaton was a specialist when analyzing the criminal mind. His fellow special agents used to kid him about how he should be the mastermind behind devious schemes instead of a man trying to track down the unseemly.

"Home is where the heart is, where a person in crisis or scared seeks comfort," Deaton said. "If we've got Alabamians involved in this, they're trying to get in front of their fireplaces as soon as possible. If we're dealing with people from other states, they're anxious to get back to familiar surroundings, too, but will definitely seek untroubled shelter along the way.

"Also, there's comfort in numbers. The smartest thing that band of thieves could do is split up, go separate ways and reunite in a week or two. But the numbers tell us wolves like that usually run together."

Worried about what his bosses at FBI headquarters in Washington would think about a wrong move, Wilcox asked Special Agent Tim Perkins to give an overview of what the most recent bulletin sent into surrounding states said.

"It's pretty simple," said Perkins, a 32-year-old native of Des Moines, Iowa. "We're telling them to stop and search almost every dark green, dark blue, dark brown, dark gray, black, white, beige and yellow sports utility vehicle they see. We're telling them the exceptions should be families traveling with children. We're telling them to use discretion because time is important and shouldn't be wasted on innocent people."

"I guess I'm from the old school, the crude way of thinking," Wilcox said. "But I've always believed everybody is guilty until proven innocent in this type matter."

"With all due respect, sir, that'll get you demoted to a desk job or banned from the FBI," Embry said with a grin.

"Thank you for the reminder," Wilcox said.

At a Waffle House in Sleepy Hollow, Tennessee, about thirty minutes from Nashville, Mills and Bass were getting started on a much needed meal. The small building that resembled a trailer was full, with all eight booths and all eight counter stools occupied, and other customers were sitting in chairs and waiting for the opportunity to eat.

The traffic on Interstate 65 remained bumper to bumper.

"This is the best cheap steak known to mankind," Mills said over the country music playing on a jukebox. "I don't have a clue why you're having breakfast."

Bass did not respond to the remark. His eyes were glued on the parking lot, where two local police officers had stopped near the crimson Pathfinder.

"How about some fresh coffee?" said their waitress.

Again, Bass did not answer. He kept his eyes on the police cruiser. They grew wider when the police officers started getting out of it.

"Damn, Ed, give the nice lady an answer," Mills said after the waitress had refilled his small cup. He tapped his inattentive friend on the arm.

"Uh, yeah, I'll — what did you say?" Bass said.

"I wondered if you want more coffee."

"Yeah, just a tap."

After the waitress poured the coffee and walked away, as Mills took another bite of steak, Bass said, "You better get ready to talk the talk and walk the walk."

Mills waited for his partner to continue.

"We've got two cops standing beside our Pathfinder in the parking lot," Bass said. "They're straining to see through the fogged windows."

"I'm not looking that way," Mills said. Instead, he looked around the Waffle House and noticed there was only one door in and one door out.

"They're coming this way," Bass said.

"Stay cool and be nice," Mills said.

"Son of a bitch," Bass said.

The waitress heard him. She was startled by the cursing. She hurried to the booth and said, "Sir, I hope there isn't a problem with your meal." She looked at the plate and noticed Bass had barely touched his cheese eggs, bacon and raisin toast.

"Oh, I'm sorry," Bass said. "My buddy was telling me an all-time best sad song and waltz story."

"I get the picture," the waitress said. "Honey, if you want to hear one worse, come home with me for a few days."

Bass was thinking a sadder refrain was about to surface.

"Who's driving the crimson Pathfinder in the lot?" the police officer said as he entered the Waffle House. His voice bellowed, causing several customers to jump.

"That's us," Mills said, raising his right arm.

"Let's have a talk," the police officer said.

"Have a seat," Mills said as he and Bass scooted to one side to make room for the police officers. "Can we buy you guys a cup of coffee."

The police officers accepted. William Fitzgerald sat next to Bass. Tommy Murphy, who had not spoken, sat next to Mills. They talked about the snarled traffic and the frigid weather, then about how good the food was, with the police officers pointing out they often took breaks at the restaurant.

The police officers looked nervous. Bass and Mills were.

"It's about as messy as it is cold, which makes our job tough on a day like this," said Murphy, who was clearly the most polite police officer.

"Yeah, and that's why we're sitting in here," Bass said.

"I noticed you've got a couple of guns in your truck, as well as a lot of other things," Fitzgerald said.

"Yeah," Mills said. "We were on our way to Brewton, Alabama for a deer hunt and got turned back by the snow."

"I can get into that," Murphy said. "Deer love to run in the snow. I got a 12-point on a day similar to this last year on the Knoxville side of Jamestown."

"That sounds like a monster," said Bass.

"Ah, he was a little scrawny," Murphy said. "But his head found a place over my fireplace, just the same."

Bass and Mills chuckled. Murphy smiled. Fitzgerald remained more serious.

"I'm sure you guys have heard about those bank robberies down in Birmingham," Fitzgerald said.

Mills was quick to reply and what he said made Bass' stomach churn.

"There's no way we couldn't hear about it," Mills said. "That's all that's on the radio. And, get this, we've got more interest in what's being said than most people."

Bass did not know where Mills was taking the conversation. Neither did the police officers, a waitress and several customers who were eavesdropping.

"Why is that the case?" Fitzgerald said.

Mills grinned and said, "Because we're employees of a bank in Western Kentucky and we're stunned something like that could happen. I mean, get real, five bank branches robbed on one night."

"You seem pretty excited, maybe too much," Fitzgerald said.

"William, ease up on these guys," Murphy said. "Who in hell ever heard of bank employees robbing a bank?"

"Well, there have been a few million dollars embezzled through the years," Bass said, making a risky bid to further disarm one of the police officers. The customers who heard his remark laughed, heartily.

"I told you these dudes are okay," Murphy said.

"Where were you guys last night?" Fitzgerald said, his voice louder.

"Come on, man, you're harassing these people," said a young man in the next booth.

"If I were you, I'd zip it," Fitzgerald said. "Now, gentlemen, answer my question."

"First of all, sir, my name is Sam Mills and this is Ed Bass. We've got identification if you want to see it."

Mills paused, just for a few beats of his heart, then said, "We got as far as Cullman, Alabama last night. There weren't any motel rooms available. We drank some whiskey and played blackjack in our truck. Then we went to sleep. We got up this morning, a little later than we would've liked, and got on the road. We'd like to get home by tonight, as long as that backed up traffic will cooperate."

"You've got a packed truck," Fitzgerald said.

"Camping in the woods and hunting deer takes a lot of equipment," Bass said.

"More than you'd believe," Murphy said.

"Why don't we take a look at all that stuff," Fitzgerald said.

The customers in the Waffle House were getting angry, obviously on the side of Bass and Mills. So was Murphy, who said, "Damn it, William, you're getting out of line."

"We've got an all points bulletin that said stop all green, black, brown, blue, white, beige and yellow sports utility vehicles and search them," Fitzgerald said. "Don't tell me I'm out of line."

The customers looked outside. So did the waitress, who said, "Officer Fitzgerald, that truck is as crimson as my blood."

"She's on the nose with that one," Murphy said. "If that's not crimson, I'm a dead Tennessee football fan."

"So you like the Big Orange," Mills said, an effort to keep the interrogation sidetracked.

"You bet, only it's more like a passion," Murphy said.

"I like Tennessee, too," Mills said. "Driving that crimson Pathfinder reminds me to hate Alabama day and night."

Bass thought his partner was getting out of hand, with good reason. Fitzgerald was embarrassed and mad.

"Let me see some identification," Fitzgerald said.

Bass and Mills stood up, fumbled through their back pockets and pulled out their wallets. The police officer looked at the drivers' licenses. He studied the addresses. He looked at the pictures, then at the faces in front of him.

"Let's at least look at the stuff in that truck," Fitzgerald said.

"William, if you want somebody to stand out there in the cold and dump a bunch of hunting equipment into the parking lot, you better get another squad car over here," Murphy said.

"Hell, we'll empty it for you if you want, all the way down to the motor and wheel lugs," Mills said, his voice rising as he made a dangerous power play. "But we want you to know we don't like the idea of catching pneumonia while you admire our outdoors gear and we'll be damn sure to let other people know we feel that way."

Fitzgerald became pensive. He knew every eye in the Waffle House was focused on him. Mills had made a strong move and the police officer seemed to be retreating.

"Fish or cut bait," Murphy said. "I'm going to the car."

Murphy took a few steps, turned around and said, "Gentlemen, I hope you have a safe trip."

"Be careful, Officer Murphy," Bass said.

After Murphy had exited, Mills look at Fitzgerald, who was standing beside the booth. The bank robber said, "Officer Fitzgerald, do we go outside with you or do we eat?"

"Enjoy your damn meal," Fitzgerald said.

Bass and Mills, plus several other people, watched Fitzgerald walk to the police cruiser and get inside. They saw the police officers arguing as they exited the parking lot.

"We'll get you a couple more plates, on the house," said the waitress.

Bass and Mills ate in silence and were amazed by how good their steak and their cheese eggs tasted.

At Inverness Corners, cameras were flashing inside five bank branches as FBI photographers took pictures of the mess produced by the explosives. They were careful as they walked. They made sure every angle was covered.

Nothing could be touched until they were finished because they were doing two things, assisting with an investigation and, possibly, recording pictures that could be used in a bank robbery trial in the future.

"Let's go across the street and get something to eat," Wilcox said as he pointed toward a Hardee's hamburger restaurant.

"I think at this moment I'd rather keep walking to that ABC Store," Embry said about a liquor establishment in the same shopping center.

CHAPTER EIGHTEEN

The photographers gave way to the laboratory experts and Inverness Corners looked like an orange grove as Federal Bureau of Investigation special agents and other law enforcement representatives wearing vests of that color over cold weather apparel swarmed in the sunlight. The temperature was rising, now that the clouds had vanished, but it remained well below freezing. Police cruiser and fire engine lights were flashing at every intersection and entrance to the five bank branches, an effort to keep onlookers from hampering the work.

The roads were becoming more negotiable, which helped investigators get into the area. However, that also brought more gawkers, particularly with television news reports growing in number and getting longer. One local station, WBRC, the Fox affiliate, was providing around the clock coverage, which meant it had to resort to senseless interviews with citizens who merely stumbled onto the scene.

The crowd was not as large down the street, at Sector, where Special Agent Paul Conrad was working closely with a fingerprint technician.

"We need prints in a big way," Conrad said to the dusting expert.

"Don't hold your breath," Tom Goldberg said. "I've already seen enough fuzz and thread fragments to know these culprits were wearing gloves and masks."

"What about body hair, chapped skin or a torn fingernail?" Conrad said, knowing he was begging.

"How is a torn fingernail going to get out of a glove," Goldberg said, adding a weak smile.

"Shit."

"None of that, either," Goldberg said. "These guys were tidy, although

I know this mess doesn't indicate as much. The wiring I've examined was waxed or cleaned thoroughly before it was brought into this building. I'm not sure I've seen a crime scene that presented so little on which to build."

"Don't give up," Conrad said.

"We won't do that because we've got a lot of debris to go through, probably two weeks worth," Goldberg said.

At American across from Patriot, a similar non-picture was being painted. At that moment the focus was on footprints, those in the snow and those inside the building.

The appearance of a Wells Fargo truck in the parking lot made onlookers gasp. A television reporter said, while on camera, "Well, it looks like somebody has come to pick up what money the bad guys left. We'll attempt to get an accounting for you."

That was the purpose of the visit by the rolling bank vault, one that arrived almost a full day too late. Two Wells Fargo employees carefully loaded change bags and boxes of cash onto the truck. The bank would not be open, they surmised, so there was no reason for them to produce an accounting at that moment. But based on prior experience, one of the men knew something important.

"Those guys, or gals, got a big chunk of loot out of this place," said the driver as he started steering the Wells Fargo truck toward the exit.

"I can't begin to imagine how much they hauled out of Sector," said the other Wells Fargo employee.

Special Agent Pat Embry was conferring with lab technician Emily Spears inside Patriot.

"Those footprints have to be worth something," Embry said.

"Yeah, heartburn," Spears said. "All I can tell you is two men were in this bank, or some oversized women. I surmise they were wearing boots, but I couldn't say that for sure. They could have been wearing loafers or sneakers just as easily."

"You'll have to explain that."

"Stand back and look at this," Spears said as she positioned a powerful light so its glow would illuminate the floor and placed what amounted to a large magnifying glass over it. Then she invited Embry to join her for an observation.

"If you look closely and perhaps imagine a little, you can see some footprints," Spears said.

"Maybe a heel here and a toe there," Embry said.

"Exactly," Spears said. "You can't really see a full image of a foot — or a boot or shoe."

"Okay."

Spears repositioned the equipment and invited Embry to take another look at a different angle. He put forth his best effort.

"It's a dirty floor with smudges on it, no real pattern," Embry said.

"You're right, a real bitch for somebody like me, even in the dust left by the explosions," Spears said. "Not only did they do a lot of shuffling back and forth through it, it appears they danced all over the place before they left in an effort to leave it like this."

"Is there any hope?" Embry said.

"Sure, there's always hope," Spears said. "I'll be at this quite a while, probably for a week. But, Pat, if you guys really want to come up with something worthwhile, you better find some boots or shoes somewhere, the real thing."

Embry looked at his watch. It was almost three o'clock, about three hours before darkness. "These boys are too good," he said. "Now they've got time on their side, too."

Team Orange looked the part. Carl McGraw and Fred Long had checked into the Maxwell House Hotel in Nashville. They had left their Pathfinder parked in a crowded lot, on the far left side, as had been planned. They were asleep in Room 203.

Team Blue appeared just as cozy. Mark Cates and Ben Bobo were in Room 452. Only they were not asleep, merely talking and drinking hard.

"The Excedrin helps, particularly with this bourbon hitting home on top of it," Bobo said.

"I'm glad — and, again, I'm sorry," Cates said.

The NCAA Basketball Tournament game was winding down, with Louisville about to put away Purdue. That pleased the men from The

Commonwealth.

"How does my nose look?" Bobo said.

"Better than those black eyes," Cates said.

"Let's get a snack from room service," Bobo said. "Tell them we want a pitcher of ice on the side."

Team Crimson, Ed Bass and Sam Mills, had deposited their Pathfinder in the parking lot, in the center section, as planned, and had just checked in. They were familiar with Nashville and had stopped by The Box Seat sports bar in the Green Hills section of town so they could watch four basketball games simultaneously. They were getting a little drunk, no doubt, after a strenuous night on another town and several cold beers at the local establishment. They contemplated a steam bath in the health club on the ground floor.

In the parking lot outside the hotel, two police officers made what amounted to an obligatory pass. The men inside the Metro Nashville Police Department cruiser, Unit 145, noticed what appeared to be a hundred sports utility vehicles.

"Unit 145 to the MNPD dispatcher," said the police officer sitting on the passenger side.

"Go ahead, 145," said the dispatcher.

"As for that FBI matter, it's clear at the Maxwell House. We'll move down the street to the Shoney's Inn and the Comfort Inn."

"10-4, 145."

"We'll come back in a few hours."

"10-4, 145, but don't forget we've got Metro Nashville to serve, too, and it could be a slippery night on the ice."

"For sure."

"10-4 — and be careful, 145."

In Birmingham, a local television affiliate, ABC 30/40, was producing one of the more interesting feature stories related to The Snowmen Project. On the makeshift set at Bruno's supermarket were store manager, Harvey Bolton, with his bald spot softened by makeup, and Susan Arenberg, with her imagination tempered by a lack of sleep and, at last count, four Miller-Lite beers and a glass of wine. The show host was

Dave Coulter, a popular 42-year-old news media figure.

"Okay, let's hear what you heard," Coulter said.

"It was like an earthquake," Arenberg said. "The roar was powerful and the ground moved."

"Have you ever been in an earthquake?" Coulter said.

"I have now," said Arenberg, who was loving every minute of the attention she was receiving. "We all stood in the store and waited and wondered what would happen next. There was a lot of anxiety, or pressure, and everybody was scared to death."

"Harvey, you had a tough night at the shop," Coulter said.

"It was more dreadful than I thought," Bolton said. "We were losing power, so we brought in some generators. Since it's our desire at Bruno's to please our customers, we wanted to make sure we were open if people could get to us. Susan, or Miss Arenberg, was there throughout the evening. She was there when we heard the first explosion and she was ..."

"Excuse me, Harvey, but let's back up," Coulter said.

"I heard this blast, a damn loud blast, a real (bleep) of a blast, if you will," Arenberg said, seeming to take charge of the show. "It was lightning and thundering at the time, but I knew there was no (bleeping) way that was the roar of thunder we were hearing."

"What did you think?" Coulter said.

"The end of the (bleeping) world, basically," Arenberg said. "Like, you know, I thought aliens had come to visit. They can do that, you know, like on the X-Files, and I thought that's what we faced, our little family down at the food store."

Bolton smiled as he listened. He had heard the same spiel.

"Anyway, like, well, you know, it ended up that we didn't have any (bleeping) extraterrestrials among us," Arenberg said. "But we might have had something just as bad, some damn bad guys stealing money from a bunch of poor folks."

Coulter was shellshocked. He said, "Let's take a short break and return to hear from Harvey Bolton, a real hero who attempted to maintain order in the face of chaos."

In the rear of the Bruno's supermarket, as well as at locations within ten miles of Inverness Corners, some grungy work was taking place. FBI special agents, including Jim Wilcox, and other law enforcement representatives, including firemen who had been drafted for a dreadful chore, were climbing into dumpsters and analyzing the trash.

That led two firemen to an interesting discovery in a dumpster not far from Sector. One pulled five pieces of recklessly sliced rubbery green fabric out of the bin. He looked at it, peculiarly, and said, "I wonder what this is?"

The other firemen analyzed the fabric and attempted to piece it together. "It's a cover for something — or maybe some packing material for a shipment of some type," he said.

"Somebody could pack a vault in something this large."

"Well, it doesn't look like anything bank robbers would use, so let's keep digging."

The FBI had a long way to go, to say the least. Dusk was approaching when the garbage detail was summoned to a meeting in front of Bruno's supermarket. Nothing of consequence had been found, but there was a lot more ground to cover the following morning.

"We'll work from seven until nine, take a break for church and start back at two," Wilcox said to the men and women who were undertaking an arduous and rank assignment. "I want the contents of every dumpster sorted and analyzed. I want you to keep your eyes on the landscape as you move from location to location.

"Take care when handling suspicious materials. Use your gloves at all times. Be sure you don't smear fingerprints.

"If you have a question about how something should be handled, get in touch with a special agent before taking any action. Remember what we're looking for: blasting caps, detonators, wires and anything that might be used to produce an explosion, misplaced tools, discarded clothing and, well, anything else somebody might need to survive for several hours on a cold evening."

The steam room at the Maxwell House Hotel health club brought blessed relief for Bass and Mills, who shared the hot box with two elderly men from Bloomington, Indiana. The bank robbers were only interested in enjoying the heat, even if it stung their skin left tender by a long stay in the elements. The travelers wanted to talk.

"I guess you two guys got sidetracked by the bad weather," said one of the men.

"No sir, not really," Mills said.

"We did, while on a tour bus junket to New Orleans."

"I see."

"You know, there's no way Nashville can be as exciting as the Big Easy, but at our age we'll do the best we can no matter where we land," said one of the men.

"I understand," Bass said.

"I'm Wilbur Sanderson and that's Frank Newton."

"Sam Franklin and Ed Dyas," Mills said.

"What brings you to Nashville?" Sanderson said.

"A convention downtown," Mills said.

"What's your line of business?" Newton said.

"Sporting goods."

"Then you must be from Kentucky," Sanderson said. "I saw an orange truck packed full of hunting and camping stuff in the parking lot after we got off the bus."

"That was somebody else, I guess, because we're from Knoxville," Bass said.

"I assume you're married," Newton said.

"Yes sir, both of us," Bass said.

"Well, with the weather like it is, you better call home as soon as possible," Newton said. "I did about an hour ago and my wife chewed me out for not calling earlier."

"That's high on my list," Bass said.

Special Agent in Charge Wilcox was already on the telephone at his house in Birmingham. A conversation with the Alabama Air National Guard let him know surveillance in flight had not turned up any suspects or leads. He had called Special Agent Bob Crawford at FBI headquarters in Washington, D.C. He was advocating an expansive roadblock plan for that evening and all of the following day.

"That's been up the flag pole once and it came down quickly," Crawford said. "The power brokers think that's an overreaction that'll turn into a public relations nightmare."

"It's our best chance, or only chance, to make up time," Wilcox said. "Those people got a head start on us."

"It doesn't look like much has gone your way," Crawford said.

"If this was a football game, we'd be behind four touchdowns after one quarter," Wilcox said, finding his usual humor near the end of a long day.

"Maybe you'll win late with a Hail Mary."

At the Maxwell House Hotel, Bass was on the telephone with his wife, Cindy, while killing time before a scheduled meeting with his partners in crime. He was standing in a long hallway that connected the lobby and a restaurant.

"Where in hell are you guys?" Cindy said, her tone menacing. "We've called all over Georgia trying to find you."

"Wow," Ed said, his eyes widening. "We've been fighting snow and ice in an effort to get home and you're jumping on me like I've done something terrible."

"That's the point," Cindy said. "You should have let us know you're safe. You've got everybody on edge up here, particularly Midge Cates. She's been on the telephone all afternoon."

"Well, exactly who did you call?" Ed said.

"We called the Georgia State Troopers office, at least six times. We called the Georgia Department of Conservation a couple of times."

Ed pounded the wall in front of him. He fumbled in a shirt pocket for a cigarette. He took a deep breath.

"Are you there?" Cindy said.

"Yeah, I'm here and everybody else is here."

"I'll pass that along," Cindy said.

"Good," Ed said. "I'll call the state troopers and game wardens in Georgia and let them know we're alive and well in Nashville. There's no reason for them to ..."

"Nashville?" Cindy said. "How can you get to Nashville from South Georgia en route to Louisville?

Ed tried to come up with a quick answer. He said, "It's a long story, Cindy, really a nightmare."

"Give me the nuts and bolts."

"Let's just say we've been following weather patterns and dodging snow and ice all day," Ed said. "We're on the right path. We'll be home at some point tomorrow."

"I'll let the other girls know."

"Please do that," Ed said. "We don't need to have people in three states looking for six men who are safe and healthy."

About two hours later, at about eight o'clock, a weary Wilcox received a telephone call at his house. Crawford was on the line with good news.

"Jim, we're going to go the roadblock route, starting within an hour," Crawford said about a decision reached at FBI headquarters in Washington. "It's a test, but at least we're making progress."

"I'm glad to hear that," Wilcox said. "If I was on the run with a load of money in my possession, I'd move around a hell of a lot more at night than during the day."

CHAPTER NINTEEN

Heightened by the unusual weather conditions that had stranded travelers, the Old Country Pub off the expansive lobby at the Maxwell House Hotel was almost filled to capacity on a frosty Saturday night. The patrons were spirited as they listened to a mix of country and rock and roll music and enjoyed libation. Several couples, some regulars and some strangers passing through the city, danced on a parquet floor around which the rest of the bar evolved.

Four bartenders did their best to care for a crowd that was more than twice the size of most they had on weekends.

There were two other smaller bars in the hotel and drinks were also served in the lobby, where there were ample chairs and tables to accommodate several dozen people. A pianist entertained those who decided to stay in that area.

Adding to the festive setting were two private parties scheduled that evening in ballrooms, formal affairs, and the men dressed in tuxedos and ladies attired in colorful gowns made a small part of Nashville look like New Orleans at Mardi Gras. Obviously, that pleased a couple of overly curious men from Bloomington, Indiana.

It was nine o'clock when Mark Cates and Ben Bobo emerged from an elevator and saw the splendor for the first time. They were an hour early for a scheduled meeting with Carl McGraw and Fred Long and Sam Mills and Ed Bass, the first for the bank robbers since they exited Birmingham.

"Damn, look at this," Bobo said as he and Cates walked through the lobby and looked for the Old Country Pub. "We've found paradise."

Cates grinned and said, "Ben, maybe we should've gone a little lighter on the booze this afternoon."

Upstairs, in Room 203, McGraw and Long were having a compelling discussion over two cups of coffee. One continued to make an unusual sales pitch.

"I'm sure you'd fit nicely in the brotherhood," Long said. "We need young men with nerve and style."

"I can't see how I could contribute," McGraw said.

"It's easy once you're connected. Basically, you become an investor and a bookkeeper. You accept money from one group and feed it to another group — after you skim a percentage off the top for yourself."

"I've got some stock, but I'm not a major player," McGraw said.

"But you would become one with the amount of cash that'd be funneled your way," Long said. "That's why you're perfect for the brotherhood. We need up and coming business people, folks who are suddenly making an abundance of money. Your company is thriving, or about to, and success like that keeps people from asking a lot of question about the investments you make."

"But I don't know good stock from bad stock."

"You don't have to know the market," Long said. "You put the damn money where you're instructed to put the damn money — again after taking a portion for yourself. You might back up a loan for a legitimate lender. You might buy a large tract of land that'll be bought by somebody else for more money in a week. You might send a big check to an organization in Central America, a tax-deductible donation, that'll come back to you twice the size in six months without Uncle Sam knowing you've been reimbursed."

"That sounds like bank money out of Birmingham."

"See, Carl, you're a natural," Long said.

Cates and Bobo were seated at the bar, quaffing Black Jack and water and looking at their watches.

"I haven't seen our buddies, nor their trucks," Cates said.

"The trucks are parked outside," Bobo said. "I took a walk while you were in the shower."

Mills and Bass had completed showers in Room 501 and were talking about something troubling.

"You know, maybe we should call the state troopers office in Georgia and tell them we're alive," Mills said.

"Hell no, not on my life," Bass said. "I don't want our names popping up for a seventh time on their telephone log."

"Do you think they have us on record?"

"Probably not," Bass said. "I'd guess they were bombarded with calls today and it's doubtful they made a record of all of them. But, either way, I'd rather them write us off as dead instead of thinking about us being on the run."

"Those damn women," Mills said. "Those damn wives."

In Louisville, Diana McGraw was working overtime trying to alleviate the suspicions of Midge Cates, who had made a move that added to her uneasiness.

"That's about as dumb as anything you've done yet," Diana said after watching her best friend place a telephone call to a female lawyer.

"Well, I told you what the message said: 'Hi, thanks for the call. I'm out of town this weekend. I'll be back at some point Sunday night.' What does that tell you?"

"Midge, that tells me the woman is out of town and will be back in town tomorrow night."

"So what did our husbands say?"

"I'm going to bed," Diana said. "I'm not going to let you implicate my husband in something not even your husband is guilty of doing."

Cates and Bobo accepted another drink at the Old Country Pub and asked the bartender to turn on the television set hanging on a wall in front of them.

"I doubt you can hear it over the music," the bartender said.

"That's fine. I'm more interested in the weather."

"What channel can I get for you?"

"CNN."

The jukebox was blaring and Bobo was checking out the action on the dance floor. He looked relaxed, tapping his fingers on the bar to the beat. But he jerked frantically when a firm hand touched his right shoulder.

"Hey," Bass said.

"Well, look at this," Cates said as Bobo regained composure.

"What brings you boys to town?"

"Snow and ice," Mills said with a smile.

"Well, by God, let's find a table and catch up," Bobo said, producing a theatrical show aimed at letting others at the bar know old friends had been reunited by chance.

"I think we should stay here and check out the weather," Cates said as he pointed toward the television set.

They looked at the screen, almost as one, and saw video tape of Birmingham as they had remembered leaving it. The focus was one bank vault, then another, from Patriot all the way to First Columbus, and the picture caused another patron seated at the bar to react.

"Hey, bartender, turn up the damn volume so we can see what's going on in Birmingham," he said, his voice booming.

The bartender was curious, too. He turned up the volume and the sound caused a relative hush to fall over the Old Country Pub. The newscaster said:

"This strange chain of events has left the FBI perplexed. The only concrete clues in the robbing of five Birmingham banks are some of the explosive devices left behind. Other than that, eyewitnesses have told authorities they saw several recreational vehicles in the immediate area at various points of the night.

"One man, Andrew Carroll, talked face to face with one of the bank robbers. He described him as being so heavily dressed he could only see his eyes, his mouth and part of his nose. He said the man, who was posturing as a security officer, was from the south. He said ..."

The newscaster paused for a couple of seconds, as if distracted by a voice in her ear. Then she said, "I'm told we're going to take a break and then go to Birmingham for a live news conference."

Several patrons in the Old Country Pub rushed toward the bar so they could better hear the newscast. A bartender quickly turned on a second television set.

"Money, so they say, is the root of all evil today," an obviously drunk man sang as he moved closer to Cates, Bobo, Bass and Mills.

"Damn, Bonny and Clyde ride again," said a female.

"Just call it Boomingham," said a man, making reference to the blasts at the bank branches.

"That's a good one," said his date.

Watching all of this from the entrance to the Old Country Pub were McGraw and Long, who were right on time for the meeting. Also in the room were two Metro Nashville Police Department officers who were giving little effort as they looked through the crowd.

"I suppose this is what the brotherhood would call a character check," McGraw said.

"If they've got descriptions to offer, yeah, you're right," Long said.

A waitress asked McGraw and Long if they were going to the bar. They had to step aside to let the police officers leave the room.

"No, not with that mob scene in place," Long said.

"But we'd like a table," McGraw said.

"One just came open in the corner over there."

"Great," Long said. "Now if you'd be nice enough to bring us a couple of Kentucky Gentlemen with a splash of water in each."

"I'm on my way."

"Ma'am," McGraw said, causing the waitress to stop. "I was wondering if the restaurant is still open."

"It's going around the clock. We've got stranded travelers and two private parties. The serving crew will be making a lot of money between now and daylight."

"We'll be here a while," Long said. "We've got four deer hunting buddies at the bar who'll be joining us."

"Then go ahead and take the big table with the picture of Winston Churchill over it," said the waitress.

Bass and Bobo were both lighting cigarettes when the news report continued. On camera from his office was FBI Special Agent in Charge Jim Wilcox.

"It's late and I'll need to be brief," Wilcox said. "Here's what we've got at this time. We've got five bank branches robbed. Explosives were used to gain entry to the buildings and the vaults. We've got only a few clues. We think we're dealing with professional criminals with knowledge of banks, their day-to-day procedures and, by all means, their security systems. We've got some materials that were left at the scene that could lead to us narrowing our focus.

"I'll attempt to answer your questions, as least the ones I'm comfortable with."

"Given that these were branches of main offices, how much money are we talking about?"

"We're talking about a substantial amount of cash because security trucks were unable to make their pickups before the snowstorm hit. The banks are attempting to review their deposit records from Friday morning and afternoon, although their computer systems took a lick from the explosives. Wells Fargo and Brinks have the cash that was left. Simple math will provide the answer to your question, provided the computer system glitches aren't too severe."

"Were the bills marked or, uh, dyed?"
"No comment."

"Are locals involved in this?"

"Most of the early indicators would point to that. Obviously, the guilty parties had knowledge of the area. But that could be the result of skillful planning, so it's still a guess about locals. If the snowstorm had bearing on the robberies, which seems likely, its sudden nature developing indicates the involvement of people who didn't have to travel far to get to where their disgusting act took place. It's not impossible to fathom, but it's difficult to believe somebody from very far away could orchestrate something like this."

"Can you give us a ..."
"Excuse me," Wilcox said. "That doesn't mean we're not focusing on

states adjacent to Alabama. You'll see evidence of that during the next several hours. In fact, we're not ruling out anybody."

"Can you give us a scenario, at least as you see it now?"

"Whew. Maybe you need a script writer for that. They come to town. They camp in an area near the bank branches. They blow up part of each building. They blow up each vault. They take the money and retreat. From there, who knows? They're either at home or trying to get there."

"Are you saying people are counting money in the comfort of their houses?"

"I'm merely saying that's possible. Like I said, I'm guessing for now. I don't expect to be guessing forever."

"You mentioned materials left at the scene."

"That's right — and I'll leave it at that."

"You said they might have been camping."

"I said might have been. Now I think I've said enough. I don't want to jeopardize what we've got working."

The CNN newscaster was quick to change directions. She said, "We'll keep you posted on developments in Birmingham. Meanwhile, U.S. troops are ..."

The patrons at the Old Country Pub had been mesmerized by the newscast. But as soon as it ended, the volume on the television sets was turned down and the jukebox was turned up. The drinking and dancing continued.

"Damn, this is unreal," Bobo said to Cates, Bass and Mills as McGraw and Long waited for them to spot them sitting at the table under the Winston Churchill picture.

"I'd like to know what kind of materials they found," Mills said. "It couldn't be much."

Bobo, Mills and Bass looked toward Cates for his reaction. He appeared to be thinking hard. Finally, he said, "It's probably a bluff on the part of the FBI. Sometimes they spring leaks to see if somebody tries to repair them."

"You seem to be lost in thought," Mills said.

"Na, not really," Cates said. "I'm just a little tired. But I was wondering if we disposed of everything properly. For instance, I'll bet my life they're looking in dumpsters all around that area."

"I'm so nervous I can't remember everything the guy said," Bass said.

"Well, there are a couple of dudes across the room who'd like for us to tell them," Mills said as he pointed toward McGraw and Long.

"Bartender, we'd like to clear these tabs and start fresh across the room with a couple of pals who dropped in," Cates said.

"I'll give you a tally in a minute," the bartender said.

"Don't mess with it," Cates said. "Here's forty bucks. That should take of it."

"I'll get your change."

"It's yours to keep," Cates said.

"Thank you, sir. I'll make sure somebody takes good care of you and your buddies the rest of the night."

CHAPTER TWENTY

William Fitzgerald and Tommy Murphy, small town police officers, were drinking coffee at the end of a double shift that had been prolonged by traffic mishaps and the need to help stranded citizens move from house to house. They were sitting in the Sleepy Hollow, Tennessee Police Department and had been watching newscasts related to the bank robberies in Birmingham. One was a little feisty.

"I told you we should have arrested those guys in that crimson Pathfinder," Fitzgerald said about their encounter with Sam Mills and Ed Bass earlier in the day at a Waffle House. "I'm betting my next paycheck those guys were involved in those bank robberies."

"Come on, William, don't let your imagination get the best of you," Murphy said. "It's almost midnight. You're tired and you're thinking way too much."

"Damn, Tommy, add it up. Sport utility vehicle — Pathfinder. Knowledge of bank security — bankers. Camping near the area of the bank branches — a truck load of supplies."

"But crimson is not green, blue, white, yellow or whatever," Murphy said. "Also, I'd estimate about a thousand sports utility vehicles roared through Sleepy Hollow between daylight and now."

"That one was full of cash," Fitzgerald said.

"They were deer hunters."

"So explain this," Fitzgerald said. "Those guys never got in the woods, or so they said, and they smelled to high heaven."

"Okay, that's a good question. But maybe the answer is something else they said, that they slept in a truck all night in Cullman, Alabama."

"Bull shit."

"Fine, William, have it your way," Murphy said. "Send a teletype to the FBI office in Birmingham and give them the names of those two guys. It's no sweat off our balls. At least we had gumption enough to question them, even though their truck was crimson."

Fitzgerald jumped to his feet and pounded a fist into an open palm. He was disturbed. He kicked a trash can. He slammed a hand against the wall and said, "Damn it, Tommy, I can't do that unless you can help me."

Murphy gave Fitzgerald an inquisitive look.

"I didn't write down their names and I can't remember them," Fitzgerald said. "I'll get fired for incompetency if I admit that to anybody, especially the damn FBI."

Murphy was kicking his brain into overdrive. He was thinking hard: Al Bailey ... Ed Miller ... Ben Baldwin ...

"I feel like an idiot," Fitzgerald said.

"I don't feel like a genius," Murphy said. "Maybe we should call the dispatcher."

"I didn't give her any information," Fitzgerald said. "I just told her we were at the Waffle House."

"Let's just call the FBI office and tell them we met two bankers from Western Kentucky we believe were involved in the bank robberies," Murphy said.

"That's a thought," Fitzgerald said. "It wouldn't be hard for them to take it from there. You know, they could check every bank in Louisville."

"Make the call," Fitzgerald said.

"You call 'em," Murphy said.

"As your superior officer, I'm ordering you to call the FBI in Birmingham," Fitzgerald said.

"Fine," Murphy said. "But I'm going to be honest with them. I'm going to tell them my partner, William Fitzgerald, questioned these guys unmercifully but didn't write down their names and didn't report the inquiry to our dispatcher. I'm going to tell them I'm not suspicious of these guys, but my partner is and he commanded me to make this call."

"You've been an obnoxious bastard since we were in grade school,"

Fitzgerald said.

"I'm just trying to keep both of us out of trouble, even if you're right about those men," Murphy said.

"Okay, I'll leave it alone," Fitzgerald said. "At least they didn't kill or hurt anybody."

Team Orange, Team Blue and Team Crimson had become Team Apprehensive while eating large steaks and drinking whiskey at the Old Country Pub in Nashville. Part of the crowd had disbursed at a dilatory hour, but they were being joined by men in tuxedos and women in colorful gowns. Also, two police officers were having coffee.

"I suggest we go a little slower on the booze and a little harder on the potatoes," Mark Cates said. "Also, I'm suggesting we make early departures for Louisville."

"No," Carl McGraw said. "The smart thing to do is to go when everybody else does, blend in with the crowd. It's my guess a lot of people will be going home late in the morning, after the ice melts."

"Then it's breakfast at nine o'clock," Fred Long said.

The bank robbers resembled outdoors men, which was their disguise, in khaki pants or jeans, plaid shirts or knit shirts and sweatshirts and snow boots or sneakers. They looked the part of travelers in distress, which is what the police officers must have thought when they walked past their table, waved and moved toward the door.

"I don't think we have to leave together," Sam Mills said.

"Hell yes, we do," Ed Bass said. "Remember, we're in a convoy from a deer hunting trip gone bad."

"I agree," Long said.

"I'm with you," Ben Bobo said.

"Damn, look at those baby dolls at the bar," Cates said.

"They're hookers — and the last thing you need is a whore out to make a buck," McGraw said.

"I'm not sure," Cates said with a smile.

"Listen, you dumb and drunk son of a bitch," McGraw said. "You've got a wife who thinks you're having an affair. The best thing you can do is cool off your tongue, or whatever."

"That's my boy — my brother," Long said. McGraw understood the underworld reference, looked at Long and nodded his head, with a smile following.

"So, Marko, what don't we know about you?" Bass said.

Cates shrugged his shoulders.

"My best pal has a wife who watches a lot of soap operas and, somehow, she intertwines their lives with the lives of the actors," McGraw said.

"That's a good way to put it," Cates said.

"Well, I hope the damn lawyer you're screwing is a female," Bobo said. "I just spent a night alone with you."

"Nobody said anything about a lawyer," Cates said.

"You did earlier today, after getting in the juice," Bobo said. "I quote: 'You know, Ben, there's something sexy about a female lawyer grilling a macho man on the witness stand.'"

The five other men chuckled and looked at Bobo. His pal, Long, noticed some war wounds. He was quick to react.

"So tell me, Ben, did you make a pass at Mark last night or did you take a blasting cap to the face?" Long said.

"Tell it, brother," McGraw said, sure Long would appreciate the mention.

"Back off my partner," Cates said. "He had a tougher night than the rest of us."

In Birmingham, the telephone lines at FBI headquarters were active as Special Agent in Charge Jim Wilcox and special agents Paul Conrad, Tim Perkins, Pat Embry and Joel Deaton discussed the case and waited for an initial report on the explosive devices that had been found at the bank branches. Despite the late hour and the fatigue they were fighting, they were summarizing the chain of events as diligently as the six bank robbers were in a more relaxed setting.

"We've got some smart cookies on our hands," Wilcox said. "But I can't believe they chose Central as a target, not with it located in such a busy area."

"That tells me we've got somebody familiar with that bank branch as a suspect," Conrad said. "They had to have liked something out of the ordinary about that location."

"Tell me more about that camp ground at Oak Mountain State Park and the wrappers found at that golf practice facility," Wilcox said.

"We'll know more tomorrow morning," Embry said. "It wasn't discovered until just before dark and we decided to wait so we wouldn't contaminate anything. The honey bun wrappers found at the golf practice facility were traced to a shipment made a few days ago to the Winn-Dixie supermarket."

"Damn," Conrad said. "There's more evidence local people are involved."

"Either that or they had enough nerve to mingle with everybody else while committing a crime," Deaton said.

A female special agent walked into the room carrying several sheets of paper. She clenched her lips and shook her head, a bad sign in the eyes of the men. She threw down the information, rubbed her face with both hands and plopped into a chair.

"So?" Wilcox said.

"There aren't any prints, at least any clear enough to give us a lead," she said. "We're just getting started tracing the origin of those blasting caps. That'll take a while. Tom Goldberg and Emily Spears will have their people back in the bank branches tomorrow morning, but neither is encouraged at this time."

"That's your summation?" Wilcox said when the female special agent quit talking.

"It's dismal, but yes."

A telephone call came in from FBI headquarters in Washington, D.C. The special agents in Birmingham learned roadblocks set up on interstate highways in Alabama, Tennessee, Mississippi, Florida and Georgia had done little more than ignite the ire of motorists.

Perkins had a lengthy telephone conversation with the Alabama Air National Guard at Birmingham International Airport. He returned to the room with a scowl on his face.

"Nothing, except deer romping in the woods," Perkins said. "The choppers are going back up at sunrise."

"Ask Carla McGuire to come back in here," Wilcox said about the female special agent they had conferred with earlier. "I want to know about those tire tracks."

As they waited for Perkins to fetch McGuire, the other special agents talked about how much cash the bank robbers might have netted.

"They weren't rapacious, not if the initial estimate is accurate," Embry said. "They left more than $125,000 in those vaults, according to the Wells Fargo and Brinks people."

"The numbers I've seen indicate they got out of there with $300,000 and pocket change," Deaton said. "That's not a big haul for four, six or eight people to split, not given the risk they've taken."

"I've been given higher numbers by accountants at Bruno's, Food World, Winn- Dixie, Kmart, Wal-Mart and other businesses in Inverness Corners," Wilcox said. "The FDIC is already ..."

Wilcox was stopped when McGuire entered the room. "You're wondering about tire tracks," she said. "Well, we're talking about the industry standard for the oversized variety — and the ones put on at the factory aren't any different than the ones bought at a store."

"Let's go to bed," Wilcox said, knowing the sports utility vehicle pool had not been reduced by that report. "I'll see you guys tomorrow at seven at Hardee's on Highway 280. I can't hear any more bad news."

At the Old Country Pub in Nashville, the bank robbers watched numerous news reports on the television set hanging near the bar, being careful not to appear overly interested, and talked about ways in which they might have gone wrong. The crowd had thinned significantly, but it was growing again because more of the men and women who had attended the formal parties in ballrooms were seeking nightcaps.

"Most of the stuff we took down there is in the bottom of a river, a lake or a pond," Long said. "The major exceptions, I surmise, are that damn green dress Carl and I took off our Pathfinder and some of the wiring we couldn't find."

"What did you do with the cover?" Bass said.

"We cut it to shreds and put it in a dumpster," McGraw said. "I don't think anybody could put it together like a puzzle and make it look like the body of a truck."

"Those damn wires bother me," Mills said.

"Hey, I wish you'd relax," Cates said, his voice firm. "Bankers know banks. Insurance men know insurance. Contractors know how to purchase and use explosives in a smart way."

"You're acting a little testy, Mark," Bobo said. "You've got your damn wallet, haven't you?"

"Hell yes," Cates said. "Why would you ask that?"

"Well, I saw you tapping on the back of your pants a few minutes ago, like you were looking for something. Then I saw you digging in your shirt pocket like you might have misplaced it there."

Cates mumbled something about Bobo being queer, jumped to his feet and pulled out his wallet. "Now, I hope you'll mind your own business," he said.

"His business is your business," Long said. "Just like his business is my business."

With that admonition considered and accepted, Long announced his intentions of calling it a night. "We're being more counter-productive than anything else at this hour," he said. "I think rest is in order."

Bobo, Bass and Mills concurred. McGraw and Cates, longtime buddies, said they were going to have one more drink before retiring to their rooms.

Actually, they had two more each and it was three o'clock in the morning before they staggered toward their beds.

"I think we're going to make it," McGraw said as they waited for an elevator in the lobby."

"Time will tell," Cates said.

"You aren't telling your best buddy something," McGraw said. "I know you. Something is bugging the hell out of you."

"I'm just worried about my extremely jealous wife," said Cates. who was really concerned about something much more threatening.

"Okay, let's a make a deal," McGraw said.

"I might and I might not," Cates said.

"When you get ready to tell me what your screw up was about in Birmingham, or whatever you have on your mind, we'll talk behind closed doors," McGraw said.

"That'll work," Cates said.

"Is this the time to talk?"

"Let's give it a rest," Cates said.

CHAPTER TWENTY-ONE

Diana McGraw, who was feeling a little guilty, was quick to greet Midge Cates with a smile when she entered the kitchen at about a quarter past seven o'clock on Sunday morning.

"Good morning, sweet lady, and I hope you slept well," Diana said to the friend she had chastised severely the evening previous. "The coffee is hot, the snow has quit falling and the weather forecast is for clear skies and rising temperatures."

"Actually, I did sleep well," Midge said. "I came to my senses about midnight and went out like a light."

"That's my girl."

"Now I want to have a good breakfast, get the children dressed and go to church."

Diana was stunned. Suddenly, the woman who had been so skeptical about her husband was a picture of contentment. She wondered if her personality was being split.

"When are the boys supposed to be home?" Midge said.

"I'm not sure," Diana said. "Cindy said they'll be rolling in at some point this afternoon. I guess it depends on the weather."

"I'm anxious to talk to Mark and Carl about those bank robberies in Alabama," Midge said. "The way I see it, a couple of contractors will be able to tell us a bunch about dynamite."

"Don't forget the two bankers who went with them," Diana said. "Maybe we need to plan a party for eight and try to get to the bottom of that mess."

"It does appear the FBI needs help," Midge said. "I felt sorry for that man during the news conference last night. He looked like a sad puppy."

"I'd say a distrustful person like you is up to the task in this case," Diana said. "Maybe you missed your calling."

Midge smiled, faintly, then said, "I'm glad you brought that up. I'm ashamed of the way I've been acting. I appreciate you taking a whip and getting me back on track."

FBI Special Agent Paul Conrad of the Birmingham brigade had decided to stay at headquarters Saturday night, choosing to work off anxiety instead of tossing and turning in his bed. He sent a Cumberland Law School underling to his house for a change of clothes and some toiletries and spent a few hours working with Special Agent Ed Samson on reports coming in from the computer lab in Washington, D.C.

After a couple of hours snoozing on couches, the two men were finalizing a report they would make to Special Agent in Charge Jim Wilcox at Hardee's restaurant on Highway 280. Already, that meeting had been pushed forward so more data could be analyzed. With things swirling at an unbelievable pace, there was a good chance the gathering would be cancelled.

"I don't think the boss is going to like this good news, bad news report any better than us," Samson said.

"You're the one who'll tell him," Conrad said. "I'm in the car and truck business."

The men had learned the explosive devices found near the bank branches had been traced to Willow Bend International, a supplier located in North Hampton, Vermont. Also, they learned the company conducts business in every state and at least ten foreign nations, that its client list during the most recent year totaled more than 31,000. More troubling, the owner said he and his associates might supply a customer in 1994 and not hear from it again until 2000.

A notation on the report said the owner should be left alone for several hours because he had become agitated when called at his house late at night.

"Screw that man," Conrad said. "He's dealing with the Federal Bureau of Investigation, not Hand Me A Nail Construction Company in Boligee.

Conrad was on edge because of some other distressing news he had learned when exploring the sports utility vehicle market. In summary, Nissan, Ford, General Motors and other manufacturers told him it would take several months, maybe a year, for them to supply the FBI with a complete list that included points of origin, dealers and first buyers.

"Damn, you'd think narrowing the colors would help cut down on the time," Samson said.

"Like the man at GM told me," Conrad said. "Just take a look the next time you're in traffic on a busy street and observe the number of sports utility vehicles around you. If you multiply that by the number of busy streets in the United States, well, you've got a billion sports utility vehicles to consider."

"But we're only interested in five or ten states," Samson said.

"So what's the difference in millions and millions and a billion?" Conrad said.

Special Agent in Charge Jim Wilcox was already hot under the collar at his house in the Riverchase area of Hoover. He was holding a bedroom telephone speaker in one hand and using the other hand to manipulate the power button on his television set remote control device. He had slept about two hours the evening previous and had a gnawing in his stomach and a chronic pain in his lower back. The stream of correspondence had come so quickly he had not been able to shower.

"I'll be a son of a bitch," Wilcox said after watching a minute of a national newscast. "Those people are freaks. They couldn't care less about what we're trying to accomplish."

"It's becoming a public relations issue," said Special Agent Carl Williams, who was on the telephone in Washington.

"Damn," Wilcox said as he hung up.

The newscaster on the television screen was explaining the picture people were watching across the nation:

"One of the first drivers stopped by these roadblocks told CNN it was something akin to a border checkpoint, that he and his wife had to get out of their Chevy Blazer while state troopers emptied the contents. This happened as they were attempting to return to Ann Arbor, Michigan from their winter home in Tampa, Florida.

"Obviously, as this scene shows, no fewer than six recreational vehicles are sitting on the side of Interstate 59 in Alabama not far from Chattanooga, Tennessee. Here is another shot that shows a few dozen sports utility vehicles on the side of the road just outside Atlanta.

"Roadblocks have been in place throughout the night on interstate highways in Alabama, Florida, Georgia, Mississippi and Tennessee. Some motorists have reported they were detained at those locations for at least two hours.

"Now it looks like the misfortune some had last night will be relived by other motorists today."

Wilcox turned off the television set and glanced at a clock on a nearby dresser. He would be late for the meeting at Hardee's if he left at that moment and drove fast, so he surmised he should make a few telephone calls and see if the roadblocks could be streamlined to include only sports utility vehicles of a certain color and those heavily packed. He knew his staff would move forward without his guidance, like to dumpsters and other dreadful locations.

His first telephone call went to Washington, where he was again hooked up with Williams. Before he could express all he had in mind, the special agent said, "Jim, they're behind closed doors talking about the roadblocks as we speak. Don't expect this one to go your way."

Nobody was eating much as Carl McGraw, Fred Long, Mark Cates, Ben Bobo, Ed Bass and Sam Mills sat at a table in Floyd's Restaurant at the Maxwell House Hotel. Instead, they were talking in whispered tones and trying to sip coffee in an effort to make their conversation look comfortable and run of the mill.

All three teams in The Snowman Project had seen news reports that showed roadblocks on interstate highways, including the one between them and home.

"Thank God for CNN because that's something we didn't think about," Cates said. "But even now that we know about those roadblocks, I'm not sure we can avoid them."

"We don't try," Long said.

"We sure as hell can't stay here another day," Bass said. "That'll create all kinds of suspicion — and I'm not sure what it'd do to our marriages."

"If you guys will try to eat a little, look relaxed, I'll tell you how we can beat this," Long said.

They all took bites.

"I don't know how far up I-65 we'll make it before we run into the first roadblock," Long said. "I'd guess it can't be far because we're practically in Kentucky. So we've got to dump our cargo somewhere as fast as possible."

"Shit, Fred, we've worked too damn hard for our money to consider that," Mills said.

"Shut up and listen," Bobo said, who had misgivings himself and thought he was blurting without reason.

Long explained he knew a lot about the immediate area because he had been to numerous insurance conventions in Nashville, not to speak of other business engagements. He said there was an undeveloped piece of property near a shopping center down the street from the hotel.

"We're not leaving money in woods and let it rot in melting snow," Bass said.

"Hey, I'm not dumb," Long said.

Long said he advocated the group driving to an out of the way area near the shopping center and taking an inventory of everything they had in the Pathfinders. He said they could bury what they did not want to keep with them, then make sure only one of the sports utility vehicles had the money in it.

"We've got too many duffle bags to do that," Bobo said.

"Maybe so and maybe not," Long said. "It'll be a tight squeeze, no doubt, but I think we can make it and still have the loot covered with something."

"Then I suppose I'll be the one who drives the Pathfinder with the cash in it through a roadblock," Mills said. "Excuse me, guys, but I'm going to the bathroom and puke."

While Mills was away from the table, Long continued his explanation. It sounded more feasible the deeper he got into it. It included a seemingly astute observation he had made on the ride two days earlier from Louisville to Birmingham.

FBI headquarters in Birmingham was getting crowded because special agents were arriving from across the state — Tuscaloosa, Montgomery, Anniston and Huntsville, among other cities. The investigation team was growing in an effort to keep pace with the bank robbers. Interviews were being conducted and several others were being scheduled.

"Sir, just take your time and tell me when you heard the first blast and what happened next," said a special agent, who was visiting with a Friday night customer from Bruno's supermarket.

"It was about three o'clock, as I remember, and I was walking to my jeep in the parking lot. It was muffled, like a quick roar of thunder. It sounded like it was about a mile away, but I'm guessing about that. Another guy, a total stranger who was scared out of his pants, ran to my side and started talking, if you can call babbling talking."

"Okay, go ahead."

"We stood there for about fifteen minutes, shaking in the cold, when across the street we saw a vehicle leaving the Food World shopping center. I felt relieved when I saw the four-wheeler because it had a yellow light on top that was flashing and a sign on the driver door. After it drove from sight, going south on Valleydale Road, I looked at my companion and said, 'Good, somebody is doing something about the power outage.'"

"Was the vehicle new or old?"

"It didn't look old."

"What color was it?"

"I think the vehicle was dark."

Every person interviewed except Andrew Carroll, the man who had conversed with Mills in the Patriot Bank parking lot, agreed the sports utility vehicles they saw were dark in color. He stuck with his white, beige or yellow description.

At that moment, a motorist was upset after a tan and black

automobile with writing on the sides and a blue light on the dash board pulled him to the side of Interstate 59 between Gadsden, Alabama and Chattanooga, Tennessee.

"Frankly, officer, I don't understand what this is about," the angry man told a Tennessee State Trooper who watched other law enforcement officers emptying the contents of a green Pathfinder and a small trailer being pulled behind it. "I just loaded this thing an hour ago. Now you ruthless bastards are taking everything we own and dumping it on the side of the highway."

"Did you say we?" the Tennessee State Trooper said.

"Yes," the man said. "My wife is about fifteen minutes ahead of me in our car."

"I'd appreciate it if you would find a place inside your truck," the Tennessee State Trooper said. "We'll come get you if you're needed. Also, we'll repack the truck."

"Damn," the man said. "I want an explanation. Do I look like somebody hauling drugs?"

"A lot of people are facing the same thing," the Tennessee State Trooper said as he pointed to long line of vehicles stopped on the side of the interstate highway. "We're doing this at the request of the FBI."

"Screw the FBI and you, too," the man said.

"Listen, you bastard," the Tennessee State Trooper said. "You're about to be arrested if you don't get your fat ass inside that truck."

The motorist hurried to the green Pathfinder. When the Tennessee State Trooper turned to his left he saw a television news crew approaching him, including a man with a camera who had been recording the conversation. The law enforcement officer rushed toward a female reporter holding a microphone and said, "Get your asses out of my face. This is sensitive business and we don't need bystanders."

"Could I ask you a question?" said the reporter. "We know this is about those bank robberies in Birmingham and ..."

"You're about to be arrested," the Tennessee State Trooper said. "Get your asses rolling."

"I'll call *CNN* and tell them we've got something hot that's ready to be aired," said the man with the camera.

Already, special agents at FBI headquarters in Washington had digested several news reports of that nature. A decision had been made. The roadblocks would stay in place until noon and only sports utility vehicles of prescribed colors would be stopped until then.

Three Pathfinders colored orange, blue and crimson were parked in a wooded area near the Festival Park shopping center not far from the Maxwell House Hotel. Several items had been buried and the sports utility vehicles looked cleaner and more orderly than they had since Friday afternoon.

"I can't believe this shit," Bobo said. "All my life I've been lucky, at least until this weekend. Now I lose a damn coin toss that has me walking in quicksand."

"It won't be bad, Ben," McGraw said after the money had been placed in the blue vehicle Bobo and Cates would drive to Louisville.

"Absolutely not," Long said. "Carl and I will be a couple of miles in front of you and Ed and Sam will be a mile behind you. Just keep on your walkie-talkie until you hear us call out the exit number. Then confirm it with a 10-4, get off the interstate and do your thing. I'm telling you that building is about four miles from here, no more than six."

"If you don't come to it before we see a roadblock, we'll tell you to bail out," McGraw said. "Ed and Sam will be there to pick you up."

Wilcox was on the telephone in his car parked beside the entrance to Oak Mountain State Park on Highway 119 near Birmingham. He was talking with Mike Sullivan, a longtime friend and ranking special agent at FBI headquarters in Washington. The tone of the conversation was something other than affable.

"I know what CNN is showing because I've watched so much of it I'm about to throw up," Wilcox said. "But, Mike, you're pulling the rug out from under us if you suspend those roadblocks."

"Jim, there must be thirty trucks on the side of the road between Chattanooga and Nashville and, damn it, I'm looking at twice that many on I-20 outside of Atlanta."

"Tell me something, Mike. Do you fuckers want to catch those bank robbers or do you want to let them drive away like ...”

“We can’t drive people crazy with these searches,” Sullivan said. “We’re on thin ice when it comes to constitutional law. I don’t think I have to explain probable cause and search warrants to you.”

“I’m on thin ice, too,” Wilcox said. “It’s my case to solve. I can’t allow my hands to be chopped off like this.”

“I understand, my friend. But the roadblocks are coming down, just like the director ordered.”

“Okay,” Wilcox said, his voice full of resignation.

“Now let me give you something else that’ll taste like crap in your mouth,” Sullivan said. “You’ve got to schedule another press conference and apologize to the public for the inconvenience.”

“Shit,” Wilcox said as he pushed the button on the telephone to disconnect the call. He threw the speaker into the floorboard, then slammed the dashboard with his right hand.

Before Wilcox could turn the ignition key on his car to drive to the makeshift camp ground the bank robbers had used two night earlier, the telephone started ringing. He took a deep breath.

“Special Agent Jim Wilcox.”

“I’ll overlook your outburst, Jim, because I know you’re under the gun,” Sullivan said.

“Thanks.”

“But I’m afraid I’ve got another order that’ll send you over the edge.”

“Fire away, like everybody else does.”

“The director has given the news media about half of an hour at ten o’clock tomorrow morning to take pictures inside the bank branches,” Sullivan said.

Wilcox could not believe what he was hearing.

“You’ll have photographers from Time, U.S. News & World Report, and The Associated Press, which will be the pool source for all others.”

“Hey, Soldier of Fortune and all of the tabloids aren’t invited?” Wilcox said, his tone sarcastic. “If I was Sports Illustrated, I’d file a protest.”

“People ask me why I love Jim Wilcox and I tell them it’s statements like that,” Sullivan said. “I’ll see you on the flip side.”

Wilcox laughed for the first time in more than a full day as he drove up a hill to the camp site. He was pleased when special agent Pat Embry, a dear friend, was the first person he encountered. Privately, he wished they were going to play a round of golf.

"What's up, chief?" Embry said.

"If I thought you wanted to know, or could handle it, I'd tell you," Wilcox said. "So what have we got here?"

"Some burned oak ashes and some dumped charcoal," Embry said.

"How have the lab folks done this morning?"

"Smudge after smudge."

"Is anybody still on garbage detail?"

"Yeah, and they found a few more feet of spotless wire and another blasting caps box. Also, the Hoover Police Department found some junk of no value in a pond near corporate buildings down Inverness Boulevard. There's something floating in the Cahaba River near I-65."

"What's new with the Alabama Air National Guard?"

"The airmen spotted a couple of sports utility vehicles between Wilsonville and Clanton. The Shelby County Sheriff's Department went in there with three units, somewhere around Lay Lake, and found a couple of deer hunters who were stuck in muck and happy to be discovered."

Wilcox paused for what seemed like a full minute?

"Next question," Embry said.

"Have you ever had a damn headache that made you think your brains were about to fly out of your ears?" Wilcox said.

"Not since this morning," Embry said.

"Well, get ready for another one," Wilcox said. "Unless we get a break later in the day, our next meeting will be in the bar at Friday's on Highway 280 at sunset. Get the damn A-Team together for that one."

"It'll be my pleasure," Embry said.

"No, Pat, on second thought, we'll meet at Connie's Cafe in the same shopping center. The federal government is about to buy my crew a delightful and expensive meal."

CHAPTER TWENTY-TWO

Jim Wilcox did not have a patent on frayed nerves as the second day of the hunt for phantom bank robbers continued. The six men from Louisville, Kentucky were apprehensive, too, as they attempted to move toward home.

They had left the Maxwell House Hotel in Nashville without fanfare. They had disposed of a smattering of evidence in woods without being seen, although after considerable debate they left blasting pads and detonators in one Pathfinder because C&M Construction needed them during the upcoming work week. Now they were on Interstate 65 wondering if the next hill or curve would be disastrous for them.

Like most everybody else in the nation, they knew roadblocks were creating havoc on main thoroughfares in five states. They did not know the dragnet was to be softened and then lifted, per orders from FBI headquarters in Washington, D.C.

Mark Cates and Ben Bobo were the men on hot seats, since they were transporting a lot of money stuffed in duffle bags. But they did not have a corner on anxiety.

"I'm about to wet my pants," Ed Bass said to Sam Mills as they drove a crimson Pathfinder through tracks left by large trucks. They were the trailing group, by design, but they could not be certain what was in front of them besides Team Orange and Team Blue.

"Team Orange will warn us," Mills said, talking about Carl McGraw and Fred Long. "Remember, if they say bail out, Team Blue hits the pavement and we pick 'em up."

The carefully spaced caravan was not far outside Nashville, maybe three miles, and the consternation was germinating as they rolled to the north without hearing McGraw or Long mentioning the exit they wanted to see as soon as possible.

Then came relief.

"Team Orange to Team Blue ... 2-7-3 ... Orange to Blue ... 2-7-3," Long said into the walkie-talkie.

"10-4, Team Orange," Bobo said with a huge grin surfacing on his face. He looked toward Cates, took a deep gulp and offered a wink.

"Did you copy that transmission, Team Crimson?" Bobo said.

"Right on, Team Blue."

Bass and Mills kept moving, still about a mile behind Cates and Bobo.

"I'd bet there are a couple of butts loosening up in that blue truck in front of us," Bass said.

"There's one getting loose in this crimson truck," Mills said.

When Cates and Bobo reached Exit 273 they were impressed by what they observed. It was exactly as Long had described, making them think he had a photographic memory of the highest order.

"Damn," Cates said. "Six miles from Nashville, like he said."

The exit was pretty much deserted. To their left, Cates and Bobo saw a BP service station and convenience mart. They were relieved to discern it was at least two hundred yards away from them. To their right, they saw a country store that was closed and boarded, an old barn with weeds growing around it, two old and rusted gas pumps in front of a concrete building that had been leveled and, well off the road and up a hill, a deserted white block service station.

"There's our gold mine," Bobo said.

"It's about to become one," Cates said.

Cates drove the blue Pathfinder around a curve and up the hill. He parked it in the back of the abandoned building. He and Bobo got out and walked toward a lubrication pit that had kudzu growing around it. They looked toward the county road they had left and saw nothing.

"Let's get that cash in the bottom of the pit," Bobo said.

Bass and Mills were sitting at the top of the exit ramp trying to decide if they should assist their partners.

"It's secluded enough for us to help Mark and Ben unload that truck,"

Bass said, his tone a tad unsure.

"That's a 10-4, good buddy," Mills said. "In fact, that'll look good to anybody who passes. You know, two pairs of deer hunters taking a break during a long journey, if only to take a leak in the great outdoors."

About three miles ahead, the mood was not so festive. Team Orange had topped a hill and had discovered three Tennessee State Trooper cars with lights flashing. Also, they saw several sports utility vehicles parked alongside the interstate.

"Well, it's just like we saw on the news, blue lights going crazy and cars strung out for what seems like a mile," Long said, trying to stay calm through the use of small talk.

"Turn off the walkie-talkie and put it under the seat," McGraw said. "While you're at it, take a look and make sure we're as clean as a whistle."

Long followed orders as quickly as he could as the orange Pathfinder approached the roadblock. A Tennessee State Trooper stepped into the middle of the interstate and began waving them to the side of the road. McGraw stopped the truck behind a cream Rodeo being driven by a solitary man. He saw a red Explorer pulling in behind him.

"I'll do the talking unless they ask you something," McGraw said. "Drivers normally do that, you know."

"I'll be damned," Long said. "Here comes a television news crew ready to put our faces on screens across the nation."

Team Blue, Cates and Bobo, had found refuge inside the abandoned service station and were delighted by something they discovered. Other than numerous spider webs and discarded tools and rags that had been left behind by the owners, the lubrication pit was relatively clean and ideal for the stashing they had in mind. It was obvious nobody had been in the garage for quite a while.

"If we put duffle bags down in the bottom of this thing and cover it with that plywood, the money should be okay for a while," Cates said while pointing at large boards leaning against a garage wall.

"It's a hell of a lot better than digging a hole in the woods," Bobo said. "I'm so weak-kneed, I couldn't dig up a ..."

Bobo stopped talking when he heard a car horn. He and Cates were frozen. They stooped to hide, but left themselves room to gaze through the shattered glass on the right side of the lubrication pit.

But they did not dare look and that led to them being startled by the voice they heard: "One damn move and I'll splatter your brains all over this place."

Bobo and Cates turned quickly in the direction of the thunderous voice. They started to run. Then when they saw Mills and Bass standing in the doorway, they went limp, dropped to their knees and, with their hearts pounding, started laughing.

"You son of a bitch, you stinking ass sorry son of a bitch," Cates said, releasing an abundance of caged energy with a couple of slurs.

"Would that be one of us or both of us?" Mills said.

Up the interstate a ways, McGraw and Long were answering questions at the roadblock. They had offered their deer hunting trip gone amiss alibi and were confident the Tennessee State Trooper interrogating them had bought into it. He had looked inside their vehicle, if only quickly, and resumed his questioning in a pleasant enough manner.

"Yes sir, that's correct," McGraw said. "We were going to Brewton, a small town in South Alabama, in Escambia County, and got turned back by the weather just this side of Montgomery. We spent last night at the Maxwell House Hotel in Nashville and, as I said, here we are."

"There's a lot of stuff in your Pathfinder, a heavy load for a weekend camping trip," said the Tennessee State Trooper.

"We work at it," McGraw said, with a smile he hoped did not appear forced. "We're city boys who like our comforts."

"Have you ever been to Birmingham?"

"Yes sir," McGraw said. "We passed through there last evening, really quite late."

"I'd like to hear what your buddy has to say," said the Tennessee State Trooper. "I assume he can talk."

"Too much at times," McGraw said, at once wishing he had kept his mouth shut, mirroring the thoughts of his partner.

The Tennessee State Trooper glared at McGraw, then looked toward

Long, who was quick to start a conversation.

"What can I add?" Long said.

"Just talk to me."

"Well, like Carl said, we came through Birmingham at a snail's pace and ended up in Nashville," Long said. "We got to the Maxwell House late in the afternoon. We drank most of the night at the Old Country Pub with some other stranded travelers. Now we're here talking to you."

"I know the place and most of the people who work there," said the Tennessee State Trooper.

"Pardon me."

"The Old Country Pub, a good place to get a strong drink after getting out of this uniform. Hell, I might head down that way tonight after this bitchy detail."

"Yes sir."

"How many hunters are there?" said the Tennessee State Trooper who flinched and scowled when he realized television news cameras were focused on him. He turned toward a cameraman and said, "Damn, sir, can you give me a break?" Then he smiled into the lens.

"There are six of us, sir," Long said. "The other guys are a few miles behind us because they had a few more drinks than us last night and, well, they chased a little trim."

"You know, I believe you guys like I've believed almost everybody else we've stopped," said the Tennessee State Trooper. "But we're going to search the truck because you're carrying a heavy load."

"Yes sir," McGraw said.

"There's some hot coffee up the road."

"Yes sir. Just let us know when we can leave."

In Louisville, Diana McGraw had skipped church, thinking Midge Cates needed the time alone, and was watching *CNN*. She started laughing when she saw a live report that showed her husband and Long being questioned by the Tennessee State Trooper. She muttered something about a star being born, then hurried to the telephone to tell the other wives.

"I'll call the other girls," Cindy Bass said upon hearing the report.

"I'm turning on the recorder in case they pop up on the screen again," Diana said. "Your guy and those other guys have to be in that crowd somewhere."

To the contrary, Bass, Mills, Cates and Bobo were isolated, to their relief, and they were working fast and furious stashing a load of money in the lubrication pit.

"I'm tempted to reach inside one of these bags and grab a handful," Bass said as he and the others tossed the last of the cash into the deep concrete hole and reached for plywood to use as cover.

"I'd like to know what we've got," Mills said. "The FBI report said at least $350,000. I'm betting there's more."

"The hell of it is we won't touch a dollar bill until it's put away some place to multiply," Cates said. "And, damn it, we won't get to do that if somebody finds it in this black widow dungeon."

"Okay, let's split," Cates said. "But not before we check the trucks to make sure we haven't left anything in them that can link us to Birmingham."

The men were careful in that quest. They took another long look at the lubrication pit to make sure it appeared unkempt. Then they returned to Interstate 65, determined to travel bumper to bumper, as if in a short caravan en route to home.

"That does it, men," said the Tennessee State Trooper as he walked toward McGraw and Long. "You can move it up the road. I'm sorry for the inconvenience."

"No problem, sir," said McGraw, who felt a fresh breath of air upon hearing the remark. "But would it be out of the question for us to ask what this is about?"

Long cringed after hearing that question. Suddenly, he was wondering if McGraw had enough discipline to become a part of the brotherhood.

"Somebody robbed five bank branches in Birmingham the other night," said the Tennessee State Trooper. "Those pompous bastards with the FBI hauled us out on a miserably cold Sunday morning to check every mother driving a truck."

"Damn," Long said. "All we wanted to do was shoot a few deer.

Somebody else got the big bucks."

The Tennessee State Trooper chuckled and said, "But we'll get 'em in the long haul."

McGraw started the orange Pathfinder, gave the Tennessee State Trooper a wave, pulled onto the interstate highway and said, "Damn, Fred Long, you're a genius. If you hadn't come up with a plan to bury a bunch of junk and stash a bunch of cash, we'd be on our way to the federal pen."

"I don't want applause," said Long, who was fast discovering his underworld savvy could not keep him cool in a real world caper. "I just want to get to Louisville, build a raging fire and have a strong drink with my lady."

Wilcox remained in need of emotional rescue as he paced nervously around FBI headquarters in Birmingham. During a series of telephone calls he had been chastised by superiors in Washington, D.C. for creating a public relations nightmare. In essence, he had relied on good instincts tempered by years of training — you better react within twenty-four hours of a crime or face a decade trying to solve it, the memorized line went — and, as time passed, he was hopelessly plodding.

Also, the special agent in charge was preparing to face a news conference mandated by FBI headquarters in Washington. He tightened the knot in his necktie, looked toward Carla Brunwig, a special agent from Birmingham, and said, "With all due respect, Big C, what the hell am I supposed to tell those people?"

"The truth will set you free," Brunwig said.

"The truth is a bunch of innocent people in Birmingham are thinking they're about to get screwed out of the money they deposited in those banks," Wilcox said.

"That's one for the FDIC," Brunwig said.

"Thank you, Carla," Wilcox said. "That F in front of FDIC stands for federal. That F in front of FBI stands for federal. I'm federal. You're federal. If this fucking case isn't solved in a timely manner, one of us won't be federal."

"That'd be you, big cheese," Brunwig said with a smile she hoped her boss would find appealing.

On Interstate 65, Cates and Bobo were stopped by the roadblock and had an interesting exchange with a Tennessee State Trooper who was familiar with their connived plight. Bass and Mills sat in their vehicle behind them.

"Let me guess, you're a couple of deer hunters from Louisville who like to drink whiskey and chase women," said the Tennessee State Trooper.

"You've got us pegged," Cates said.

"Well, you better get moving because your buddies have a headstart on you."

"With pleasure — and thank you, sir."

The timing could not have been better. The FBI had just sent out word that the roadblocks should be suspended. So Team Blue and Team Crimson were free to roll without having blasting pads and detonators discovered in one of the trucks.

"I don't know if we're rich, but we're blessed," Cates said.

"We'll be wealthy enough after Long and his boys get finished washing and restacking the cash," Bobo said. "Also, we've got one hell of a story to tell."

"Only we can't tell it."

As her husband breathed a sigh of relief and joked with his partner in crime, Midge returned home from a refreshing church service and heard a telephone message from Diana. Her minister had talked about family values, with emphasis on spouses supporting each other in times of weakness, and the words had renewed her faith.

"But I thought they were going to South Georgia," Midge said after hooking up with Diana by telephone and learning two of the bank robbers had made television appearances beside an interstate highway.

"That's not what Carl told the state trooper," Diana said.

"Well, last night Ed told Cindy they were returning from Brunswick, Georgia and got sidetracked."

"I'll keep the video tape in case we need it in divorce court," Diana said, following the remark with a chuckle.

"Hey, don't hang up now," Midge said. "Remember, you're the loving wife with nothing to fear, the one who told me I had lost my mind when I became suspicious."

Wilcox was standing in front of a bank of microphones with cameras recording his every move. He had been nervous when he walked to the podium and he appeared tired. He rubbed his face, vigorously, then started his televised address:

"I've been asked by colleagues at the FBI to bring you up to date in our investigation of the robbery of five bank branches in Birmingham, Alabama. While there is not a lot to report at this time, at least from a positive standpoint, let me summarize what has transpired.

"On Friday night, an undetermined number of individuals set up camp just outside Oak Mountain State Park near Birmingham. They left little or no evidence at that location.

"At some point between 11 p.m. Friday and 7 a.m. Saturday, these individuals robbed five bank branches in the Inverness Corners area of Shelby County. They used forced entries, explosives, and they left with an undetermined amount of cash, probably between $300,000 and $500,000. An accurate accounting should be made during the coming week.

"The culprits used off-the-road vehicles, recreational trucks, if you will, during the commission of these crimes. We assume they spent some time hiding at the Pro Learning Center golf facility on Valleydale Road, not far from the bank branches. That's based on numerous individuals seeing off-the-road vehicles in that area after hearing muffled blasts.

"We don't have suspects at this time. However, we think between four and eight people were involved. We know they're skilled when using explosive devices and have knowledge of bank security systems. If you have information to share, contact the FBI office nearest you.

"As part of our effort to catch these criminals, the FBI has utilized roadblocks on interstate highways and other major thoroughfares in five states. Also, we've used helicopters supplied by the air national guards in those states.

"In summary, we're involved in a tedious process that requires the cooperation of numerous individuals, not the least of which are motorists on the aforementioned roads. With that in mind, the FBI apologizes to those innocent people who have been placed under hardship because their vehicles were stopped at roadblocks and they were forced to endure the bitter cold weather while searches were made. We're appreciative of the patience most individuals have displayed. We're announcing the roadblocks have been suspended.

"I won't be able to answer any questions at this time."

Wilcox hurried from the room as reporters screamed questions he did not solicit. It was obvious to fellow FBI special agents he was not amused by the mandate to interrupt the use of roadblocks. That opinion was heightened when he uttered to nobody in particular, "I hope the director and those damn lawyers at the Justice Department are satisfied because without those roadblocks we're facing one hell of a challenge."

Long before sunset on a white Sunday afternoon that was melting back to normal, McGraw, Long, Cates, Bobo, Bass and Mills were at their respective houses in Louisville, after stopping for a cup of coffee at a Shoney's Restaurant to make sure each was on line as it pertained to their alibi. They decided to tell their wives they made it to South Georgia, discovered snow and ice, heard dreary weather forecasts, traveled across South Alabama and drove up Interstate 65 through Montgomery and Birmingham to Nashville, where they spent the night at the Maxwell House Hotel.

But one of them had something else to explain as he went about the business of putting away his portion of the deer hunting and camping equipment.

"Have you been in a fight? Frances Bobo said.

"No, I slipped in the ice and jammed my face against the back of the truck," Bobo said. "I wouldn't be surprised if my nose is broken."

"Let's go to the emergency room."

"No. I'm going to bed and forget that stupid trip."

CHAPTER TWENTY-THREE

Every office at Federal Bureau of Investigation headquarters in Birmingham, Alabama was crowded on Monday morning, a few hours more than two days after the bank robberies in Inverness Corners. Dozens of special agents were busy compiling information that was coming in at a fast pace, data related to explosive devices, sports utility vehicles, fingerprints and anything else they deemed important.

There was not a lot of good news to be found.

In one office, three special agents poured over sales records and determined it would be almost impossible to trace the blasting caps and wiring used to blow holes in the walls at Sector, First Columbus, Central, American and Patriot. During the most recent year alone orders had been placed and filled in every state except two, Hawaii and South Dakota.

Down the hall, in a conference room, five special agents looked over sales records provided by General Motors, Ford, Nissan and other manufacturers and were amazed to discover the number of sports utility vehicles owned by United States residents living in Alabama, Florida, Georgia, Mississippi, Tennessee and other nearby states.

In a laboratory, four special agents looked at smudged fingerprints and footprints and shrugged their shoulders. All they could determine was the criminals were men or, as one said, "one massive woman."

Meanwhile, Special Agent in Charge Jim Wilcox and Special Agent Pat Embry were talking in the office occupied by the boss. Begrudgingly, they were preparing to meet the press, so to speak, getting ready to work with photographers who had been given clearance to photograph the debris inside the bank branches. Obviously, the ranking special agent was not in a good mood.

"Jim, before we quit I've got something I need to tell you," Embry said, his tone sincere.

"If you're going to jump on my ass for yelling at you yesterday, save your breath," Wilcox said. "I'm sorry I've been on edge. I should never take out frustration on a ..."

"Excuse me, Jim, but I want to apologize for coming up with that roadblocks course of action. Obviously, that has added to your woes."

"It was a good idea," Wilcox said.

"I agree, so I'm willing to take the rap for it," Embry said. "Tell the bastards in Washington to ease up on you and start firing shit at me."

"That won't be necessary," Wilcox said. "It's over now. But damn it, Pat, I'll go to my grave thinking we would've had those guys locked up if we had maintained a strong position on those interstate highways."

"Yeah," Embry said. "We should be grilling those bastards instead of them having the time of their lives."

Actually, Mark Cates was not having such a nice meeting with Midge Cates. His wife was back on a rampage, with her suspicions fueled by the strange path the bank robbers had traveled over the weekend.

"Don't give me that shit," Midge said as her husband attempted to dress for work in their bedroom. "One minute you tell me you're in Georgia. The next minute you tell me you're in Alabama. Then, lo and behold, you're at a hotel in Tennessee."

"I haven't lied to you," Mark said.

"Sure. What you're telling me is about as logical as me going to the supermarket by way of Indiana. Damn, Mark, you go through Atlanta going and you go through Birmingham coming. Now you're talking in broader circles."

The husband was becoming agitated. He had been greeted by a loving wife the afternoon previous. Now he was being interrogated.

"Look at a damn road map and you'll see there isn't much difference in drive time," Mark said. "With the damn weather like it was, we did the right thing."

"I suppose Sandra Brewer thought so, too," Midge said, bringing up the female lawyer.

"Shit."

"Listen, Mark, I was about over that fling you had with her until you went out of town, to Nashville, and she went out of town, too. I won't tolerate ..."

"It was a kiss, not an affair," Mark said, his voice rising.

"Fine, have it your way."

"I will have it my way because that's what it was, a cheap kiss from a drunk woman at a party."

Midge started crying and walked briskly from the room, slamming the door behind her.

At Inverness Corners later that morning, Embry and two other special agents were escorting photographers from a couple of magazines and *The Associated Press* from bank branch to bank branch. Already, they had taken pictures at Sector, First Columbus, American and Patriot, an ordeal that had taken more than an hour. Now they were in the lobby at Central and were flashing bulbs in rapid order.

The debris was situated the same way it had been since blasts gutted the building, although that was scheduled to change the following afternoon when cleaning crews were to arrive. The frustrated lab experts had completed their work, earlier than expected and to no avail, and bank executives were anxious to start the repair process.

"You guys should go get some lunch," Embry said to the other two special agents. "I'll ride this out."

"We'll get you a footlong tuna at Subway and wait for you across the street," said one of the special agents.

"I won't have time for that," Embry said. "I've got to catch a flight to Washington early this afternoon."

A couple of minutes after the other two special agents departed in search of nourishment, a couple of bulbs flashed simultaneously.

"Wait a second," Embry said as he stared at a pile of rubble. Then the special agent said, "That's it, folks. It's time to leave."

"Give us a few more minutes to work the vault area," said a photographer from *Time* magazine.

"No," Wilcox said. "Pack your stuff and get out of here."

"But the folks in Washington said we could take shots of every lobby and every vault."

"That was Washington talking," Embry said, his voice boisterous and rising. "This is Alabama you're in now and I'm telling you you've got fifteen seconds to get your butts out of this building."

The photographers left in a hurry.

Embry took a few steps, stopped by a pile of debris and squatted to take a closer look. He stared at the rubble and could not believe what he perceived he was seeing. The cloth he was observing did not seem to fit with the torn wall frame, the splintered wood and the slashed paper that was surrounding it.

"Damn," Embry said.

The special agent paused for a few seconds.

"Damn, a breakthrough, I think."

CHAPTER TWENTY-FOUR

Jim Wilcox looked around the table on the fourth floor at Federal Bureau of Investigation headquarters in Washington, D.C. and was amazed by the distinguished individuals who had gathered for a meeting early on Tuesday morning. He had been joined by Mike Sullivan, a ranking special agent, four other special agents, Carmen Norris from the Central Intelligence Agency and Ben Eubanks from the International Trade Commission. A noted absentee was Special Agent Pat Embry, who had stayed in Birmingham to oversee an important inquiry.

"We've had three frustrating days to remember, that's for sure, and this one doesn't figure to be much better," Wilcox said as he started a presentation related to the bank robberies. "We're trying to throw a net around some crafty birds."

"I assume everybody has read the report," Sullivan said. "So, Jim, is there anything else new to relate before we get into some questions and answers?"

"Yeah," Wilcox said. "I received a telephone call this morning from the FDIC. It looks like they got out of there with a minimum of $480,000."

"Jesus," Eubanks said in disbelief. "Whatever happened to the Birmingham we used to know, the city known for rednecks, pawn shops and good college football games?"

Wilcox explained Shelby County to the group, focusing on that financially blessed portion. He told the others routine pickups by bank security trucks had not been made because of the snow and ice. He indicated that had to have been a part of the master plan designed for The Snowmen Project.

"That points to locals," Sullivan said.

"Yeah, as well as people who utilized a lot of surveillance before they went into action," Wilcox said. "Also, the fact they left the cash laced with dye in the vaults tells me they know the banking business."

"I assume you're conducting interviews," Sullivan said.

"Yeah, much to the anger of some high-profile individuals in that city," Wilcox said. "We're being discreet for obvious reasons. But we're covering all of the bases, from executives to janitors."

"And ..."

"So far we haven't found many people from the banking industry who own sports utility vehicles. That's a Maxima-to-Lexus crowd."

"We're barking at empty nests," Sullivan said.

"Unless Embry comes up with something worthwhile, that might be true," Wilcox said. "But that's why the CIA and the ITC are here. Our best chance of catching these people will come if they get careless handling the cash."

"That's an excellent point," Eubanks said. "Sometimes bankers are too smart for their own good."

Ed Bass and Sam Mills were not surprised when they arrived at First Commercial Bank in Louisville, Kentucky on Tuesday morning and found fellow workers still talking about the bank robberies. After participating in such conversations the day previous, at least cautiously, they had decided to be more assertive.

"You know, I hope to high heaven we're conducting a thorough review of our alarm systems," Bass said as several officers sat down to begin a routine second-day-of-the- week meeting. "It's beyond me how that many bank branches can be so lax."

"Frankly, Ed, I'm not sure our system would hold up under such extreme weather conditions, at least those at our branches across the state," said Wilbur Haskell, the vice president of operations. "We're insulated in this large building. But those tiny buildings in the rural areas are another story."

Bass shook his head, trying to exhibit disbelief, even while knowing the alarm system at First Commercial was similar to the ones he and the others had shortcircuited.

"What's more troubling to me is the ease with which they blew apart walls and vaults," said Eddie Maple.

"I agree," said Margaret Cummings. "I don't know a darn thing about dynamite, nor do I believe most people do. So I'd guess the men who did that have more than token knowledge about such things."

Cates and Carl McGraw were chatting in a more private environment at C&M Construction Company. They were concerned about how to fetch the cash they had stolen and how it would be handled by total strangers. Also, they were worried about inquisitive wives.

"Diana talked my ear off again last night," McGraw said. "She has a fixation about those bank robberies."

"I've heard the same thing," Cates said. "Except Midge suddenly wants to become an explosives expert."

McGraw mentioned the enthusiasm the women were showing might lead to them talking too much in country club circles. Specifically, he feared somebody in the social crowd might put two and two together and figure out he and Cates were out of town that weekend.

"But there is some good news from the girls," McGraw said. "They know much more than we do about the progress the FBI has made and, partner, all I've heard sounds damn good to me."

Cates nodded, smiled and said, "Yeah, it looks like our next hurdle is getting that money to Louisville and letting that damn Sid Wieckhart take it off our hands."

McGraw quickly opened a desk drawer, pulled out a notes pad and said, "It's Winestein — Sid Winestein."

"Whatever," Cates said while shrugging his shoulders. "The Jewish laundry man — and, Carl, I think you should commit the name to memory and burn that paper."

McGraw tore the page from the notes pad and put it in his shirt pocket. He saw Cates grinning.

"You look amused," McGraw said.

"I wouldn't call it amused," Cates said. "Midge thinks both of us had affairs last weekend because we stayed overnight in Nashville."

"Oh no, it's the old Sandra Brewer syndrome," McGraw said.

"Yeah, and the hell of it is I didn't screw the woman," Cates said.

"Okay, fine," McGraw said. "I'll believe that if you think it'll help you get through a guilt trip."

"But you'll admit she's a stick of dynamite," Cates said with a smile.

Explosive devices were a hot topic of conversation as the meeting continued at FBI headquarters in Washington. In fact, the authorities agreed their best shots at catching the bank robbers were finding some way to trace the path followed by blasting caps and taking advantage of a bungled money exchange.

"The problem with zeroing in on the owner of the blasting caps is it doesn't take that much firepower to do what those guys did," said Special Agent Micky Miller. "A guy could have much less than that laying around a warehouse for five years."

"The numbers are stacked against us, given all of the customers that supplier has had during the most recent year," said Special Agent Martha Knight. "We'll do a lot of whistling in the dark."

"Hell, it's an economics thing as much as anything else," Sullivan said. "We can't go that route. We'd spend a million dollars trying to get around to 5,000 customers. We'd be better off letting the FDIC return the money to the banks than running all over the country for a year."

"Don't tell me you want to give up," Wilcox said.

"No, not at all," Sullivan said. "But the blasting caps search is as unfeasible as the sports utility vehicles search. We've got to draw some tighter boundaries."

"Carmen, we're going to need your help," Wilcox said. "The same with you, Ben, and your associates at the ITC."

"We've got every bank in Switzerland under our surveillance as we speak," Eubanks said.

"The laundering of money is always near the top of our priority list," Norris said. "The mafia keeps us hopping to the tune of what seems like a jillion cases a year."

"So what would those guys do with five hundred grand?" Wilcox said.

"I'm betting they'll move slowly and let it grow," Norris said.

Dressed in a business suit and carrying a briefcase, Fred Long walked into a swank office building in Louisville. He rode an elevator to the fourth floor and entered a smartly and expensively decorated receptionist station located behind two large glass doors.

"I'm Fred Long from South World Insurance and I'm here for a meeting with Edgar Swartz," Long said.

"I don't see you on his calendar," said the receptionist.

"You might want to remind him we've got an appointment to discuss health insurance programs."

Two minutes later, Long was seated in front of a smiling Swartz, who had made sure his office door was closed tightly before directing his visitor to a sitting area on the far side of the spacious room.

The host looked magnificent for a 64-year-old man, slim and tanned with a full head of black hair that might have been touched up a bit and a moustache that was showing a few gray whiskers. His appearance grew more grandiose when he smiled broadly and said, "You told me you guys had it planned properly, but I must admit I'm more than a little impressed."

"It was cold and at times unnerving," Long said.

"It looked that way on television," Swartz said. "But, damn, you're still three or four steps in front of the feds."

"We've still got a little problem to overcome," Long said.

"Hey, don't bring your problems here," Swartz said, suddenly becoming surly. "I only want your money."

Long stayed cool and explained the money was stashed in a lubrication pit near Nashville. He said it would be retrieved in the near future. Swartz reacted in a pleasant enough manner, then hurried to a nearby telephone.

"Sid, this is Edgar," Swartz said. He paused for a few seconds and smiled as Sid Winestein reacted.

"Yes, I'm delighted, too. But that cash from The Snowmen Project will be delayed getting to us." Swartz paused again, this time for a longer period of time.

"Wow, I didn't know the wheels were turning like that," Swartz said. "We'll have the dough by no later than next Monday, less than a week from now." He paused again.

"Sure, those guys are as good as gold. There's no reason to believe they won't deliver. Hell, I think we've seen evidence of that."

Long took a deep breath, relieved, and watched as Swartz listened to Winestein.

"I'm told the numbers are about right," Swartz said. "We'll take ten percent off the top, as agreed, and turn it loose. Then we'll get another share when it comes back in a bundle."

Swartz talked a few more minutes with Winestein, about another project, then hung up the telephone. He looked at Long and said, "Fred, high noon next Monday. No earlier and, by God, not a minute later."

"Where?"

"There's a warehouse at the corner of Elm and Westwood, down by the railroad tracks. That's a couple of miles on the back side of East Louisville Airport, the private strip."

Long nodded and waited for more information. Swartz said, "You'll see my blue BMW and you'll see a white van. Back up your truck to the rear of the van."

"We'll all be there," Long said.

"Hell no," Swartz said. "I don't want to see anybody except you and one of those contractors. It's too early in this manhunt for six bad guys to be traveling in a group."

Wilcox was shaking his head when he returned to the meeting at FBI headquarters in Washington after being summoned to the telephone. He appeared more stressed than before. He seated himself and took a deep breath. Then he tried another breath he thought might work.

"You don't look good," Sullivan said.

"We got a call from a country bumpkin police officer in Middle Tennessee who said he and his partner spent several minutes Saturday morning questioning a couple of guys in a tightly packed crimson Pathfinder," Wilcox said.

"That's a start," Sullivan said.

"No, it's another dead end," Wilcox said. "The dumb son of a bitch didn't record a name or a tag number."

"Damn," Norris said.

"Don't be too hard on them," Wilcox said. "Our records indicate we stopped a similar vehicle Sunday afternoon — or at least we passed them off as deer hunters and waved them through a roadblock because we had orders to quit stopping people."

Wilcox cut his eyes toward Sullivan, who knew the point his fellow special agent was attempting to make.

"Don't start in on me," Sullivan said as Wilcox shifted uneasily in his chair. "What's done is done."

There was a silence that lasted several seconds. Then Sullivan said, "Let's use the next hour and a half to take care of other matters. Then Jim can tell us what Pat Embry is working on in Birmingham."

"With all due respect, I'd like to talk to you about that privately," Wilcox said. "We'll probably need some assistance from the CIA a little later, but I don't want to move too fast on what might be our only prayer in this deal."

CHAPTER TWENTY-FIVE

The headline in the Wednesday morning edition of *The Birmingham News* was astonishing: "Bankers Will Be Probed In Local Robberies." The story went on to explain how the Federal Bureau of Investigation was zeroing in on distinct suspects, having questioned many local bank officials at length the previous day and had several more interrogations scheduled.

The FBI had interviewed several people, some of them Birmingham socialites, but the interrogations had been conducted in an effort to detect suspects, not to grill individuals who already fit into that category. For obvious reasons, feelings had been put to tests and the moods in the offices where special agents Paul Conrad, Tim Perkins, Joel Deaton, Pat Embry and Carla Brunwig made inquiries became tense.

More than three dozen people had appeared. The range the first day was similar to the range set up for the second day, from bank employees who had been terminated like Jesse Caylor, senior tellers like Marilyn Howlett, security truck drivers like James Bronner, janitorial workers like Ralph Sandburg, alarm systems installers like David Blalock and, to the dismay of a lot of folks, bank presidents like Patrick Wood.

The inquiries were brusque at times, as well as leading, and the smarter people being asked questions had lawyers at their sides.

Conrad went face to face with Caylor in a small office while a stenographer recorded questions and answers.

"Were you upset when you were terminated by Central Bank?"

"Yes sir," Caylor said. "I was extremely angry."

"You don't like the bank president do you?"

"No sir, not particularly, but ..."

"You don't, uh, excuse me."

"But if you're suggesting I'd rob a bank, well, you're way out of line," Caylor said.

"I didn't say anything about you robbing a bank. But I would like to know where you were last weekend."

"I was at home."

"Were you alone?"

"Yes sir. My wife and I are separated and she and my children are in Florida with her parents."

"I'm sorry to hear that, Mr. Caylor."

Caylor did not respond. He looked toward the floor.

"Mr. Caylor, did your termination have anything to do with your wife leaving you?" Conrad said, being a bit too relentless to satisfy the stenographer assisting him.

"It could have, yes," Caylor said, bristling a bit. "She's accustomed to a certain style of living and our money has gotten tight."

"What kind of car do you drive?"

"I don't understand why you'd ..."

"Just answer the question, Mr. Caylor."

"A Ford Explorer, for now. I might be in a used up heap if things don't get better."

"Let me ask you a few hypothetical questions," Conrad said.

"Fine."

"If you wanted to open a bank vault, you'd know how wouldn't you?"

"Certainly. I've done it several times through a normal course of business. But I wouldn't know how to blow open a vault, if that's your next question."

The riveting interrogation of Caylor was interrupted by a sudden clamor inside an adjacent office, where Howlett became so upset over the persistent questioning by Perkins she grabbed her chest and fell to the floor. When she went into convulsions, paramedics were summoned. After a quick evaluation, they concluded the 44-year-old woman had suffered a heart attack. She was barely moving and her pulse was fading when they carried her to an ambulance parked outside.

Immediately, Perkins was summoned to the office of Deputy Special Agent in Charge Carl Monroe.

"What triggered that collapse?" Monroe said, obviously concerned about possible inappropriate behavior.

"She started getting shaky after I asked if she had ever had dealings with anybody who had been convicted of a crime," Perkins said. "She told me her brother had done four years at Holman Prison after being involved in a series of house burglaries. Several times after that, she kept going back to how she didn't tell the folks at First Columbus Bank about that when they interviewed her."

"She's worried about losing her job," Monroe said.

"I'm worried about her losing her life," Perkins said.

"I assume you don't consider her a suspect," Monroe said.

"I didn't after the first five minutes of our interview," Perkins said. "But I thought I should ask some more questions after hearing about that damn brother."

"Where is the guy?"

"He's living in a rural area just outside Trussville after being paroled about two years ago."

"Check him out," Monroe said.

Bronner, a licensed Wells Fargo truck driver, was dealing with questions offered by Embry, who at that time was more interested in dealing with a possible piece of evidence he had discovered than interviewing a security officer.

"It's normal for you to make pickups at bank branches on Friday afternoon, but you didn't do that," Embry said, offering a statement that sounded more like a question.

"I didn't last Friday afternoon because I received a radio dispatch that told me the people at Sector requested I get there in fifteen minutes or forget the pickup," Bronner said.

"Why couldn't you get there?"

"We run strict routes, sir, and it was impossible. I was on the other side of I-65, on Highway 31. So the dispatcher told me to forget Sector and try to make it to Patriot and American, two of our other clients."

"But you didn't make those pickups," Embry said.

"I stopped by at my normal time," Bronner said. "They were like Sector. Everybody had gone home because it was starting to snow harder by the minute. Finally, I radioed the dispatcher and she told me every bank had closed early, that I should suspend my route and go on about my business."

"I thought your business was driving for Wells Fargo."

"Yes sir, but like I said, the ..."

"Let me ask you a few more questions."

"Yes sir."

"Don't you routinely go in and out of bank vaults?"

"Yes sir."

"Don't you know the three branches we've talked about like the back of your hand?"

"Not really," Bronner said. "All banks start looking pretty much the same after a while. You don't pay attention to details. You go in, get the money, go out and keep rolling."

"But, Mr. Bronner, I think it's safe to assume a guy like you would be able to move around in one of those bank branches better than most people, even if it was dark outside."

"Is that a question?"

"Yes, you can consider it one," Embry said.

"Sir, I think I better call my boss and see if he can get a lawyer in here before I answer any pointed questions like that."

"Why do you need a lawyer, Mr. Bronner?"

"Because you're starting to accuse me of something I didn't do or wouldn't dream about."

"You don't need a lawyer, Mr. Bronner," Embry said as he walked toward the office door and opened it. "Thank you for taking the time to come in for a visit."

"I hope you mean that because you were starting to get a little too pushy," Bronner said.

"We'll see, Mr. Bronner," Embry said while thinking the man he had questioned was probably correct.

The office door at C&M Construction Company in Louisville, Kentucky remained closed and the front entrance was locked as Mark Cates, Carl McGraw, Ben Bobo, Fred Long, Ed Bass and Sam Mills shared drinks poured from a bottle covered by a paper sack and discussed their next steps. They had seen enough and read enough to know they had the FBI baffled, at least at present, and they knew they would lose a high stakes game only through a series of stupid errors.

Long had reported the information he received during his meeting with Edgar Swartz, so the bank robbers knew the money had to be delivered in less than a week. It was a few hours away, in an abandoned lubrication pit, at least they hoped, and they agreed getting it back to The Commonwealth was a little more risky than they would have liked. Ultimately, it was determined McGraw and Cates would make the trip.

"I wouldn't drive a Pathfinder down there," Long said.

"Damn, Fred, sometimes I think you think I'm stupid," Cates said as he poured more bourbon into a glass. "To set your mind at ease, we'll take one of our oversized pickup trucks and a thick cover of canvass.

When the conversation turned to explosive devices, McGraw made the group feel more at ease. He told his partners in crime the blasting caps used were leftovers from a Rocky Ridge Mall project completed three summers earlier. He said the FBI could never trace the materials to C&M Construction because he and Cates had bought additional boxes from Cagle and Associates in Frankfort, Kentucky, that purchase orders would indicate all of the blasting caps in question had been used.

"I could kiss you," Bass said.

"Don't think about trying," McGraw said.

After reading newspaper reports about the FBI focusing on sports utility vehicles, the men debated the merits of unloading the Pathfinders they had recently purchased.

"I can't get rid of mine," Cates said. "My damn wife loves that truck."

"Yeah, probably more than she does you," McGraw said, offering a private joke his friend did not appreciate.

After another round of drinks laced with idle chatter, the six men decided they should meet again Sunday afternoon to count money.

"This is as good a place as any," Long said. "But make sure we've got a good calculator. The people we're about to deal with don't want to see bad bookkeeping."

"What are they expecting?" Mills said.

"They'll be pleased with $300,000," Long said.

"Did you say they'll be pleased or you'll be pleased with them?" McGraw said.

Long laughed, heartily, as did the other five men. He realized they knew he would double dip along the way, a price they would have to pay for his money laundering connections. But he grinned when he said, "See, Carl, like I've said, you're as sharp as a tack. The brotherhood could use a guy like you."

There were no chuckles to be heard at FBI headquarters in Birmingham, where Wood was being questioned by Special Agent Ed Samson in connection with the robbery of American Bank, which he served as president. Also present was his lawyer, Eddie Maples, who continuously attempted to establish some guidelines for the interrogation.

"Mr. Wood, I know you're growing impatient with us," Samson said about an hour after Deaton had completed his questioning of janitorial worker Ralph Sandburg and as Brunwig continued her inquiry with alarm systems specialist David Blalock. "We only have a few more questions."

"With all due respect, Special Agent Samson, my client has been humiliated for quite a while, for more than two hours," Maples said. "You've teetered on the edge much of that time."

"We can continue this tomorrow," Samson said.

"No," Wood said, in a snap. "I want this senseless debriefing to end by no later than tonight."

Samson looked at Maples, who nodded.

"Mr. Wood, it's our understanding you're closely acquainted with contractors in the Birmingham Metro Area," Samson said.

"I don't understand."

"Do you count as your friends many large construction company owners?"

"Yes sir."

"Have you made sizeable loans to some of them?"

"Yes."

"Do you occasionally socialize with them, like on the golf course or for a few drinks at the Country Club of Birmingham?"

"Yes sir, I do."

"Have you ever had business dealings with them, such as investments in projects related or unrelated to your banking business?"

Maples jumped to his feet and said, "That's far enough. That last question was a direct hint at a wrongful act. My client has done nothing wrong and I won't ..."

"Mr. Maples, fifty per cent of the people in Birmingham know your client has screwed up in the stock market and is having financial distress," Samson said.

"We're leaving now," Maples said.

"Fine. But if you leave, we follow."

"I can't let you drag a fine, upstanding man through shit like this," Maples said.

"We're trying to get to the bottom of a sensitive case," Samson said. "Somebody who walked into those bank branches knew a hell of a lot about the business."

Wood held up his right hand to stop the bickering. He glanced at his lawyer, told him to sit down and looked at the special agent. "Go on, Mr. Samson," he said.

"Thank you," Samson said. "Mr. Wood, through no fault of your own, or at least a minimum of blundering, you're in a precarious position financially. What we're attempting to determine is whether you're capable of orchestrating a ..."

"That's it," Maples said. "We're out of here. You either file formal charges against Mr. Wood or forget this painful, lingering and obnoxious line of questioning."

In Louisville, a different form of interrogation was developing as the six bank robbers started winding down their meeting at C&M Construction.

"That's correct," Long said while reacting to a question provided by

Cates. "After six months, we get twice as much as we give them to invest
— or put on loan with them. After a year, we get back at least three times
as much."

"Is this mafia related?" Bass said.

"I don't know any other place where money churns and resurfaces in
numbers like that," Long said.

Cates reactivated his calculator. He smiled when he looked at the
numbers it produced. He explained it to the others, based on $300,000
being placed in dirty hands.

"It's a good deal," Bobo said.

"It fucking sucks," Bass said. "I just spent three years in three days for
peanuts."

"If this works, or rather when this works, there's a future for you
guys," Long said.

"I'm worried about now, not tomorrow," Mills said.

"Well, gentlemen, let me offer an apology to any man who doesn't
like this deal," Long said. "Now that I've done that, let me offer an
observation."

The other five men waited.

"I know the brotherhood," Long said. "I know how deep we're into
this, to the man. I know the groundwork that has been established.
Gentlemen, to back out now is to lose some fingers, hands, legs, lives and
loved ones."

The silence was sickening until McGraw said, "Fred, tell your pals
we'll have the money for them and we'd like to flush it through the system
for a year."

"Carl, you're wise beyond your years," Long said. "If everybody shares
that opinion, there isn't any reason for us to be concerned."

A man worried about his future was Blalock, the bank security systems
guru being questioned by Brunwig at FBI headquarters in Birmingham.
She had become a bulldog with a growl and he had become a puppy.

"Yes ma'am, there's no doubt I could bust into one of those vaults in a
manner of minutes, provided somebody handle the blasting for me,"
Blalock said.

"Have you ever been tempted?"

"Sure, I've thought about it — normally after about six strong vodka and tonics."

"What kept you from trying?"

"Honesty."

"You're telling me, Mr. Blalock, that honesty has kept you from capitalizing on your knowledge of alarm systems to the tune of one million dollars."

"That's right, Ms. Brunwig. With a little help I could probably make a lifetime fortune robbing banks on a single weekend. I know alarm systems from bottom to top. I know the non-deluxe models aren't flawless, to say the least, that they'd go dead in a second given the weather conditions last weekend in Birmingham."

"You know a lot," Brunwig said.

"Yes."

"Well, since you mentioned it, what about those alarm systems in Inverness Corners?"

"I would've given them a much better than even chance of surviving in that kind of weather — and, ma'am, I've got a feeling I know what happened to them."

"Let's hear it."

"The telephone lines either failed or got cut," Blalock said. "I'd guess some power lines were taken out, too, including those connected to motion sensors."

"Just what else do you know?" Brunwig said.

"More than anything I know I'm a good person, a deacon in my church who sings in the choir, a man who wouldn't steal from people."

Brunwig stood and stared at Blalock. She looked toward the stenographer. Finally, after several seconds, she said, "Thank you for your cooperation and what I perceive to be your honesty."

"Ms. Brunwig," Blalock said.

"Yes, Mr. Blalock."

"I'm going to be embarrassed if my son and daughter see any of this in the newspaper."

"I'll do what I can to keep it quiet. But, Mr. Blalock, the FBI stands a better chance than you of being embarrassed in this matter."

"I assume the bank robbers didn't leave anything behind that's helping you get to the bottom of this."

"They left very little, Mr. Blalock."

Brunwig had no way of knowing, but a smattering of hope was surfacing on the floor above her office. Special Agent in Charge Jim Wilcox was back in town after a quick trip to Washington, D.C. and he was visiting with Embry and laboratory experts Emily Spears and Tom Goldberg. They were seated around a circular table. In front of them was an oversized red bandanna in a plastic bag.

"If this pans out, Pat Embry will get a promotion for giving the FBI its break of a lifetime," Wilcox said with a smile.

"Then call it almost blind luck," Embry said. "Those cameras flashed and I saw about a quarter of an inch of red sticking out of that rubble by the vault."

"I'm telling you there's no reason to be that optimistic, at least right now," Spears said. "We've got a long way to go, even if we knew where we were headed."

Already, Spears and Goldberg had told Wilcox and Embry the red bandanna was extremely damp and soiled when they took possession of it, that the fingerprints found on it were severely smudged. But, they said, the pool of suspects was significantly smaller than was the case with sports utility vehicles and blasting caps.

"I'll take 10,000 possibilities over 500,000," Wilcox said.

"That's about where we are," Goldberg said.

"Could the red bandanna belong to a bank employee who simply left it at Central?" Embry said.

"We don't have a fingerprint match like that," Spears said. "Also, we've discovered a lot of smoke stains, which means the owner spent time near a fire at some point."

CHAPTER TWENTY-SIX

Winter commenced giving way to spring on the sixth day after the bank robberies. The sun was glowing and the temperature started ascending, both in Birmingham, Alabama, where it reached 72 degrees, and Louisville, Kentucky, where it reached 65 degrees. The snow and ice that had led to a hideous crime was a distant memory for most people, the exceptions being Federal Bureau of Investigation special agents and others saddled with deciphering a baffling case.

Mark Cates and Carl McGraw were so enlightened by the change in climate they left work crews under the direction of on the site foremen and departed for home early. Of course, they had business to attend to on Saturday morning, a drive back toward Nashville, and they concurred a marvelous Friday evening of rest would serve them well. Already, they had packed the bed of a large pickup truck with concrete so their trek into a potentially dangerous territory would be more comfortable, even if just as a state of mind.

At about four o'clock, Midge Cates poured her husband a glass of red wine and said, "Honey, I wondered if we'd ever see a nice day again."

"I agree," Mark said. "I was beginning to think we'd never get in a full day of construction until summer."

"I hope you aren't working tomorrow," Midge said. "Diana and I thought it'd be an ideal time for the four of us to take in a Saturday afternoon movie followed by a stroll through Kingsdale Mall."

"Where are the kids?" Mark said after suddenly realizing their children were absent.

"This is Spring Fling Week at the church," Midge said. "They're at camp — in good hands from the youngest to the oldest."

Midge paused, then said, "So what about tomorrow?"

"That sounds great, baby, but Carl and I have to spend the day on the road," Mark said. "We're going to Tennessee to pick up some discounted concrete mix and a few other supplies we'll need next week."

Midge was crestfallen. She was attempting to start over, at least in her mind, after accusing her husband of infidelity. Now the mere thought of him going back to Nashville was tormenting.

"I thought they delivered stuff like that," Midge said.

"Not with the type discount we're getting," Mark said, quick on his feet while wishing he did not have to continuously be untruthful. "Besides, we've got to have it Monday morning and they can't get it to us that quickly."

Midge pouted as she took a couple of sips of wine. She forced a smile and told Mark she understood, that she would telephone Diana and see if they could make it another in a long line of female only outings.

"I've got to call Carl about something else," Mark said as he jumped to his feet and hurried toward the telephone. "I'll let you talk to Diana after we're finished."

Mark and Carl completed their telephone conversation in a few minutes, making sure their stories about the impending trip matched, and hooked up their wives. As Midge walked toward the den, she handed her husband a copy of the latest issue of *Time* magazine and said, "While Diana and I chat, you might want to read this article about the bank robberies in Birmingham. I've just got started on it, but it's interesting stuff, even speculation that bankers and contractors are involved."

Mark wasted little time before fetching the magazine. He quickly thumbed through the pages to get a good look at the pictures. He studied the details as he chugged one glass of wine and poured another. His eyes grew wide when he noticed what he thought might be a small portion of an oversized red bandanna resting in the rubble just outside one of the bank vaults.

"Shit," Mark said as drank the second glass of wine and moved toward the liquor cabinet.

As Mark poured a glass of bourbon on the rocks, his mind swirled:

"That's a distinctive bandanna. If Midge notices this and discovers mine is missing, I'll be in for some interesting conversation."

Mark attempted to remember where Midge had purchased the red bandanna with a matador embroidered on it. He recalled her giving it to him as a gift to celebrate C&M Construction Company landing a Rocky Ridge Mall project. He took three swallows of bourbon and refilled his glass. He hoped so little of the uncommonly colored cloth was visible in the picture that she would not notice.

But Mark knew what that speck of red was because he recalled wiping perspiration from his face while standing in the lobby of Central Bank.

"Maybe our old check registers or credit card records will let me know where she bought it," Mark said under his breath as he walked upstairs to a bedroom he utilized as an office.

Mark fumbled through old financial documents in rapid fashion for at least a quarter of an hour. He became frustrated because none of the addresses seem to signal the purchase of a large handkerchief. Also, he noticed the alcohol he was consuming at such a fast pace was causing his head to spin. He decided the search would have to wait, carefully replaced the documents, closed the desk drawer and walked downstairs to fix another drink.

When he arrived in the kitchen, Mark was surprised to see Midge sitting nude on an island the family used to eat breakfast. Her luscious body, trim and tanned, looked good to him. Also, he noticed she had completed some artwork on her pubic area, a neat trim in the shape of a heart, and he was aroused by the sight.

"I want you to make love to me like you've never made love to me," Midge said before she licked a finger and ran it across a bare nipple. He could smell the fresh splash of cologne. He wanted to lick it from the inside of her thighs. "I want you to control me like you used to, take me in your arms and drive me out of my mind."

Mark began undressing while keeping his eyes on his wife. His face felt flushed when she licked a finger and gently started massaging her clitoris. "This is where I want you to go tonight, something like this," she said. Then she stretched out on the island, spread her legs, put her hands on her knees and said, "I want you here, right now. I want you to screw me, with passion. I don't want to make love. I want to screw."

Mark obliged her, with pleasure and without foreplay, which neither really needed at that point, and he was much more whipped than Midge when the act was over.

"Get a shower and I'll be waiting for you in bed," Midge said. "I've got champagne chilled."

"Damn, what got into you?" Mark said.

"You just did, baby, and I want it again," Midge said. "This time we'll move a little slower."

The pace was decreasing at Federal Bureau of Investigation headquarters in Birmingham, too. All of the out of town visitors had gone home for the weekend and, the overnight shift notwithstanding, only Special Agent in Charge Jim Wilcox, Special Agent Pat Embry and Special Agent Paul Conrad and Special Agent Ed Samson were at the office. They were in a conference room, putting the wraps on a frustrating week of service.

"What's left to do tonight and what's on tap for the weekend?" Embry said as he looked at a clock that said it was a quarter until nine.

"I want you guys to rest tomorrow," Wilcox said. "I've got to meet with the managing editor at *The News* in the morning and four lawyers in the afternoon. On Sunday afternoon, we're playing golf."

"I've got a few things you can tell that managing editor," Conrad said. "For starters, tell her to get the facts right, to at least ask us what's going on instead of taking the word of a bunch of irate citizens we just happened to interview for the sake of clearing their damn names. Then tell her to ..."

"I'll handle the newspaper," Wilcox said. "I'll make sure our side of the story is in print Sunday morning."

Wilcox paused and winked at Conrad. Then he said, "What I need help with is dealing with those greedy lawyers who are threatening lawsuits because the newspaper printed what their damn clients said about our interviews and how we conduct our business."

"I'd tell them that and leave it at that," Samson said. "I've got a law degree. I know it's difficult for the plaintiff to win a slander lawsuit when the plaintiff is the one who took the objectionable information to the public in the first place."

"I'm an accountant," Conrad said. "But I'd bet the matter related to that woman collapsing is different."

"It is to an extent," Samson said. "The woman had an anxiety attack because she had lied to a potential employer. Besides, she's fine now, which points out the difference in a heart attack like *The News* reported she had and a bit of apprehension."

Wilcox was amused by the fiery ways of Samson. He looked at the special agent and grinned.

"So do you want me to go with you tomorrow?" Samson said.

"No, absolutely not," Wilcox said. "All I want you guys to do is keep your mouths shut about that red bandanna. Six people in this office know about it. Two people in Washington know about it. We've got to keep the circle tight until we're ready to move on it."

The following morning, as Wilcox prepared to go to the newspaper office, Cates and McGraw were moving toward Nashville in a large pickup truck with C&M Construction Company painted on the doors. After listening to their wives talk long and hard about it the evening previous, they discussed the article in *Time* magazine.

"I haven't had time to read it because Diana hogged it all night," McGraw said. "But it looks like they've got every criminal justice guru in the nation on the case."

"Yeah, including a few of those guys who let O.J. Simpson slip through the net," Cates said.

"Well, it looks like we're home free if we can get that cash back to Louisville," McGraw said. "Then it'll be time to sit and wait until the spoils start rolling in."

Cates did not respond. He sat in silence. McGraw could tell he was preoccupied, but he chose not to ask why. He turned up the radio to let the Rolling Stones come through more clearly. After that song, they listened to a large portion of a Pink Floyd song before the driver turned down the volume.

"I've got to tell you something," Cates said.

"I thought so," McGraw said. "Don't make it bad news."

"I don't know how bad it is now or how bad it can be. But I screwed up inside Central Bank."

Cates told McGraw about losing the red bandanna and seeing it in the *Time* magazine photograph. He watched his friend shift uncomfortably in the passenger seat.

"How much did you use it before you lost it?" McGraw said.

"If you're wondering about fingerprints, I'd guess they've got some," Cates said.

"Shit."

"But it might not be as bad as I think because I gave that damn handkerchief a workout that night. I'm hoping all the times I wiped the fog off of those Pathfinder windows and cleaned up the vodka Bobo spilled distorted the fingerprints."

"How wet was it?"

"When I wiped my face with it inside the bank, it was soggy and extremely cold."

"That's the good news," McGraw said. "We'll have to live with it, a secret between you and me."

"Thank you."

Cates and McGraw kept rolling along Interstate 65 in the direction of Exit 273. When they got into Tennessee, they noticed an unusually high number of state troopers on patrol, at least six cruisers within fifteen miles of each other. They decided to stop at a truck stop for a cup of coffee with the hope they could find out why so many law enforcement officers were in the area.

Conversations with a few truck drivers did not yield an explanation. But they were happy to acknowledge they had not seen a Tennessee State Trooper in quite a while as they drew nearer to their destination.

They continued at a safe speed until they reached Exit 273. Almost simultaneously, they looked to their left and saw the abandoned service station. To their right, in the distance they saw the BP service station and convenience mart.

"If there's anybody watching us, they're tucked in the woods," Cates said, his way of dealing with fears of an around the clock surveillance. "I think it's safe to take a look."

"Get the truck up to that service station before I puke," McGraw said, his way of alleviating apprehension.

In Louisville, Ed Bass and Sam Mills were playing racquetball, Ben Bobo was getting his nose straightened and Fred Long was working on the blueprint for another scam.

In Birmingham, Wilcox was unloading his fury on a defenseless managing editor who had summoned a reporter to the meeting so the FBI's side of a controversial story could be prepared for printing.

Cates parked the pickup truck well out of view from the highway and joined McGraw on a careful approach to the lubrication pit. They resembled cats sneaking up on mice. Once there, they pulled back the plywood like children reaching into a candy jar. When they saw the duffle bags in place, exactly as they had been left, they smiled broadly.

"Bingo," Cates said. "Let's get that cash out of there and get home."

"I think you forgot something," McGraw said. "We've got a ton of concrete to unload first."

By the time the two men had stacked several dozen bags of concrete beside the pickup truck, they were wet with sweat. But their energy levels remained elevated as they loaded the duffle bags into the bed and carefully covered them with the cargo they had brought, including the canvass cover.

When the task was completed, they looked toward the road and watched an older pickup truck roll past the abandoned service station. They waited until it was out of sight, exchanged nods and got into their larger and more modern pickup truck.

"I'm thirsty, the result of wine mixed with bourbon and champagne," Cates said. "Let's stop by that BP for a cola."

"Over my dead body," McGraw said. "If you die of dehydration before we get up the road a few miles, I'll leave you on the side of the road and get this truck home as fast as I can."

Cates and McGraw did not converse much as they moved along the interstate. They were acting as if they were transporting explosives that might erupt in a snap, which was understandable given the money they had in tow. For the most part they listened to music and kept their eyes on the canvass cover to be make sure it remained in place.

"Where did you get that damn bandanna," McGraw said, breaking a long silence.

"Midge gave it to me," Cates said. "I'm a son of a bitch if I know where it came from."

"That's why I asked," McGraw said. "You need to get another one as soon as possible."

Cates was miffed by his stupidity that had come back to light. He pushed hard on the accelerator and rode for at least ten miles without saying anything. The partners were thinking laboriously and neither noticed the exits they were passing in North Tennessee.

"Damn," Cates said after he glanced in the rear view mirror and observed a Tennessee State Trooper with the blue light on his cruiser flashing. "We're cooked, baby. There's a cop on our tail and he's reeling us in."

"Slow this thing down and see if he comes past us," McGraw said.

"No chance, buddy. He's zeroing in on us."

"Just stay cool," McGraw said. "Remember, we bought the concrete at Abbott and Sons in Nashville."

Cates pulled the pickup truck to the side of the interstate and through the rear view mirror watched as the Tennessee State Trooper pulled in behind him. He saw the trooper talking on the radio in his cruiser.

Then Cates starting getting out of the pickup truck.

"Driver, stay in your seat," said the trooper over a speaker. "I'll tell you when to get out."

Cates closed the door.

The Tennessee State Trooper approached the pickup truck cautiously, even with his right hand on his revolver. "Gentlemen, put both hands on the top of the dash and stay put," he said as he reached the rear bumper. The state trooper looked inside the cab of the pickup truck, saw nothing out of the ordinary and said, "Gentlemen, you seem to be in a hurry."

"Yes sir, it's my mistake," Cates said. "We were talking and the speed sort of got away from me."

"It's the Final Four," McGraw said. "We're anxious to get back to Louisville in time for both games."

"I'm not sure a judge would like to hear two guys are driving a pickup truck like a freight train because they want to see basketball games on television," said the state trooper.

"Yes sir," Cates said. "But we love our basketball in The Commonwealth and we've got Louisville and Kentucky still in the tournament."

"Let me see your license."

After looking over Cates' license, the state trooper said, "Do you know the new fine for speeding in Tennessee?"

"No sir."

"It's $175 for the speed you were going. If you had been going five miles faster, you'd be looking at $250."

"Yes sir."

"I assume you work for C&M Construction Company?"

"Yes sir — and this is my partner, Carl McGraw."

"Well, we've been alerted that there's a lot of drugs being run from Alabama to Kentucky through Tennessee. So tell me what you're doing down this way with two basketball games on television."

"We've been to Nashville to pick up ..."

"Wait a minute," said the state trooper, who leaned toward his cruiser so he could better hear the dispatcher: "Attention all units, there's a Code Seven Orange at Exit 296 on I-65. Attention, we have a Code Seven Orange and an officer is in need of a backup."

Then they heard another Tennessee State Trooper respond: "Unit 32 will take that."

"Roger, 32. If there's a DEA representative in the area, please respond with Unit 32."

"Now you see what I mean," said the Tennessee State Trooper as he returned his attention to Cates and McGraw. "We've got drugheads all over America."

"Yes sir, it's bad," Cates said.

"Mr. Cates, I'm going to give you a ticket for speeding," said the trooper. "You'll need to come with me to the patrol car."

Cates got out of the pickup truck and started following the Tennessee State Trooper to his cruiser. When they were almost there, the trooper said, "Wait a minute. I want to know what you're hauling in the back of this truck."

"Concrete mix," Cates said.

"Let's take a look under the canvass," said the trooper. "Untie this rope for me."

In a sudden reversal of form, McGraw was more nervous than Cates. He was tempted to leap from the pickup truck and run. He wanted to light a cigarette but concluded that would draw too much attention to his anxiety.

Cates felt his knees trembling as he attempted to stay cool. The Tennessee State Trooper stood and watched as the rope was being loosened.

Cates reached for the canvass cover and folded it back, about two feet. On top of the duffle bags of cash, the trooper saw bags of Solidify Concrete Mix.

"That's not good enough," said the Tennessee State Trooper. "It looks too orderly. Pull back the canvass and let me have a look."

Cates tried to buy time as he started untying the rope at the far side of the pickup truck. McGraw felt a more forceful urge to run.

"Sir, with all due respect, I'd just about be willing to let you arrest us and let somebody else unload this damn truck," Cates said. "It was a bitch getting this concrete in here."

"I'll decide what we do from ..."

The Tennessee State Trooper was stopped before he could complete the statement by the voice of the dispatcher coming through his radio speakers: "Attention all units. Shots have been fired and an officer is in need of assistance at Exit 296. Attention all units. Shots have been fired at Exit 296 on I-65. An officer is down. I repeat, an officer is ..."

"Those damn fuckers," said the angry Tennessee State Trooper as he ran toward his cruiser. "Those damn drughead bastards. Those damn ..."

Cates and McGraw watched as the state trooper leaped into the cruiser. They saw him grab the radio and they heard him say, "Unit 43 will answer. Unit 43 will respond."

"Roger, Unit 43," said the dispatcher. "The officer down has been hurt bad. Do you copy, Unit 43?"

"Roger. Unit 43 is en route."

"Attention all units in the area of Exit 296 on I-65. An officer is down and has been hurt bad. Unit 43 is ..."

As the Tennessee State Trooper slammed his door and started putting his cruiser into gear, Cates threw up his arms as if to ask him what he should do.

The trooper responded by pointing toward Louisville, his way of telling Cates and McGraw they were free to leave.

Cates and McGraw watched the state trooper depart at a high rate of speed with his blue light flashing. They were frozen by the sight.

"Damn," McGraw said after getting out of the pickup truck and placing his hands on the side of the bed. He could not say anything else. He closed his eyes, bowed his head and shook it furiously, like a dog would after a bath.

"Carl, help me tie down this damn canvass," Cates said. "It's time for us to go home."

Special Agent in Charge Wilcox was drawing the same conclusion as a meeting with the managing editor at *The News* wound down. He had made the FBI's points in the matter, skillfully he thought, and a reporter had recorded them.

"Special Agent Wilcox, thank you for a good lesson in how the FBI conducts its business," the managing editor said. "I didn't know the bureau could be so warm and caring."

"Similarly, thank you for letting me know how a newspaper article develops, especially one when the stakes are enormous and interest is high," Wilcox said. "I'm sure we'll be a more open with our information in the future."

"The only way to get both sides is for both sides to talk to us," the managing editor said.

"I agree," Wilcox said. "But, ma'am, the only way a person or an organization can defend itself after being accused is if the newspaper asks to hear its side."

"Are we going where we've already been with this conversation?" the managing editor said.

"I think so," Wilcox said. Then he smiled and said, "But contrary to public opinion about the news media, the FBI has the last word."

CHAPTER TWENTY-SEVEN

Jim Wilcox, Ed Samson, Pat Embry and Paul Conrad were sitting in golf carts at Riverchase Country Club just outside Birmingham, Alabama. The Federal Bureau of Investigation special agents were embarking on a playful Sunday morning of work, something they needed badly after a full week of utter frustration related to the bank robberies. The weather was overcast, but mild, and their dispositions were balmy, yet improving because they had read their side of the story earlier that day in *The Birmingham News*.

The group was three foursomes away from teeing off on the first hole, which gave them several minutes to talk before their game began. Also, the time allowed many of their fellow club members to ridicule the four men they knew were disheartened by the week just ended.

One by one the special agents took turns providing updates on the areas of the investigation each was leading.

Samson reiterated what had become obvious, that the tracing of blasting caps would take a miracle.

"The investigation would be too broad and too costly," he said. "In my opinion, Mike Sullivan and the others in our Washington headquarters are correct. It's a fruitless endeavor."

Conrad talked about the lack of information and damaged reputation that came from the interviewing of a few hundred local residents.

"Basically, we don't have anything to show for it, other than the black eye we got in the public relations area," he said. "Frankly, I don't think the crooks are from the Birmingham area and I wouldn't be surprised if they're from out of state."

"You remember to tell those bastards in Washington you've come to that conclusion," Wilcox said. "If it's interstate flight, they got away on highways with the same name because we didn't use roadblocks."

Embry discussed the tracing of sports utility vehicles, in the process making his boss madder.

"Did you know we have as many wives driving those type trucks as we do husbands?" Embry said. "By the time we finished peeking in garages, we'd be too old to testify against the bank robbers."

Wilcox grabbed a driver from his golf bag and took a few practice swings. The others got out of the golf carts and followed his lead. The special agent in charge took a towel in hand and said, firmly, "They screwed up somewhere along the line or they will at some point."

At their residence in Louisville, Kentucky, Midge and Mark Cates were having an interesting conversation. The wife was pulling clothes out of a dryer and the husband was searching for his car keys.

"Honey, I haven't seen your red bandanna for several days," Midge said. "I hope you've left it at the office."

Mark was shaken by the remark. He regained his composure and said, "I thought it was in the wash."

"I'm on the third load and I haven't seen it."

"I'll look at the office."

Midge had expected them to attend church together, a perfect conclusion to what had been a couple of enjoyable evenings of revived lust and rediscovered affection.

"I can't believe you're going to the office on Sunday morning," Midge said. "I was hoping we'd be able to ..."

"I don't have a choice," Mark said. "I've got to get out that concrete Carl and I picked up yesterday so Sammy Calhoun can load the truck with equipment his crew will use tomorrow morning."

"Well, I hope you'll take time to look for the bandanna. It came from overseas and it was fairly expensive given the letters I wrote, the calls I made and the ..."

"Damn it, Midge, put a lid on that talk about the bandanna and help me find my damn car keys," Mark said in such a fiery tone he bit his lip after being so blunt. He hurried to his wife, put his arms around her and said, "I'm sorry, honey. I'm just in a rush."

Midge nodded, not at all convincingly, and said, "I think I saw your keys on the floorboard of the Pathfinder."

Midge watched her husband hurry toward the door. She rolled her eyes and said, in a mumble, "Lord, please tell me this nightmare isn't unfolding like it appears to be."

She waited several seconds for a comforting response, which never came, walked past the kitchen table that had a *Time* magazine on top of it and, to her surprise, thought how good it would be if her husband had been out of town having an affair instead of doing something totally out of character and stupid.

Mark was thinking hard, too. But by the time he arrived at C&M Construction Company and exchanged pleasantries with Carl McGraw, Fred Long, Ben Bobo, Sam Mills and Ed Bass, he had convinced himself his wife was talking more out of coincidence than the realization her husband was running the risk of being sentenced to prison.

"I can't believe you guys couldn't wait for me to start counting the money," Cates said.

"Just stand over there and wait until we get a total — or start stacking the bills in those other duffle bags," Long said. "We're piling them five hundred bucks at a time, no matter the face value."

The six bank robbers were not being frivolous as they took care of a joyous chore. They resembled enthusiastic tellers in the happy room at a Las Vegas casino.

This went on for more than three hours, cigarette after cigarette and tally after tally, until it was time to calculate a total. The adding machine McGraw manipulated buzzed until the result was printed in black ink on white paper.

"I'll be a son of a bitch," McGraw said. "We're sitting on top of $532,352."

"Damn," Bass said.

Cates giggled like a little boy and said, "What's the minimum amount we've got to pass along to Eduardo Martinez, the goon who works for Sid Winestein?"

"Three hundred grand," Long said. "The more we give them, the more they return to us in multiples of two or three, possibly four or five."

"I'm voting we skim a little," Bobo said.

That prompted a serious debate, a blistering argument on occasion, until they went back to the calculator before reaching a decision.

The bank robbers decided to take $2,352 off the top, leaving $530,000 to pass along to the brotherhood.

"We can take our wives out for a fantastic dinner and evening on the town for $392 each," Mills said.

"We'll be able to take them on a dream cruise in a year," Long said.

"Also, each of us will have the option of turning it over again and making the pile deeper."

At Riverchase Country Club, Wilcox, Conrad, Embry and Samson were ready to discuss a different kind of trip as they walked to the 19th Hole from the eighteenth green. After they were seated around a table in a back corner of the large grille, with vodka and tonics in front of them and sandwiches on the way, they started talking about Madrid, Spain.

"I assume we're in agreement that the only quiet and efficient way to track down that red bandanna is go over there and talk to the supplier," Wilcox said.

"That's the ticket," Conrad said. "If we call over there asking questions or tell them we're coming, the news people will have the story out for public consumption in a snap."

"Also, there isn't a guarantee those folks in Madrid will want to work with us on this," Samson said.

"It isn't going to be easy, anyway," Embry said. "Already, we've had calls from people in Idaho, Virginia, New York and Arkansas who recognized that bandanna from the picture in *Time* magazine."

"Just what color is that damn thing?" Wilcox said.

"It's a touch of cardinal, a touch of crimson and a touch of orange, as best I can tell — one strange and bright shade of red," Embry said.

"Who'll be going to Spain to check it out?" Samson said.

"Maybe all of us and maybe two or three of us," Wilcox said. "I won't know until I'm finished with that meeting tomorrow in Washington."

CHAPTER TWENTY-EIGHT

Edgar Swartz was attempting to look cool, but his smile gave him away as he closed the door on the van parked behind his BMW beside an old warehouse in Louisville, Kentucky.

"We'll do the final accounting later, but it looks like you gentlemen did well," Swartz said as Mark Cates and Fred Long gazed at the duffle bags full of cash.

"You've got $530,000 on the nose," Cates said.

"We'll count it again," Swartz said.

Swartz turned toward Eduardo Martinez and said, "Get it out of here. Take it to hangar three."

Martinez looked at his watch. "You've got fifteen minutes to get it on the airplane," Swartz said.

The driver got into the van, turned the ignition key and started driving cash taken from five bank branches in Birmingham, Alabama into the underworld.

"Thank you, gentlemen," Swartz said. "We'll be in touch."

"Don't we get a receipt?" Cates said, a remark that made Long flinch.

Swartz glared at the contractor. He took a deep breath and said, "Gentlemen, and I'm using that terminology loosely in regard to one of you, there's no reason to worry. In six months, maybe earlier, you'll have about a million dollars to split six ways. If you want to wait a year, you'll have about a million and a half and probably much more."

"I assume I'll be your contact for The Snowman Project," Long said.

Swartz nodded and said, "That's right, Fred. But there's no reason for any of us to talk about it for at least four months. I trust this guy and the others know that."

"What happens if you or Fred dies?" Cates said.

Swartz was not enamored by the statement. He did not respond for several seconds. Then he said, "Fred, take this guy to lunch and explain the valor involved in international trade done underground. Tell him there are no more honest dishonest people in the world than those who'll be handling this bundle of petty cash."

Lunch was being served in a conference room at Federal Bureau of Investigation headquarters in Washington, D.C., where a meeting that had started two hours earlier was continuing without interruption. But five other individuals had been excused and only three remained, Special Agent in Charge Jim Wilcox, Special Agent Mike Sullivan, the highest ranking officer on the case, and Carmen Norris of the Central Intelligence Agency.

"Unless these crooks start spending money foolishly, and I mean in an extraordinary fashion, we've got one good shot at catching them," Sullivan said. "The red bandanna is our ticket and the odds are getting longer by the minute."

Sullivan was referring to computers in a laboratory that continued to spit out possible matches to the smudged fingerprints found on the bandanna. At last count, the number had skyrocketed from a seemingly manageable 10,000 to more than 80,000, about a fourth of them residing in the Deep South.

"I don't understand how there can be so many people with similar fingers," Norris said.

"It's the smears that's driving the computer nuts," Wilcox said. "There are two strong lines on the right bird finger that have it cranking out names at a baffling pace."

"How appropriate — a screw you," Norris said.

The men chuckled, welcoming some comic relief.

"Also, I guess it's appropriate I'm still here," Norris said. "An investigation headed for Madrid, Spain needs a CIA touch."

Sullivan quickly told Norris such decisions would be made by the FBI, not the CIA. He was reacting because the two federal agencies often had trouble cooperating. He was determined to stay in charge.

"Could I make a suggestion?" Wilcox said, attempting to take a sharp edge off of the proceedings.

"Wait a minute, Jim," Sullivan said. "Carmen, what I'm saying is I don't want the CIA stumbling in front of the FBI and causing us to trip."

"Well, we've both had our ankles sprained and our knees scraped on occasion," Norris said.

Wilcox was squarely on the side of his superior officer, a 58-year-old veteran of many important cases, as he sparred with a brilliant and feisty 32-year-old lady. But he was caught in the middle and made a move to settle the issue.

"I'd like to make the trip and I'd like for three men from my office to accompany me," Wilcox said. "Also, I think it'll be helpful if Carmen joins us. After all, she'll be a good coach when it comes to diplomacy and communication."

"I've got an open mind," Sullivan said, maintaining his position of power.

"Can your folks speak Spanish?" Norris said.

"All four of us — at least to some extent."

"French?"

"Pat Embry."

"German?"

"Paul Conrad."

"Is there a secretarial type in the group?"

"Pardon me."

"Somebody capable of handling an enormous paperwork load."

"Ed Samson."

Since she was asking all of the questions, Norris attempted one more try for authority. She said, "Who'll call the shots, the FBI or the CIA?"

"Damn it, Carmen," Sullivan said.

"Fine," Norris said. "But you can count me out if those guys won't listen to my suggestions."

"Then let's pack," Wilcox said.

"Not so damn fast," Sullivan said. "We've got to stay on top of this red bandanna thing by moving skillfully and cautiously, at times slowly."

"I agree," Wilcox said.

"Then the first order of business is to get Embry, Conrad and Samson to Washington to meet with the three of us," Sullivan said.

"They're in the health club downstairs waiting for me to summon them," Wilcox said.

"That's pretty damn cocky," Sullivan said to Wilcox as Norris pounded the table and laughed.

"That's my way of moving quickly and cautiously," Wilcox said.

At her house in Louisville, Kentucky, Midge Cates was conducting her own investigation. She had rummaged through clothes pulled from a bedroom chest of drawers and had not found the red bandanna with the matador on it. She had looked at the picture in *Time* magazine at least a dozen times and each examination added to her anxiety.

Midge walked into a bedroom down the hall and grabbed a magnifying glass. She returned to the magazine and took several up close looks at the picture. She walked downstairs to the kitchen, pulled out a map of the southeastern portion of the United States and examined it. With a finger she traced possible travel routes between Brunswick, Georgia and Louisville, focusing on any that would go through Nashville, Tennessee.

A drive through Birmingham, Alabama did not seem to fit.

CHAPTER TWENTY-NINE

Fred Long was dressed in a turtleneck shirt and silk sports coat as he sat at the Two Frogs Bar in Louisville, Kentucky and waited for his expected guest. It was quaint joint, an old wooden bar with thirteen stools in front of it, a dozen tables with two chairs at each and a music box in the rear of the rectangular room that played old rock and roll records.

Long looked at his watch and wondered. He was getting impatient. Reluctantly, he ordered another glass of gin and grapefruit juice.

Then he saw Carl McGraw in the doorway. He got out of his chair and said, "My man, I was starting to worry."

"I'm sorry, Fred. I got caught in a four-car bumper-bender a couple of miles away."

Long and McGraw talked for maybe ten minutes about The Snowmen Project before the subject grew more serious.

"Carl, I've always thought you have what it takes to be a brother," Long said.

"I've noticed that."

Long smiled and said, "I've got an indoctrination for you that could be worth a half million dollars."

McGraw took a few seconds to gather himself.

"There's a heist in the works on Long Island that could be easy cash for you, Sam Mills and Ed Bass," Long said.

"What about Mark Cates?" McGraw said.

"Forget that dumbass," Long said.

"Excuse me?"

"He's an idiot, as a recent *Time* magazine picture proves."

"Okay, I noticed."

"Noticed," Long said, his voice crisp. "Carl, your screwed up business partner has all of us in jeopardy."

McGraw nodded and took a slug of whiskey and water.

"Also, the dumb fucker is having an affair with a divorced lawyer, a hot chick named Sandra Brewer." Long said.

McGraw recoiled and said, "But we don't know that."

"Hell yes we do. They're meeting at the damn Galt House, of all places. Why not the Red Roof Inn?"

"I'm listening," McGraw said.

After stating that the ungovernable ways of Cates did not appear to be an obstacle, at least not at that moment, Long laid out a new course of action for McGraw.

Long told McGraw there was a diamond exchange on Long Island, New York that housed roughly $28 million dollars in stones that were ready to be taken. He said six security officers normally worked the night shift, from eleven o'clock to seven o'clock, and they had agreed to take a lengthy snooze at a cost of $20,000 each. He said the rare gems were stored in vaults similar to those at Sector, First Columbus, Central, Patriot and American near Birmingham, Alabama.

Long told McGraw he wanted him, Ed Bass and Sam Mills to get the diamonds out of the warehouse and to deliver them to a transport vessel in the Atlantic Ocean.

"Why me and the two bankers?" McGraw said.

"Because you're a brother," Long said. "I like the other two guys more than I did a couple weeks ago."

"What about Ben Bobo?"

"Ben is too unstable. Cates is too dangerous. I'm too old for the on the scenes shit. That leaves three."

"Give me the menu."

Long raised his glass, drank the final two swallows and ordered another round. He winked at McGraw and laid out the details:

"I want you, Bass and Mills to arrive at O'Hare Airport in Chicago on Wednesday afternoon, the 21st of April and go to the Hertz Rental Car counter. We'll have a small truck waiting for you that's loaded with what you'll need.

"I want the three of you to drive to New York, arriving no later than the 23rd of April.

"I want the three of you to arrive at the diamond exchange on Long Island at one o'clock in the morning. You'll have security guards waiting for you. They'll open the damn vaults and help you load the truck. You'll drive the truck to the transport vessel. You'll go back to the diamond exchange, put to sleep the security guards with a mixture in their coffee machine, shortcircuit the alarm system and blow open the six vaults that at one time housed the jewels.

"You'll get into a car waiting in the parking lot for you, drive to Philadelphia and catch an airplane to Louisville.

"Again, Carl, your take will be a half million dollars each, with more to come at the end of the project."

McGraw was impressed. "Basically, we blow up the place and leave," he said.

"That's about it."

"I've got questions," McGraw said. "I mean, there isn't any doubt we can pull off this if you do your part. But ..."

"Shoot," Long said.

McGraw took a gulp and lit a cigarette. He listened to the music, at least sort of, and thought hard.

"We've got a rental car agent to deal with in Chicago," McGraw said, his apprehension showing.

"Bought," Long said.

"We've got security guards on Long Island."

"Bought. All you've got to remember to do is stay away from that spiked coffee. They'll be out for six or eight hours after drinking it."

"We've got a car at the diamond exchange."

"Bought — and listed as stolen.

"We've got airport security in Philadelphia."

"Be cool. We'll probably arrange the flights to Louisville so two of you travel together, Bass and Mills, and you fly solo."

"How do I deal with my friend Mark Cates?"

"Pay him, if you want. But keep the son of a bitch a thousand miles away from Long Island."

"But he helped me a lot planning The Snowmen Project."

"That's why he's still able to walk. If he keeps moving in the circles he's running in now, well, that could change."

"I hope the brotherhood isn't pissed at him," McGraw said.

"The brotherhood doesn't know what you and I know. I hope we're able to keep it that way."

McGraw thought for several seconds, then said, "Let's do it."

"Will Bass and Mills play?"

"With that kind of money on the line, yeah, you bet."

"Remember, Carl, this is your baby, your baptism into the brotherhood," Long said. "Don't let Mills get reckless. Don't let Bass talk too much."

"I won't let you down," McGraw said.

"As I recall, you like your steaks bleeding out the butt," Long said.

"With a lot of bread and onions on the side."

"Then let's go across the street and have dinner."

CHAPTER THIRTY

Jim Wilcox, Pat Embry, Paul Conrad, Ed Samson and Carmen Norris were seated in a large suite at the Posada Valenzuela, an enormous hotel in Madrid, Spain. They had returned from a delightful dinner downstairs, replete with a sauntering venda that entertained them with a variety of music, and they were planning an unwavering next day. At their disposal they had two rental cars, economy class, and an interpreter they hired in the event communication became a problem.

"Let's have a toast to expected good fortune," Wilcox said as he and the others lifted one shot of tequila.

"Bueno verdaderamente," Embry said.

"I'm going to check that one out with the interpreter," Norris said with a smile.

"There's no need," Wilcox said. "Good indeed, bank on it."

Their plans for the following morning had been made. They were to appear unannounced at the Calusso Woven Goods International headquarters, the manufacturer listed on a tag on the oversized red bandanna they had with them. They were to introduce themselves as Federal Bureau of Investigation special agents from the United States, seize and examine mail order records from the previous three years and begin linking citizens to the evidence through the use of the fingerprint records they had in hand.

Few people knew they were traveling overseas, only a smattering of special agents and Central Intelligence Agency representatives, because the surprise element was a hole card. They knew some natives might be reluctant to help law enforcement officials from the United States.

"We'll show up at the address we have and let Carmen take the lead,"

Wilcox said. "It'll be a woman-to-woman exchange because we believe Constantina Maria Calusso runs the business. If her husband, Jorge, gets involved, we'll let Paul deal with him."

"Remember, what we want is access to their mail order records," Norris said. "That should be easy for them to understand, registro correo, and for the life of me I can't see why they'll be apprehensive."

Norris paused for a few seconds. Then she said, "I don't think I have to remind you guys to leave behind your macho personalities. These are innocent people, not crooks, and we've got to make them feel comfortable, assure them they're helping us catch some bad guys."

"In other words, be nice to the senor and senora," Conrad said. "We don't need to shoot the doves when we've got hawks driving us nuts."

"That's a bit eloquent, but yes," Norris said.

The special agents chatted for about an hour more, mostly about the strangeness of the investigation plan they were initiating. As Wilcox said before they retired to bed, "We're accustomed to running background check after background check on people before we meet them. But we don't have any idea what to expect when we hit the streets tomorrow."

The only eyes they had belonged to Maria Valequez, the interpreter who met them in the hotel lobby at nine o'clock the following morning to start a trek across town. The men occupied one rental car. The women occupied the other and, armed with a city map and some local knowledge, they led the way to 615 Camino Ruiz.

"I'm not sure what to expect, a major manufacturing facility or a sweat shop," Norris said.

"Nor do I," Valequez said. "But I do recall that as a warehouse area."

Madrid was bustling for a morning hour. Buses and taxi cabs were the normal modes of travel, but there were numerous pedestrians who thought little about stepping into the streets. Horns were blowing. People were screaming.

"This is a mini-New York City," Norris said.

Valequez shook her head as if to say she did not understand.

In the second car, the men were going over plans.

"Ed, we need a copy of every piece of paper in that building," Wilcox said to Samson. "I don't care if it takes a month, we're going to leave Madrid with a name and an address for every person who ordered a red bandanna from the Calusso Family."

"They don't sell wholesale, or at least we think, so they've got have a lot of paperwork in their possession," Samson said. "The mail order business is like that, although not that orderly at times."

"That depends on what kind of records they keep," Embry said. "They don't have to answer to the IRS."

The caravan turned left, traveled for a couple of miles on a boulevard and turned right onto Avenida Emmanuel, the thoroughfare leading to Camino Ruiz. The traffic was thinning. The anxiety was growing.

"We can't be far from that place," Conrad said as he looked at a city map. "It looks like four blocks to Ruiz Road."

"What's your guess on the ages of these people, Constantina and Jorge?" Embry said.

"I'm betting middle of the road," Wilcox said.

"I'm betting on down the road," Samson said.

Norris parked her car curbside at 603 Camino Ruiz and Wilcox parked his car directly in front of it. They looked around and saw a village of sorts, a somewhat modernistic redesign of what had obviously been a warehouse district. There were numerous boutiques and cafes, as well as several pubs. A little more than a block away they could see a curbside vegetable and fruit market.

"Welcome to New Orleans, the French Quarter," Embry said. "This is a party district, not the kind of place a woman would labor over a sewing machine."

Further proof of that was found when they looked down Camino Ruiz. Sitting just beyond several nondescript buildings they saw a massive nightclub called Guatemala Bay.

"I don't like the looks of this," Wilcox said as he and others started walking briskly in the direction of 615 Ruiz Road. "Either the Calussos operate a quiet business or they don't spend money on storefront exposure."

His fears were founded when they got to 615 Camino Ruiz and

discovered the entrance to Guatemala Bay, which had the appearance of a spacious, ritzy and popular gathering place.

"Este es un celebrado lugar," Valequez said.

"It might be a famous place, indeed, but this isn't what we wanted to find," Wilcox said.

Conrad walked to the front door secured by a chain and lock and looked inside, putting his eyes against the tinted glass to improve his badly distorted view.

Embry strolled down the sidewalk, passing the Guatemala Bay II Bar, a small building adjacent to Guatemala Bay, the Moonlight Cafe and Aparicio's Fine Jewelry, which appeared to offer nothing of the sorts.

Wilcox, Norris, Samson and Valequez simply stood and gazed in silence until they heard a car horn behind them. They turned quickly and saw a taxi cab driver smiling and pointing toward the back seat. They waved him pass and looked across the street, where they saw three young boys on bicycles and a farmer bartering with a customer at a fruit stand.

Conrad joined them and said, "It looks like a fun place to visit, but nobody in there is making bandannas."

Embry returned to the group, shrugged his shoulders and said, "Folks, we better hope the Calussos relocated for the sake of progress on this street."

"Let's take a shop each and start asking questions," Wilcox said. "I'll need Senora Valequez with me since I'm the least fluent in Spanish."

Information related to the Calussos was less than sketchy, summed up by consistent revelations that the area around Camino Ruiz had been remodeled two years ago and not a single person they encountered had met Constantina and Jorge or was familiar with their woven goods business.

Also, the special agents from the United States heard a familiar refrain, "Perdon, pero no le entendi" — sorry, but I do not understand you. It did not take skilled investigators to know more people than not were simply trying to brush them off by using a language barrier as an old and trusted means.

However, they received some encouragement when Wilcox and

Valequez learned Ferdinand Ballesteros, the owner of Guatemala Bay, would be arriving later in the day. After all, he owned the building once occupied by the Calussos.

"We've got six hours to kill," Wilcox said.

"Then let's talk to everybody we can within four blocks of this place," Norris said. "Somebody has to know something about those people."

Wilcox, Conrad, Embry, Samson and Norris and Valequez spread out and started fanning the area they soon learned was known as Aldea Utopico, Utopia Village, because of its fine restaurants and entertainment value. But it was nothing of the sorts for them, particularly since they found everything from a small church to a prostitution house within the expanse they covered on foot.

Interestingly, it was the Madam from the prostitution house two blocks from 615 Camino Ruiz who provided them with the most insight into Constantina and Jorge Calusso.

"Yes, I knew Senora Constantina and Senor Jorge," the Madam said through skillful interpretation by Valequez.

"Did you say you knew them?" Norris said.

"Yes, bless his soul," the Madam said. "Jorge passed away four years ago. Life got oh so rough for Constantina. She no longer could take care of the warehouse alone. But she kept sewing until it became too much."

"I assume they lived in the warehouse."

"Yes, but only on the bottom floor."

"How old were they?"

"At least 75, perhaps 80."

"Is Senora Constantina still alive?"

"I do not know," the Madam said. "She sold her warehouse at a cheap price and moved to the Montego Hotel when the revitalization work started. That is the last I heard from her."

"Did she continue making bandannas?"

"Yes, I heard she did for at least one year. Her hands were tired and they hurt with arthritis. She was frail. She often said she must quit soon."

"Did they have children?" Norris said.

"I know one son was killed in a street fight. It pained her so bad. I never heard her talk about other children."

Norris and Valequez thanked the Madam for her time and prepared to leave the house of prostitution.

"Excusar," the Madam said.

Norris and Valequez turned around to let the woman continue. She said, "Do you want to see a gift Senora Constantina gave to me?"

Norris nodded.

A few minutes later the Madam returned clutching an oversized red bandanna, holding it to her heart until she handed it to Norris. It was like the one shown in *Time* magazine, the one she had in her purse.

"Is this the only type bandanna she made?" Norris said.

"Yes, sadly," the Madam said. "She made them all red. I told her, 'Constantina, you make much more money if you make some blue, green and other colors. Some people like something other than red.' But she liked red only."

"Gracias," Norris said.

"Adios," the Madam said.

By the time Norris and Valequez arrived at Guatemala Bay, Wilcox, Embry and Conrad were inside visiting with Ballesterors and Samson was waiting to greet the women in front of the building.

"They're visiting with the owner now," Samson said. "He's a jovial guy. I think he'll try to help us."

"We'll need it," Norris said. "We've got one deceased Calusso and one terribly old and fragile Calusso, at best. Other than that, there are no other Calussos we know about."

CHAPTER THIRTY-ONE

Dinner at the Posada Valenzuela was tasty to the visitors from the United States, although each agreed the sauces were a little strenuous on their nervous stomachs. Also, there was too much conversation during the meal as the special agents attempted to communicate over a steady stream of music provided by locals who were more interested in tips than merely being charming hosts.

The group returned to the large hotel suite weary, full, perplexed and with a lot more to do before going to sleep. Their interpreter, who liked the food better than them, stayed to participate in a serious discussion.

Jim Wilcox announced he and Paul Conrad would continue their discussion with Ferdinand Ballesteros. The Guatemala Bay owner had excused himself that afternoon, pointing out he had customers to serve. He agreed to answer more questions the next day if the special agents would allow him to host them for dinner and an evening of good music.

"I think he'll help us all he can," Conrad said. "He's a delightfully funny and personable man."

"Also, he's a smart businessman or a hard one," Ed Samson said. "He talked that poor lady into selling him that warehouse for a handful of pesos, not more than $15,000. I bet he could get two hundred grand for it now without anybody saying, "Es desasiado caro.""

"Okay, Ed, fill us in," Pat Embry said.

"It's too expensive."

"But that's not our problem," Wilcox said. "We've got to get our hands on that inventory Ballesteros claimed when Constantina Calusso moved out — her sewing stuff, her bandannas and, more than anything, her damn sales records."

"We don't know if she took any of the paperwork with her to the Montego Hotel, just that she continued to sew after moving in the place," said Carmen Norris.

"Let's don't assume she's dead, not just yet," Wilcox said. "But if that is the case, I want you and Maria Valequez to put your hands on anything she left at that damn hotel."

Based on a tip provided by a woman from Iowa who had telephoned Federal Bureau of Investigation headquarters in Birmingham, Alabama, Embry and Samson were to conduct interviews at a Travel and Leisure magazine sales office.

"*Travel and Leisure* sounds familiar," Conrad said.

"It's the American Express magazine sent to customers," Embry said.

"Hell, I'm a subscriber, I guess, but not much of a reader," Conrad said with a smile.

"That magazine is our link to the United States," Norris said. "They'll have sales records for sure."

"Mail order houses aren't always so efficient," Wilcox said.

"Pardon my language, but screw el casa de ventas por correro empleo," Embry said in a huff.

Valequez laughed and appeared a little embarrassed.

"Okay, Maria, what did I say?" Embry said.

"Senor Embry, you said you wanted to do something wicked to mail order houses," Valequez said.

"We understand better than you think," Conrad said. "If there's an international trade that drives the FBI and the CIA crazy, it's mail order — guns, drugs, pornography and, in this case, oversized red bandannas."

The next morning at just after nine o'clock, Norris and Valequez walked into the Posado Montego and found nobody in the small lobby. The short registration desk was empty, except for a small bell, and the place smelled musky, as if nobody had been inside the building with five floors in months.

"This place is creepy," Valequez said as Norris grabbed the small bell and shook it ferociously. She waited several seconds and shook it again, this time harder.

At last, a tiny old man walked from a small office behind the registration desk. In his native tongue he said, "We take boarders only, not tourists."

Valequez informed the desk clerk that they were from the Federal Bureau of Investigation in the United States. Before she could tell him they were seeking information about Constantina Calusso, he said, "No tan aprisa" — not so fast. We have good people here, no trouble."

Valequez assured him nobody had anything to fear. Then she asked about the woman they were seeking. Hearing the name made the man perk up. "Hermoso, hermoso, hermoso, senora," he said.

Norris quickly looked toward Valequez, who said, "A lovely, lovely, lovely lady."

"Is she here?" Valequez said. She could tell by his facial expression Norris was about to hear something she dreaded.

"She died about eight or nine months ago," the man said. "A lovely, lovely, lovely lady."

Norris pulled the red bandanna out of her purse and asked the man if he could answer some questions for them. He agreed and suggested Rose Alou, "a dear friend to Senora Constantina," be included in the conversation.

At the *Travel and Leisure* magazine sales office in an upperscale building in downtown Madrid, Embry and Samson were in a conversation with Emerson Montgomerie a native of London, England who managed operations in Spain. The office manager was aware of Constantina Calusso and her bandanna business, but he summoned Frank Weatherspoon to the meeting because he knew the woman better.

Weatherspoon, a portly man with an infectious smile, entered the room carrying a red bandanna in one hand and a folder in another. The special agents were encouraged when they saw the paperwork he had with him. "If you want to talk to me about Miss Constantina, you better have all day," he said.

"We've got a month," Embry said.

It did not take long before Embry and Samson had a better understanding of the fondness Weatherspoon had for Constantina.

"Miss Constantina telephoned our office and said she wanted to place an advertisement in *Travel and Leisure*," Weatherspoon said. "She said she was from Calusso Woven Goods International and she wanted to sell her red bandannas with a matador on it to Americans and Englishmen. I thought, 'Wow, this is a smash hit for an advertising salesman, a huge commission based on the placements of a massive international company with a lot of money to spend.' But I found out that was not exactly accurate.

"I went to see Miss Constantina at her warehouse. She said she could spend what amounted to $100 in United States currency. She was so charming and determined I didn't have the heart to tell her our cheapest advertisement sold for $300, a tiny paragraph in our international speciality goods section. I told her it cost $100 for a placement like that, drew up a contract and helped her write the copy.

"I ended up giving her an advertisement three times that size for $100.

"Here is the paperwork."

Weatherspoon pulled the contract and the advertising copy from the folder. He handed it to Samson, who read it aloud:

"Oversized hand-crafted bandanna, finely woven with matador monogram embroidered ... 24 inches x 12 inches ... red only ... $50 U.S.A., check ... Calusso Woven Goods, 615 Camino Ruiz, Madrid, Spain 4E-U2361."

"Damn," Embry said.

"I understand fully," Weatherspoon said. "I thought that lady wouldn't sell a single bandanna, which made me feel bad for her. But two months after the ad ran I went to see her and she said she had sold 430 in the United States. I told her, 'Miss Constantina, I guess we better raise your advertising price to $300.' She wouldn't have anything to do with that. She said, 'Un negacio perona un negacio' — a deal is a deal."

"If my math is correct, Senora Calusso paid $100 and sold at least $21,500 worth of red bandannas in a quarter," Embry said.

"That's correct," Weatherspoon said. "Other than getting chewed out for selling her the space so cheaply, the only thing I got from that deal was a great sales pitch."

"I assume she's still advertising with you," Samson said.

Weatherspoon looked shocked, as well as pained. "Oh no, Miss Constantina died after only two quarters in our magazine, la primavera (spring) and el verano (summer). I'm sorry. I thought you knew she had departed."

"No, we didn't," Embry said. "Also, I'm afraid to ask you my next question."

Weatherspoon waited without speaking.

"I'm fearful you don't have a record of her sales, that she simply took orders in at her warehouse and shipped them out," Embry said.

"Correct," Weatherspoon said. "Also, when I tried to get her to advertise in other publications, like *European Holidays* and *El Riviera,* both which accept credit cards, she refused to do so. In fact, she said, 'Senor Weatherspoon, you are my only partner in business.'"

"This is too damn bizarre to be true," Embry said.

"I'll call the post office," Samson said.

"While you're at it, you might as well call the Montego Hotel and Guatemala Bay and let the others know Constantina Calusso has been dead for a while," Embry said.

By that time, the news had already spread. Norris and Valequez had left the Montego Hotel and were en route to Maria Angelica Cathedral a few blocks from 615 Camino Ruiz. Before their departure, they had telephoned Wilcox and Conrad at Guatemala Bay, at which time they told them about the death and informed them that Constantina Calusso had retired from the bandanna business not long after moving out of the warehouse. Also, they informed them she did not have Calusso Woven Goods International sales records with her when she changed her residence from a warehouse to a posado.

Wilcox and Conrad were drawing blanks, too.

"Like I said, sir, the senora left everything here except her clothes, a rocking chair and her sewing machine," Felipe Hernandez said as Wilcox and Conrad interviewed him and Fernando Ballesteros sat and listened. "I said, 'Ma'am, you have boxes of paper, some furniture and some other household goods. You should let us deliver them to you.'

"Senora Constantina looked at me eye to eye, dropped her head and said, 'Senor, I have nobody left to give this to and my hands are tired and my eyes are weak. I will sew a little more, but you should take what you want and throw away the rest.'"

"What did you keep?" Conrad said.

"I took home a bed, a table, two cabinets, four chairs and a picture," Hernandez said. "My family is grateful to Senora Constantina."

"I'm afraid I know the answer to ..."

"Oh, sir, I am sorry," Hernandez said. "She gave me three beautiful bandannas for my sons."

Wilcox nodded and shook his head. He felt tears forming in his eyes. Conrad looked away, too. Then the special agent in charge said, "What did you do with everything else, particularly the papers she left behind?"

"We took all that was left to a junk yard outside of Madrid and burned it," Hernandez said.

"Who burned it?" Conrad said.

"We did, sir, at least most of it. The rest of it we dumped."

Wilcox slumped forward and lightly pounded his head with both fists. He looked toward Conrad and shook his head. It was apparent both special agents were extremely frustrated.

"Can I open the bar and get you a strong drink?" Ballesteros said.

"Gracias modo," Wilcox said, declining the kind offer. "But Senor Ballesteros, you'll have five very drunk Americans and a delightful Spanish woman in here tonight."

Ballesteros threw out his arms, smiled broadly and said, "How do you say it, my friends from the United States, it will be libre, mi gusto" — on the house, my pleasure."

As Wilcox and Conrad stepped onto the sidewalk outside Guatemala Bay, the ranking special agent looked at his friend and said, "We're back to suspending those roadblocks, Paul. We had 'em and we let 'em get away. Now we're running into barricades every way we turn."

CHAPTER THIRTY-TWO

Although the door to Mark Cates' office at C&M Construction Company was closed, Belinda Wilbanks could hear the voices loud and clear as she sat at her desk in the reception area. Her bosses were having a heated discussion and, rather than eavesdrop, she interrupted the conversation and asked if it would be okay for her leave early.

"Yes, and I'm sorry," Carl McGraw said. "As you know, it has been a tough day."

"No doubt," Wilbanks said.

"Before you go, Belinda, please call Mercy Hospital and see how Dan Thomas is doing."

Thomas, one of the laborers at C&M Construction, had fallen from scaffolding while working on an office complex. The early diagnosis was a broken back and doctors were trying to determine if there had been spinal damage. McGraw had not been able to locate Cates all afternoon and that was why he was giving his friend a fiery piece of his mind.

After a few minutes, all spent in silence, Wilbanks returned to the office and said, "He's going to be fine, at least in time. The doctors are saying six months in a brace will do wonders."

"Fine, and thank you," McGraw said.

After Wilbanks had left the building, McGraw continued his assault on Cates. He did not skip over any low points.

"Damn it, Mark, I know where you've been, piled up at the Galt House with that woman."

"Screw you," Cates said. "You don't have any idea where I've been."

"Yes, I do. So does Fred Long, who told me about your affair a few days ago."

"You didn't call Midge looking for me?" Cates said.

"Hell no, I wouldn't do that to her or to you," McGraw said. "But, pal, I'm not going to conduct business this way. If you're off screwing, I want to know the place and the room number."

"That's fair," Cates said.

"Okay, now let me tell you about something I'm going to do."

McGraw told his partner he would need to take a few days off to conduct some extracurricular business. When pressed for an explanation, he told Cates a shallow version of the deal Long had presented to him, Ed Bass and Sam Mills.

"Wait a damn minute," Cates said. "I thought we were partners."

"That we are, as well as damn good friends," McGraw said. "But, Mark, you've screwed up as far as Long and his associates are concerned."

"Just because I'm having a little fun on the side?"

"Well, yes, that plus the fact you left some cargo in Birmingham."

"I can't believe you told him about that."

"I didn't, McGraw said. "He saw *Time* magazine, too. He remembered that damn red bandanna from a planning meeting we had downtown. He put two and two together and, guess what, he nailed a four."

"I'm a dead man hobbling," Cates said.

"No you aren't," McGraw said. "But the only reason you aren't impaired in some way is Long hasn't talked to anybody about this."

Cates sat speechless. He was sweating. He reached for a pocket and pulled out a white handkerchief.

"Damn, you're talking about pocketing a lot of money for a guy who'll be out of town three or four days," Cates said.

"Yes sir," McGraw said. "As a show of good faith, I'll cut you in for fifty grand."

"Thank you. I feel much better."

"But, Mark, watch your step with that damn Sandra Brewer. You've got a wife who's suspicious by nature. You never know when she'll be the one who needs to find you and can't."

"I'll break it off," Cates said. "I'll call her tonight."

"Wait until tomorrow," McGraw said. "We're going to Mercy Hospital tonight."

"I better call Midge."

"Yeah, and I'll cover for you this time."

Jim Wilcox was on the telephone waiting to be connected with Mike Sullivan at Federal Bureau of Investigation headquarters in Washington, D.C. He and the other special agents were having drinks in the hotel suite in Madrid, Spain. They had reconstructed the events of the day, sadly, and were on go for another round of interrogations the following morning. The mood was somber, to say the least.

"Hello, Jim Wilcox," Sullivan said. "Tell me how you folks are doing over there."

"Well, we're getting ready to get smashed out of our minds, if that tells you anything."

"That doesn't sound good."

"Mike, you wouldn't believe this fucking story if you lived it," Wilcox said. "In summary, our star witness is dead and it appears all of her records are ashes, by honest means. And, adding to our grief, we've got some jackals at the Madrid Postal Service who laughed when we told them we needed their help."

"It sounds a little too unreal."

"But it's true, all the way down to a lovely lady named Constantina Calusso giving more than $55,000 in United States currency to her church."

"Let me guess," Sullivan said. "That money was the result of the lady selling a bunch of oversized red bandannas with matadors on them to people in the good ol' U.S.A."

"You've got the picture."

"Well, I'd say you're on a camino angosta running the risk of hitting a comino cerrado," Sullivan said.

"Don't frustrate me with that bunk," Wilcox said as interpreter Maria Valequez snickered.

"I said you're on a road heading to a dead end," Sullivan said.

"We've made contact with something hard, by all means," Wilcox said.

"Does a damn roadblock sound familiar to you?"

Sullivan said he would overlook that remark. Then he told Wilcox he should be glad he is not in Birmingham, Alabama, where quacks were coming out of the woodwork.

Wilcox asked to hear more.

Sullivan told him people were calling FBI headquarters and confessing to the bank robberies. He told him there were scuba divers in the Cahaba River looking for money other callers had said they saw floating in the water. He told him people from Florida to Maine were threatening to sue the federal government for invasion of privacy, the result of the fruitless roadblocks that had stopped traffic.

"How can anybody sue a nation so far in debt?" Wilcox said.

"That's not the case," Sullivan said. "That was before our boss Bill Clinton made a successful run."

There was a period of silence.

"But we need a plan, not humor," Sullivan said.

"I don't want to do it before our work over here is completed, if it isn't already, but I think we need to seriously consider leaking the Madrid, Spain story to the news media," Wilcox said.

Sullivan thought for several seconds without speaking. Then he said, "That might have some merit. I sort of like the idea of using the bastards who have tried to destroy us."

"Let's see what happens tomorrow," Wilcox said. "If we don't make progress with the damn mail people and the damn church people, pardon the adjective, I'll be ready to cut loose everybody except Carmen Norris."

"Don't rush it," Sullivan said. "You guys have been through a ringer. Have some fun while you're away."

Wilcox, Norris, Pat Embry, Paul Conrad, Ed Samson and Valequez did enjoy themselves that evening at Guatemala Bay. Ferdinand Ballesteros was a delightful host, to the extent he kept attractive female and handsome male dance partners coming their way until well past midnight. The nightclub owner loved seeing his guests from the United States having so much fun. The native sons and daughters, regular patrons, found the visitors charming and enjoyable.

"Que sesea usted" — what do you wish? Ballesteros said repeatedly. The cheerful one was quick to tell his regular customers the foreigners were an on a highly complicated secret espionage mission.

The drinks were served and consumed quickly. The hours moved just as fast. It was difficult to tell whether the men were having more fun than the women as the music played and bodies moved across the dance floor.

"Hey, boss, I'm thinking about taking a leave of absence with that beautiful senorita over there," Embry said to Wilcox at about two o'clock in the morning. The special agent in charge observed the senora, smiled and nodded.

"We'll meet at one o'clock tomorrow afternoon," Wilcox said. "From the looks of it, I'd say Carmen and Maria have plans until then, too."

Embry looked toward the dance floor and saw Norris and Valequez cheek to cheek and appearing cozy while dancing with two men. When the pace of the music quickened, they were amazed and aroused when the Central Intelligence Agency representative in the crowd dropped to her knees and then onto her back and gyrated.

"Damn," Wilcox said. "She's pretty at breakfast. She's damn beautiful on the floor."

"I'll spread the news — a meeting at one," Embry said.

"I'm out of here," Wilcox said. "One of us has to maintain some degree of sanity."

Wilcox thanked Ballesteros for his extreme hospitality and left the building. He was met by a driving rainstorm and the sound of a taxi cab horn summoning him. He crawled into the back seat and told the driver he wanted to go to the Posado Valenzuela.

"On second thought," Wilcox said, "I'd like to take a slow drive through this village."

After some charades, the taxi cab driver nodded and, through the use of charades, told his passenger to point the way.

Wilcox made several notes as he rode through the village, trying hard to find a place where someone might know more about Constantina Calusso — more importantly, something related to her customers in the United States. After about fifteen minutes of looking and thinking, he knew he was taking stabs in the dark. He told the taxi cab driver he was ready to go to the hotel — "Lleveme al Posado Valenzuela."

Once there, Wilcox gave the taxi cab driver what amounted to $20 in United States currency and said, "Guarde el cambio."

The taxi cab driver grinned broadly, thanked him for his generous tip and said, "Prostituir, senor?"

Wilcox understood clearly. He thought for a moment and, surprising himself, said, "Si, agradar, gracias." Then he showed the taxi cab driver his room key and walked into the hotel.

"Damn, what have I done?" Wilcox said as he ambled down the hallway to his room and opened the door. About twenty minutes later, he found what he had ordered, an extraordinarily beautiful senorita who smelled wonderful and smiled enchantedly. She put her arms around him and rubbed his back and the rear of his neck. She blew warm air into his right ear, creating a tickling sensation throughout his body. She pulled back and began undressing.

No doubt, Marguerite Ramone had a lustful touch. Also, the prostitute, who appeared to be in her early thirties, had penetrating charcoal eyes and a sensational body that held Wilcox spellbound until she moved toward him and starting taking off his clothes.

After leading Wilcox to the kingsize bed, Marguerite rubbed his body, starting with the legs, moving to the shoulders and stopping at his most private part. She massaged it until he was about to explode. Then she stopped, giving him a needed break, and walked to a large bag with draw strings she had brought into the room. She pulled a bottle of wine from it and walked toward a sitting area to get two glasses.

"This I drink in honor of a wonderful man and to a wonderful evening together," Marguerite said.

"Likewise," Wilcox said.

When they finished the first glass, Marguerite kissed Wilcox as passionately as he had ever been. They kissed again. But when he attempted a third time, she pushed him back onto the bed, crawled on top of him and snaked her way down to his most private part. She performed oral sex until he was about to explode, then stopped in the nick of time.

"Drink a few more swallows with me before we complete our journey," Marguerite said.

The first journey was blissful, to say the least, and after they shared a hot bath, they drank another glass of wine and started the second journey.

"Oh, you American men are more gentle than most," Marguerite said as they cuddled and moved toward sleep. "Also, sir, you have much style in that you respect a woman of the night like me."

Wilcox pulled her close and they went to sleep.

At a quarter until ten the next morning, Wilcox kissed Marguerite, paid her handsomely, $500 in FBI money, and sent her on her way.

"Wow, I'm glad that's over," Wilcox said as he moved toward the bathroom and a hot shower.

Little did the special agent in charge know.

"Holy cow," Conrad said as he got off the elevator to go to his room and saw the beautiful woman coming out of his boss' room. "It looks like the man in charge did much better than the rest of us."

In Louisville, Midge and Mark Cates were watching television, the *Today Show*, with their two children, Courtney, age seven, and Bradley, age five. The kids were waiting for the school bus to stop in front of their house. The father was expecting a prospective client to telephone him. The mother was thinking it was a rare treat having all of them together at just after breakfast.

"I'm so thankful that worker won't be paralyzed," Midge said about the man who had taken a fall the afternoon previous. "I mean, that could've been much worse."

"I know," Mark said. "He just stepped off the plank and into the air. Two hundred feet later, he hit the ground."

Midge was about to respond, but she stopped when she heard television host Katie Couric say, "After this break, we'll be talking to an FBI special agent from Washington about those incredible, unsolved bank robberies in Birmingham, Alabama. As you can see by this video tape, there's still a lot of debris to clean up down that way."

Midge reacted to the statement immediately. She glanced at the television screen, then at her husband. When she saw him jerking his head in the same direction, she felt nauseated. She had what seemed like a million questions dancing through her head, as had been the case for a few days, and she chose the wrong one to ask at that moment.

"Mark, did you ever ask Carl about that bandanna?" Midge said. "I've looked all over this ..."

"Midge, can't you focus on something else," Mark said in a harsh tone, causing his daughter and son to look at him. "I told you I'd see if anybody found it. It isn't like I don't have other things to do with my time."

Mark jumped from his chair and started leaving the room. He turned and said, "I probably lost the damn thing on that hunting trip that got screwed up."

After Mark had stormed out of the kitchen door, obviously too upset to remember the telephone call he was waiting to receive, his daughter turned toward her mother and said, "Is daddy mad at us?"

"No, Courtney, your father is just extremely worried about losing his big red handkerchief with the matador on it," Midge said with her voice cracking and moisture forming in her eyes.

CHAPTER THIRTY-THREE

After five more days of a lot more fun and a smattering of work that produced little to help the Federal Bureau of Investigation solve the case, Jim Wilcox and Carmen Norris dropped off Paul Conrad, Pat Embry and Ed Samson at Madrid International Airport and said farewell to Maria Valequez. After renting a front end loader and digging through rubble in a large junk yard and filing petitions with the Spanish Postal Service seeking clearance to examine parcel mail records and to interview employees, the investigation team was dwindling to two and all it planned to do was make repeat calls in search of pertinent information.

"Don't leak anything to the news media until we have a conference call," Wilcox said at the airport.

"We'll fill in everybody who needs to know what has transpired over here, prepare a detailed report, and wait for instructions from you," Conrad said.

"Don't expect much new," Norris said. "Unless we're able to make a power play, I doubt we'll be here more than a week."

"That's stretching it," Wilcox said.

The group enjoyed a few light moments while reflecting on the nasty labor they had completed at the junk yard before the public address system made the first call for Air Europe Flight 1320.

"Well, that's us," Embry said. "Good luck — and adios."

After the group started walking toward the departure gate, Conrad hurried back to Wilcox and Norris. He motioned for the special agent in charge to step to the side with him. He leaned forward and said, in a whisper, "That was one fantastic looking woman you had in your hotel room the other night."

Conrad laughed when he saw the shocked look on Wilcox's face. Then he said, "Don't worry, Jim. I won't leak that to anybody either."

Norris had noticed Wilcox's stunned reaction, too, and she quickly became inquisitive.

"It has nothing to do with what we're doing here," Wilcox said. "It was something about another tough case we're working on in Birmingham."

Wilcox and Norris departed the airport in a rental car and immediately went back to what had become a tiresome pattern of work — interviewing familiar faces, talking to a few strange faces and dealing with smiling faces at Guatemala Bay, where they had become cult heroes.

The Postal Servico Madrid would not budge.

"Senor, you are requesting the impossible," said the tall and slim director at the main office on Camino Saint Christopher. "We do not register every piece of mail that comes through our office. Do they do that in the United States?"

"No sir," Wilcox said. "We just thought your clerks at the post office nearest to Camino Ruiz would remember unusual packages sent to the United States, maybe a city or two on the address labels."

"I think not, sir. No luck. I asked and they remember the senora you speak about. But they say she put stamps on the packages and dropped them off, sometimes one at a time or four at a time."

"Okay, I understand what ..."

"They say she sent packages all over the world — London, Paris, New York and Leningrad. They know no more than that and I cannot take more of their time asking them stupid questions for the United States, what do you say, TCI."

"FBI, senor, the damn FBI."

At the Montego Hotel, Wilcox and Norris spent time talking to Rose Alou, a younger women who had befriended Constantina Calusso. She kept the elderly lady company from time to time and helped her clean her small room on the fourth floor. There were occasions when she would stay overnight to prepare a nourishing dinner and provide companionship.

"Si, senor, Senora Calusso spoke proudly about how her red

bandannas were being purchased worldwide," Alou said, with Norris interpreting most of her remarks for Wilcox. "She was a glorious lady, yet humble among her friends."

"Do you recall any of the cities or the states?" Norris said.

"London, si. El Paso, si. Mexico City, si, no doubt."

"Let's focus on the United States," Wilcox said.

Alou appeared confused. She said, "No hablo ingeles."

"Fine, Rose," Norris said. "Let me name some for you and see if they have a familiar ring." Al

ou nodded, but still looked perplexed.

"Alabama." Alou looked puzzled.

"Birmingham."

"Si, Birmingham," Alou said, a smile surfacing as if she wanted to hear encouragement. "Miss Constantina shipped many to England."

Wilcox and Norris appeared as if the air was coming out of them. Their eyes glistened when Birmingham was mentioned, then dimmed when England followed.

"Florida? ... Tennessee? ... Georgia? ... Mississippi? ... Louisiana? ... Kentucky?..."

Midge Cates was on the telephone in Louisville, Kentucky placing a telephone call she had dreaded. In fact, she felt stupid as she dialed the number for Imperial Surveillance Services, a company she had found in the Bell South Yellow Pages. When a husky voice answered the ring — "ISS, this is Ike speaking" — she quickly hung up.

After a minute or two, Midge redialed.

"ISS, Ike speaking."

"Hello, this is Midge Cates."

"Yes ma'am."

"I just called and hung up on you."

"That's how I figured it. It happens all the time. What's your problem?"

"Well, you see, I'm thinking ..."

Carl McGraw, a veteran of The Snowman Project and now a part of The Treasured Gems Project, was seated in first class on a U.S. Airlines jet destined for Charlotte, North Carolina and on to Louisville. He wondered how Ed Bass and Sam Mills were faring since they had departed the City of Brotherly Love about three hours before him.

Fresh in McGraw's mind was the bewildering sight of security guards asleep at their stations, as well as the view of crewmen on an impressive wave runner boat who had accepted the cargo the trio had delivered to them. Also bracing was the fear he had felt as the masked men wielding rifles thanked them in muffled voices and told them to get out of the area as quickly as possible.

"Yes, I'd like a bourbon on the rocks, your choice," McGraw said to the flight attendant who was serving him and about a dozen other travelers in first class.

"Are you feeling well?" she said. "With all respect, Mr. Sadler, your face appears flushed."

"I feel great, at least as good as a man can after eight days moving up and down the East Coast."

"I'll get you a drink, a swallow of our miracle nervous stomach medicine and a steak and biscuit."

"That's a grand trifecta — and thank you."

At Maria Angelica Cathedral in Madrid, Wilcox and Norris were conversing with several nuns and other individuals who knew Constantina Colusso and admired her. They spent several hours with Sister Monique Sanches, who had known the lady best and had handled her funeral arrangements and final personal matters.

Wilcox noticed a recklessly perceived resemblance between Sister Monique and Marguerite Ramone and quickly dismissed it as a guilt trip.

"As I told Miss Norris on our first meeting, Constantina was like an angel to us," Sister Monique said without needing any translation. "She was at church every Sunday, even when the weather was bad and her tender bones ached, and she had to make a long trip from the Montego Hotel to get here. Then, bless her glorious soul, she astounded us with a most generous gift at the time of her death."

Sister Monique chanted something in Latin, smiled and said, "Sainthood awaits Senora Calusso."

"Did her will or anything she said provide a reason why she would be so generous, other than her devotion to God, of course," Wilcox said, with his stilted delivery drawing a smile from Norris, a devoted catholic since birth.

"The only stipulation was that we use a portion of the money to fight gang violence, the evil that killed her son," Sister Monique said. "We have started a Pequeno Auxiliador program that has done much good."

"Sister, I want you to think hard about this," Wilcox said.

"Sir, I try to think hard every day."

"Yes ma'am, I'm sorry."

"I accept the apology."

"Thank you, ma'am. But we're looking for every piece of information that could explain where Senora Constantina mailed her red bandannas."

"I comprehend."

"We think one of her customers in the United States left one of those oversized red bandannas with a matador on it at the scene of a bank robbery. We want to catch that person who stole from others, totally innocent people, as well as those who were involved with him."

Sister Monique did not respond for several seconds, almost a minute. Then she said, "Father, forgive those who have made bad judgements. Let their lives become pure."

Wilcox glanced toward Norris. The Central Intelligence Agency representative gave him a look he understand, an expression that told him to be patient.

"Senor Wilcox, I am not as naive as you might think," Sister Monique said. "I watch television, too, and I see bad people hurting good people. I know the type people you are chasing and I hope you find them, if that is God's will."

In Louisville, in room 431 at the Galt House, Mark Cates was preparing to exit after spending a couple of lustful hours with his female lawyer friend.

"I hope I'll see you in a couple of days," Sandra Brewer said.

"You will, no doubt," he said.

McGraw was in the air with money on his mind.

In Central America, just outside a seedy bar, two drug smugglers were making purchases with money that had been taken from five banks in Birmingham, Alabama.

"Senor Wilcox, you do not have to play on my sympathy for those people who lost money," Sister Monique said in Madrid, continuing her previous thought. "I know everybody in the world is not as nice as most people in the world."

Wilcox smiled.

Norris laughed.

"And, sir, I am sure I know where you might find most of the clues you need. But I am not sure I will allow you to look for them in such a treasured place."

"Excuse me?" Wilcox said.

"Constantina had large maps of the countries in which she sold her beautiful red bandannas," Sister Monique said. "They included one from the United States. She had it colored brilliantly, marking almost every city from which she received orders. She said it helped her learn more about the world, the places she would never visit."

"Now at last we're getting somewhere," Wilcox said.

Norris was not so sure.

"Sir, that map and the others were buried with Constantina," Sister Monique said. "They are a part of her grave with her Bible, one of her red bandannas, a picture of her blessed husband, Jorge, and a copy of her will with a thank you note from Maria Angelica Cathedral attached to it."

As soon as Sister Monique paused, instincts kicked in with Wilcox, who looked toward Norris in disbelief. He was quick to respond, knowing a period of reflection is often needed at such an emotional point in an interrogation.

"Sister Monique, would it be possible to continue this inquiry tomorrow morning?" Wilcox said.

"This is not an inquiry, merely a conversation," Sister Monique said.

"I respect that," Wilcox said. "Still, can we talk more then?"

"My time is your time, as long as your time comes after eleven o'clock and before three o'clock."

CHAPTER THIRTY-FOUR

The desk clerk at Posada Valenzuela saw Jim Wilcox and Carmen Norris walking through the lobby and quickly excused himself from the two businessmen he was checking in. He rushed through a small office and emerged in front of the special agents just before they made a turn down a hallway to a bank of elevators.

"Senor Wilcox, you have had several urgent calls from a Senor Mike Sullivan," said the desk clerk. "He requests you telephone as soon as possible."

Wilcox told the desk clerk thank you and picked up the pace toward the elevator. He was moving so fast, Norris had to struggle to keep up with him. Neither said a word until they got to the spacious suite and dialed the hotline number at Federal Bureau of Investigation headquarters in Washington, D.C.

"Have you seen the news?" Sullivan said.

"No."

"Well, we've got one for the ages and it might be related to the case you're investigating."

"Let's hear about it," Wilcox said.

"How does $28 million in diamonds and other gems missing from the Atlantic Shore Diamond Exchange sound to you?"

"Impossible."

"That was my first reaction," Sullivan said.

Sullivan told Wilcox and Norris how the heist had occurred. He talked about the security guards that had been discovered unconscious at their stations. He talked about how the front door of the building had been blown open and the vaults inside had been blown open. He talked about a presumably stolen car that had been scrubbed clean and left unattended on the Temple University campus in Philadelphia. He talked about a helicopter pilot seeing a mysterious boat in the Atlantic Ocean a couple of hours before daybreak.

"Damn," Wilcox said. "Where are the clues?"

"There aren't any, at least not many," Sullivan said. "But, Jimbo, the technique used in the blasting process was exactly the same as the one used in Birmingham. Also, the security system was extremely similar to the ones that failed at those bank branches."

"How did they get around? I mean, somebody had to have rented a car or a truck."

"A truck was rented in Chicago by a guy with bogus identification, a G.H. Nichols from Fordyce, Arkansas. The guy doesn't exist."

"Where is the Coast Guard?"

"Zooming across the Atlantic Ocean looking for a fast boat."

"How did the security guards get conked?"

"Somebody planted some laced coffee packets in the snack room."

"That's good," Wilcox said. "Inside jobs are easier to solve than strangers coming in and out."

"Perhaps, but we're talking about honorable people who ..."

They talked for several minutes more, at last getting around to the latest report on the quest for the oversized red bandanna with a matador on it. Then Sullivan returned the conversation to the heist on Long Island.

"Is Carmen with you?" Sullivan said.

"Standing two feet away," Wilcox said.

"Good, because she might want to check in with the CIA," Sullivan said. "This one smells like terrorists who are connected with some strong glue — and, at this point, I don't think we can rule out them being involved in the Birmingham case."

"I'm betting the mafia," Wilcox said.

"That could be," Sullivan said. "But terrorists are terrorists."

"We've got to check out that old and trusted mafia trail — New Orleans, Birmingham, Knoxville and New York," Wilcox said. "The parameters fit perfectly."

"Get those sales records," Sullivan said.

The following day, at about noon, Wilcox and Norris were back in front of Sister Monique Sanchez. She had heard about the diamonds being stolen in the United States. She had empathy for what the special agents were attempting to accomplish.

But, she said, "I think not, Senor Wilcox. "That blessed lady deserves better, the chance to rest peacefully after a life of hard work."

When Sister Monique paused, Wilcox considered explaining to her how he might be able to get a court order to have the body of Constantina Calusso exhumed. He thought the better of it, however, because he knew that might not be possible because of the international scope of the investigation.

"Sister Monique, seeing that map appears to be our only chance of solving the bank robberies," Norris said, her tone soft and more pleasing to the nun.

"From what I understand, I do not think the map in the casket will help you," Sister Monique said. "It had markings on it all across your nation, far too many for you to chase after."

"Were there names with the markings?" Norris said.

"No, most definitely not. Constantina just marked the map. I must say last night I thought about that and concluded most of her customers were from Texas, Montana, Colorado and others that do not come to mind."

"Could you recreate the markings on a map?"

"No, not with accuracy."

Do Louisiana, Alabama and Tennessee come to mind?" Wilcox said.

"I do not comprehend," Sister Monique said.

"Do you remember seeing Alabama on the map?" Wilcox said as he reached into a briefcase and pulled out a map of the United States."Were there markings in this area?"

"Yes, but not many," Sister Monique said.

"Then that makes it more important for us to see her map," Wilcox said. "There are fewer people to check out."

Sister Monique stood and said, "Excuse me, please." She walked from the room. After a quarter of an hour, Wilcox looked at Norris and said,

"Is Sister Monique coming back?"

"I'd guess she's looking for divine guidance," Norris said. "Sometimes, that takes a while."

Wilcox mentioned the possibility of attempting to get a court order. Norris laughed at the thought and said, "Jim, my CIA experience let's me know you can forget that."

Wilcox nodded and said, "I understand — and, frankly, I'm not sure that's proper in this case."

Another fifteen minutes passed before Sister Monique returned to the room. Wilcox had already put the map of the United States and his notebook in his briefcase. She had tears in her eyes when she looked toward the special agents.

"I do not see a reason to disturb Senora Constantina from her blessed rest," Sister Monique said.

"Nor do we," Wilcox said. "It would be wrong for us to bother such a nice lady who really might be an angel."

"You are a good man, Senor Wilcox," Sister Monique said. "As for Senora Constantina Calusso, she is a saint."

"How do you say angel in Spanish?" Wilcox said.

"Angel is angel, no matter the language."

"I should have known," Wilcox said. "Un million de gracias. Ahora si entiendo. Adios, delicaco senora."

As they exited Maria Angelica Cathedral and made their way back to the rental car parked about two blocks away, Norris complimented Wilcox for the nice remarks he had made as they prepared to bid farewell to Sister Monique.

"I was just being honest," Wilcox said. "Sister Monique is an extremely nice lady who made me realize tampering with a grave isn't worth it."

"After some initial reservations, I've got to admit you aren't so bad yourself," Norris said before giving Wilcox a kiss on the cheek.

"Put the mushy stuff on hold," Wilcox said. "We've got a lot to do and need to get back to work."

"No," Norris said. "Jim, we've run into the final roadblock. It's time for us to visit Ferdinand Ballesteros one more time, pack our bags and start a long trek home."

"Let's go down to one of those quaint cafes beside the lagoon and have a cocktail lunch," Wilcox said.

"So you are willing to mix pleasure with business," Norris said.

Wilcox smiled and said, "But this won't be business. This afternoon won't be on my expense account. It's all on me."

Norris giggled and said, "Then let's add a boat ride to the agenda, maybe at sunset."

"You're the boss," Wilcox said.

"I don't want to be. I'm starting to have too much fun playing the role of underling."

"Good," Wilcox said. "Just stay in line after we get home."

Carl McGraw had arrived at home and the following morning he reported to work early at C&M Construction Company. The clock on the reception area wall said it was a quarter past six, so he figured he was the only person in the building. But he smelled fresh coffee and flinched when Mark Cates greeted him with a huge grin.

"Damn, you make building a snowman look like a small undertaking," Cates said. "I'm up early so I can hear about it."

McGraw grinned and looked around to make sure nobody else was in the building.

"So should I call you G.H. Nichols the rest of our lives?" Cates said.

"Put a lid on it, Mark, and bury that name," McGraw said. "Ask me no questions and I'll tell you no lies."

"So where have you been the last couple of days?"

"Dallas and Phoenix," McGraw said.

Cates laughed, boisterously, and said something about having some hush money coming his way.

"Exercise a little patience," McGraw said.

"It must be in the washing machine."

"Some of it, yeah."

"It seems like all I do is sit around and wait."

"Are you going to the bank this morning?" McGraw said.

"Sure."

"Well, I've got something for you to put in our safety deposit box," McGraw said as he reached into a pants pocket.

McGraw handed Cates a cloth pouch with a draw string. When he looked inside, he saw six large uncut diamonds.

"I figured you might skim a little off the top," Cates said. "I know you aren't the brother they think you are."

"Just call it a mini-heist," McGraw said. "After seeing what I did on Long Island, I'm positive they won't miss it."

CHAPTER THIRTY-FIVE

Almost six months to the day after Mark Cates and Carl McGraw agreed to attempt The Snowmen Project on a snowy deck in Louisville, Kentucky, the families were together again in the same place for a Saturday night dinner. On this occasion the men were grilling humongous steaks while their wives and children played in the back yard.

It was warm and dry, ideal for construction work, and business had been good, including that conducted above board and that conducted in shadows. A sudden influx of cash from the Long Island caper had the husbands feeling generous and they were ready to surprise their wives.

Mark and Carl called Midge and Diana to the deck. They mixed them a couple of drinks and refreshed the ones they had been tending.

"We've had some good fortune selling stock we've been sitting on for quite a while," Carl said. "So how would you wonderful ladies like to take the children on a cruise?"

Midge and Diana were delighted. They had talked about traveling to Cancun, Mexico for years. They hurried to their husbands and gave them warm hugs.

"Are you sure we can afford this?" Diana said. "I mean, you guys are sinking a lot into C&M Construction and ..."

"Hey, we're the prudent ones in the crowd," Mark said.

Midge was thinking hard. She saw the sweet dream as the revival of a recurring nightmare. Thoughts about the missing red bandanna did not come as frequently as they had in the past, but they remained painful. Also, the Sandra Brewer matter preyed on her mind.

In Washington, D.C., Mike Sullivan, Jim Wilcox, Pat Embry, Paul Conrad, Ed Samson, Carmen Norris and Ben Eubanks from the Federal

Trade Commission were seated at a conference table. With all of their efforts leading nowhere, the special agents were ready for the Federal Bureau of Investigation to attempt an uncanny course of action.

"I never dreamed the news media would become our chief ally," Sullivan said.

"It's our last shot," Wilcox said. "As time passes, people forget bank robberies and think about airplane crashes. We've got to remind the public of what happened in Birmingham. Also, at the risk of sounding like a broken record, those bastards owe us something after ruining my roadblocks plan."

"You don't forget," Norris said.

"I don't forgive either," Wilcox said.

"Then tell me how to say I love you in Spanish," Norris said.

"Amor tu," Wilcox said.

"Well, I'm glad to see you two getting along," Sullivan said. "But I'm too nervous to ask how close you got while in Madrid."

Wilcox and Norris smiled. They decided to let the others wonder about their last evening together overseas.

"Let's talk business," Sullivan said. "It's your stage, Ben."

"No news is bad news," Eubanks said. "There hasn't been an influx of new cash in the foreign market, at least none remotely related to bank robberies or stolen diamonds."

"It's under ground, buried," Norris said. "The CIA believes that cash has touched a dozen hands. It'll come back as clean as powdery snow."

"That's a hell of a way of putting it," Wilcox said.

Embry reported there remained about 20,000 suspects based on the fingerprints found on the red bandanna.

Conrad said there were 50,000 sports utility vehicles that needed to be checked out.

"Like we said, it's the news media or bust," Sullivan said. "Let's get the game started."

In Louisville, Ben Bobo and Fred Long were watching a minor league professional baseball game with their wives and a group of children from the local Boys Club. The homestanding Cardinals were in a thriller, leading two-to-one in the top of the seventh inning.

As the children marveled over superstars and dreamed of becoming some, Long noticed a man walking along an aisle. He turned toward Bobo and said, "Let's go get a few bags of peanuts for the kids."

Bobo started to object, wanting to watch the game, but noticed Long looked determined. So they hustled through a portal and moved swiftly toward a concessions stand.

"I'll do the talking," Long said.

"That's fine since I don't know who we're going to see," Bobo said.

In a couple of minutes he started figuring it out.

"Well, you never know who you'll run into at the ball park," Long said.

"How are you, Fred?" Edgar Swartz said.

"I'm doing fine, my friend. I hope you are."

"Everything is going great, all around the world," Swartz said. "It couldn't be better."

Swartz hurried into the crowd.

"Let me guess," Bobo said in a low tone as he and Long moved toward the concessions stand to buy peanuts. "That's a member of the brotherhood."

"You heard him," Long said. "The laundry business is booming. The cash is flowing at a good pace."

At FBI headquarters in Washington, Wilcox was asked to read a proposed script to be used at a news conference. The other special agents wanted to gauge its impact.

"Okay, I'll give it a whirl," Wilcox said.

The special agent in charge started reading:

"The FBI is pleased to announce a possible breakthrough in our investigation of the bank robberies about six months ago in Birmingham, Alabama. At the scene of the crime we uncovered an oversized red bandanna produced by a company in Madrid, Spain and mailed to a customer in the United States. The name of the company is Calusso Woven Goods International, which is on the label of the bandanna. The bandanna is distinct in that its color is an unusually bright shade of red and there is a matador embroidered on it.

"Calusso Woven Goods International is out of business and the owner, Constantina Calusso, is deceased. So is her husband, Jorge Calusso, and there are no other members of their family. There are some records of sales made in the United States, but some were destroyed two years ago.

"Here is the oversized red bandanna. It is 24 inches by 12 inches. It has tightly woven edges that make it durable and heavier than most bandannas. The dimensions of the matador on the bandanna are two inches by two inches.

"After conducting an extensive investigation in Madrid, Spain, with some success, the FBI needs your assistance in this matter. It is our intention to question anyone who owns one of these bandannas. So if you own one, know someone who owns one or have seen one in the possession of an individual, please contact the FBI. Our toll free number is 1-800-324-2265. The number on the screen is 1-800-FBI-BANK.

"The FBI appreciates your assistance."

"Bravo, el matador," Norris said.

"Si, hermoso senora," Wilcox said.

"Damn," Conrad said.

"Jim called Carmen a lovely, seductive lady."

"I didn't say seductive."

Norris giggled as the others laughed.

"I want to get the news conference arranged promptly," Sullivan said.

"I'll get on it," Samson said.

"Also, I've got something to say to Jim Wilcox and Carmen Norris," Sullivan said. "I want the damn soap opera to end."

In Louisville, Midge Cates was on the telephone with Ike Alexander of Imperial Surveillance Systems.

"If you're sure, ma'am, I'll pick up the pace," Alexander said.

"I'll be out of town on those dates," Midge said.

"I've written them down."

"How is my escrow account doing?"

"You're still way ahead, ma'am. We'll chat when you get back from your cruise."

CHAPTER THIRTY-SIX

A casual observer would have thought a space flight was in progress or, to a heavier degree, a presidential assassination had taken place had he or see walked into the executive offices at First Commercial Bank in Louisville, Kentucky. Any employee who could take a break had his or her eyes riveted on the television screen as the *Cable News Network* aired a Federal Bureau of Investigation news conference.

Similar scenes were developing in Birmingham, Alabama, where at Sector, First Columbus, Central, Patriot and American people were digesting the latest developments in a bank robbery case that had hit squarely at home.

People were chattering in both cities at an impressive pace as the newscaster in Atlanta, Georgia prepared to switch the focus from her to Special Agent in Charge Jim Wilcox in Washington, D.C.

"I'm told we're less than a minute away from a startling announcement in the bank robbery case in Birmingham, Alabama," said the newscaster. "The FBI has been quiet about this for several weeks. We do not know if it has anything to do with the unsolved diamonds heist at the Atlantic Shore Exchange on Long Island."

Ed Bass and Sam Mills were among the bankers watching the television in an office on the eighth floor. They joined in juvenile laughter when fellow workers made jokes about the newscast. But their hearts were more heavy than light, if not tugging at their throats. Suddenly, from their point of view, the room temperature felt ten degrees warmer.

"I've got 20-to-1 that says it was a six-year-old who masterminded this," said one man.

"You're on," said one woman. "It'd take somebody at least ten years old to come up with such a plan."

"Hush," said another man. "Here we go."

They watched as Wilcox made his lengthy spiel. They reacted in whispered tones as he told the story of Constantina Calusso and her oversized red bandanna business. Few of them believed what they were hearing, as their reactions showed. They laughed when they saw the telephone number:

1-800-FBI-BANK.

"Get real," said a man standing next to Bass and Mills. "Can you guys believe the FBI is begging us to help it crack a case?"

"Elliott Ness is spinning in his grave," said a woman.

Bass looked at the man, smiled and shook his head. He looked at Mills, who appeared pale.

"That damn Calusso woman sounds like a character Walt Disney might create," said a man.

"It's a case for Super Chicken," said a woman.

"Well, it's time to get back to the real world," Mills said as he started walking toward the door. Behind him he could hear the television, with reporters firing questions at Wilcox. Beside him he could feel the presence of another person. He did not have to look to know who was making an exit with him.

It took Bass and Mills about a minute to seclude themselves in a bathroom lounge down the hall. They looked inside two stalls to make sure they were alone.

"Do you know anything about that bandanna?" Mills said as the bankers pretended to be washing their hands.

"Not a damn thing," Bass said. "But I'll know something about it by tomorrow morning."

Mark Cates was in a mall purchasing a birthday gift for his wife when he was attracted to a bank of television sets in a department store. Numerous customers had gathered to watch the news conference. He joined them and attempted to determine what was going on by their remarks. His stomach turned a flip when video tape of Central Bank appeared on the screens.

"Now, we'll repeat the statement issued by FBI Special Agent in Charge Jim Wilcox," said the female newscaster. The crowd listened until the end:

1-800-FBI-BANK.

Cates' mind was being blitzed. He hoped his wife was not watching, but he knew it was a matter of time. He ambled aimlessly, or so he thought, but his instincts were working because he ended up in the outdoors department.

"Can I help you?" said a sales representative.

"Yeah, I hope so. I'm looking for some large handkerchiefs, something colorful that kids might enjoy."

"Those would be in the men's department."

"No, I'm talking about camping handkerchiefs, something like a Boy Scout would use."

"Oh, I think you mean a bandanna."

"Maybe. As long as a bandanna is large."

Cates was led to a part of the department that featured hiking gear. The sales rep showed him numerous bandannas of several colors, some with prints and some solid. He felt one, unfolded it to check its size, about 16 inches by 12 inches, and said, "Do you have anything larger?"

"No, that's fairly standard, certainly large enough for a boy."

"Fine," Cates said. "I'll take three red ones, two green ones and two blue ones, all without designs on them. Better yet, make it four red ones."

"You're taking care of an entire troop," said the sales rep.

Midge Cates was driving home after picking up her children at school. She had on the car radio at the top of the hour and heard the newscast starting: "A strange red bandanna might be all the FBI needs to solve a bank robbery case. We'll have the details after this commercial break."

Midge felt her legs weaken. Her stomach tightened. When her children became restless in the back seat, she turned and screamed, "Hey, keep your mouths shut." She wanted to cut out her tongue as soon as she had said that. Her heart was already bleeding. "I'm sorry," she said to the children. "I just want to hear this news report."

Actually, Midge did not want to hear anything like that. Nor did she want her children to digest anything related to a red bandanna, not after all they had already absorbed at home. She turned down the volume and listened intently.

After driving to their house, Midge let the children run free for about half of an hour and secluded herself in the master bedroom. She cried like an infant. Her fears about the past were founded, that much she knew. But the future was more troubling because she figured it was just a matter of time before a special agent knocked on the front door.

Midge flinched when the telephone rang. She waited for several seconds before answering it.

"Hello, baby, how are we this afternoon?"

"Fine, Diana," Midge said, feeling much more calm.

"Have you been watching television?"

"No, not really. I've been cleaning the house."

"Well, tell me if I'm wrong, but didn't you buy that beautiful bandanna for Mark from a place in Madrid, Spain?"

"Yes, the one with the matador on it," Midge said. "In fact, I just got it out of the dryer and folded it."

"Well, honey, that's damn fine because I just saw ..."

Telephone calls were pouring into FBI headquarters in Washington, too, more than forty in the first fifteen minutes after the news conference. Some were pointless after their descriptions of red bandannas had been recorded, but some appeared worth tracking.

Special agents Ed Samson and Paul Conrad were reading notes provided by telephone operators and processing the information as quickly as possible. The computer room was getting a workout as data was being typed into the system.

"Boom, Tyler, Texas," Samson said as he worked. "Boom, Laramie, Wyoming. Boom, West Point, New York. Hey, boom-boom, Atlanta,

Georgia. Boom, boom, boom, Dadeville, Alabama."

"We've got to move fast," Conrad said. "We don't want people running for cover."

"Don't get too hasty," Samson said. "Nobody can hide that damn oversized red bandanna because we've got it."

"That's a good point," Conrad said. "But we've got to contact FBI offices in all of these locations and give them some direction. If I was a crook with anything tying me to what went down in Birmingham, I'd take a long vacation."

Wilcox entered the room in a huff and said, "I swear I'm going to kill one of those bastards."

Samson and Conrad looked at him, perplexed, and the former said, "I thought the news conference went well."

"Obviously, you didn't hear the question that idiot from *ABC News* asked," Wilcox said.

"I left during the q-and-a."

"He said, and I quote, 'Won't it be hard for a federal prosecutor to make a case if a person said he or she simply lost the bandanna?' Hell, we've got leads coming in from all across the nation and that son of a bitch is playing defense lawyer for the bad guys."

Conrad looked at Samson and raised his eyebrows. Then he said, "I don't like the stiff any better than the boss does. But he's right. I've never heard of anybody being put in prison for losing a handkerchief."

"Listen, Paul, if that's your idea of sick humor, zip up your damn lips," Wilcox said. "Somewhere out there we've got some bastards who are finally feeling heat and I'm not going to let them get away without scorching their asses."

Mark Cates walked into C&M Construction at a brisk pace. To his right he saw Carl McGraw on the telephone looking at him through a doorway while seated at his desk. He walked to his secretary, and rubbed the upper part of his right leg in an effort to draw her attention to the area. She took the bait and saw about two inches of a red bandanna sticking out of one of the pockets on his khaki pants.

"I'm glad you're here, Mark, because the telephone has been ringing off the hook," Belinda Wilbanks said. "Here are the message slips. Some sound urgent."

"I hope we don't have an on-the-site problem," Cates said.

"I don't think so," Wilbanks said. "A Ben Bobo called and said he needed to talk to you as soon as possible. The same with Ed Bass, although I think Carl is on the line with him. Also, I just got off the telephone with Midge."

"Does she have a problem?"

"I don't know. She said it wasn't anything important, but she sounded troubled to me."

"Are all of the crews in?"

Wilbanks looked at the clock, peculiarly, and said, "No, it's still a little early for that."

"I guess so," Cates said. "But, Belinda, let's see if we can get everybody together for a meeting at seven o'clock tomorrow."

Cates had some explaining to do to Bobo, Bass and Mills and he was not looking forward to it. Nor was he anxious to talk to Long, who was already aware. He wanted to see them face to face, in an out of the way tavern or behind closed doors at his office. So he telephoned Midge and told her he was sorry but would be late for her birthday dinner.

"Take your time," Midge said. "We'll go to Pizza Hut and cut the cake and ice cream as late as nine o'clock."

"I hope you understand," Mark said.

"I understand more than I really care to and I don't want to talk about it on the telephone," Midge said.

Midge slammed down the telephone at about the time McGraw walked into Cates' office.

"What in hell do you want?" Cates said, his tone causing Wilbanks to jump at her desk.

"Excuse me," McGraw said as he closed the door. "Maybe I should back up and try this again."

"I'm sorry," Cates said. "If there's anybody in the world I need right now it's you."

"You've got that."

"Damn, life in the fast lane," Cates said.

"Whatever. All I know is it's definitely moving at a quick gait."

Cates stood to give McGraw a good look at the red bandanna protruding from the pocket of his pants.

McGraw smiled and said, "Hey, I must admit it looks good enough at first glance."

"Good," Cates said. "I don't plan to take part in a strip search."

Cates paused, then said, "But I'm not sure the other four guys will let me live after this blunder. I've got to talk them, face to face, the sooner the better."

"I've handled that for you," McGraw said.

"So ..."

"I can't say they're pleased. But it isn't the end of the world, nor the end of a partnership."

"The goons might feel differently."

Cates would have liked to have heard the conversation taking place on the far side of Louisville, where Long had answered a telephone call placed by Edgar Swartz.

"Fred, I'm calling to find out what the fuck is going on with your guys," Swartz said.

"I thought I'd hear from you."

"Go on with it — and be forewarned I'm recording this for people higher up the ladder."

Long gave Swartz a detailed explanation of how Cates had wiped his brow in the Central Bank lobby and had misplaced the red bandanna in the process.

"That's pretty sloppy," Swartz said. "But I guess it's understandable."

"I'm heightened by your reaction," Long said.

"Hey, I've talked to our lawyer. He says that's circumstantial evidence, that there isn't any proof the man took the damn handkerchief to Birmingham, especially since he was hunting deer in South Georgia."

"Super."

"But, Fred, we're only cool about this as long as it remains comfortable on your end."

"There won't be any other surprises," Long said. "I've been assured of that by my pal."

"McGraw?"

"Yeah."

"He's a hell of a worker for us," Swartz said. "See if you can find something else for him."

"Are you serious?"

"Hell yes, I'm serious. There's never enough capital floating around in our business."

The next thing Long heard was a dial tone. Swartz had spoken his peace and hung up.

CHAPTER THIRTY-SEVEN

Mark Cates and Carl McGraw stood in front of their employees at C&M Construction Company and started making what amounted to a motivational speech. Their audience numbered more than a hundred as one of the partners paced in front of the crowd, at times awkwardly, to make sure most of them saw the red bandanna protruding from the right front pocket of his pants. He looked like a fashion model, turning left and turning right. He was in a good mood after hearing he had been forgiven by the brotherhood.

"Ladies and gentlemen, our company is doing well," McGraw said as Cates walked. "We're into this mall project just over the Indiana border and we're working on a couple of office buildings in East Louisville. We've got some others waiting for us. With that progress comes new demands, most of them tied to deadlines. Because of that, we've got incentives we'd like for you to consider."

McGraw looked toward Cates, who with the fervor of an evangelist yanked the red bandanna from his pocket and wiped sweat from his mouth. Then he said, "We've got only a few months to complete the Indiana-Kentucky Mall project. That's a tall order, but we can do it if you're willing to work. If we get it finished on time, we'll give each of you three extra days of paid vacation and we'll consider bonuses."

The men and women hooted and hollered. Cates yanked out the red bandanna and wiped his face, like a politician who had made a good point. Then he said, "That includes all of you who are working in the preliminary stages on the office complexes. In summary, we're asking you to work overtime, maybe on some weekends."

Again, Cates pulled out the bandanna and wiped his forehead.

McGraw thought his partner might be overdoing it.

"Are there any questions?" McGraw said.

"As I understand it, we'll get three extra days of paid vacation if we bring in the mall on schedule."

"Right on."

"Does that include your lowly secretary and the remainder of the office staff?" Belinda Wilbanks said.

"Of course."

"What kind of raise are we talking about?"

Cates looked at McGraw, who shrugged his shoulders and said, "I'd guess at least a quarter an hour, perhaps a half dollar."

Cates noticed a man in the rear of the room holding up a hand, a veteran bricklayer who was one of their favorite employees.

"Rufus, do you have a question?"

"It's more of a statement."

"We should've known," McGraw said with a smile.

"Mr. Cates, I just want you to know you made me mighty happy when you pulled that red bandanna out of your pants pocket," Rufus said.

"Why is that?" Cates said.

"Well, last night on television they said those guys who robbed all of those banks down in Birmingham left a large red bandanna like yours on the scene."

"Does that make me a suspect?" Cates said, prompting laughter.

"No sir, it doesn't," Rufus said. "You've got your bandanna stuck in your pants pocket."

"I guess I understand," Cates said. "Anyway, let's go back to work and get that damn mall finished."

As the construction workers left the warehouse, Cates looked at McGraw, who gave him a comforting wink.

During the next two days, things were not so peaceful at Federal Bureau of Investigation headquarters in Washington, D.C. or, for that matter, at other offices across the nation. At least two dozen individuals had been summoned to answer questions related to oversized red bandannas purchased from Calusso Woven Goods International.

"I'd like to know where you got that bandanna," said a special agent in Atlanta to a 42-year-old man.

"A woman gave it to me."

"I assume you can put us in touch with her."

"No sir, I can't. She was a broad I met at the Fulton County Rodeo two years ago. She was passing through. We had a pleasing fling."

"But she gave you an expensive gift?"

"Yes sir and no sir. I didn't get the bandanna until later. It came in the mail at my office with a short note. She said she had a nice time and signed it."

"What's her name?"

"Angie."

"Where did the damn package come from?"

"Denver, I think. Maybe it was Boulder. All I know it wasn't Flagstaff, which is where she told me she was from."

"Sir, I want you to listen to me closely," said the special agent. "A neighbor of yours said you have an oversized red bandanna with a matador on it and that you were out of town the weekend those banks got robbed."

"Yes sir."

"Have you ever been to Birmingham?"

"Sure, bunches of times. My buddies and I stay at a Holiday Inn there when they have car races in Talladega."

"Were you in Birmingham the weekend of those bank robberies?"

"Sort of, yes."

"What in hell does sort of mean?"

"I passed through Birmingham on the way to Philadelphia to do some gambling."

"Sir, that doesn't make sense," said the special agent. "I think you mean Atlantic City. Regardless, you don't go through ..."

"I don't need for you to tell me what in hell I mean," said the man, now growing angry. "I was in Philadelphia, Mississippi gambling at the casino there. I went straight through Birmingham, Alabama on my way."

"Let's get back to the red bandanna."

"Hell, here it is in my hand," said the man. "I don't see how it can be the one you've got if I've got it with me."

"Maybe you had two."

"Sir, I don't guess it's my place to assist the damn FBI, but if you're wondering if I was in Philadelphia, Mississippi when those bank branches got rocked, call the damn Shamrock Hotel and ask them if James Lee McCurdy was there from Friday night until Tuesday afternoon."

"I think we'll do that," the special agent said.

About fifteen minutes later, a special agent returned with news that James Lee McCurdy had told the truth. The interrogating special agent, obviously embarrassed, said, "Sir, you're free to go. I'm sorry about the inconvenience."

McCurdy started toward the door. He stopped, turned toward the special agent and said, "Sir, this was a real pleasure. I've heard for months you guys don't have a clue about what went down in Birmingham. But I never realized just how screwed up the FBI is until now."

"Mr. McCurdy, how would you like to have your ass kicked up one side of this room and down the other?" said the special agent.

"I'm not interested," McCurdy said. "All I want to do is get in front of a television camera and tell this nation how rude you guys can be when dealing with innocent people."

Similar results were achieved by the FBI in headquarters across the nation, which meant another public relations monstrosity was developing. That became apparent to Special Agent in Charge Jim Wilcox when he arrived at his office and read a revealing teletype.

Wilcox learned a fight had broken out between a veteran special agent and a young man in Lincoln, Nebraska. The interrogating law enforcement officer was hospitalized. No charges were filed because probable cause was determined.

Another incident, this one in Tyler, Texas, resulted in a lawyer leaving FBI headquarters with a client and going directly to the local newspaper for an interview.

Wilcox was not digesting good news.

In Louisville, Kentucky, Mark Cates discovered something he

perceived to be more encouraging after taking Midge and their children to the airport to begin their cruise vacation. He returned home to shower and shave before work. When he reached into a cabinet for a clean towel, he felt something unusual. He gathered the materials and gazed at the *Time* magazine article with a sealed envelope clipped to it.

Nervously, Cates opened the envelope and began reading the handwritten words of his wife:

Dearest Mark —

First of all, I want you to read this note twice, digesting the words carefully. Then I want you to burn it so nobody will ever see it.

I love you.

I haven't said anything about the attached magazine or the missing red bandanna because we've had far too much turmoil in our marriage in recent months. Obviously, you realize I know about your involvement in the bank robberies in Birmingham. I assume Carl McGraw was there, too, and I feel as sad for him as I do you.

I haven't discussed this with Diana, except I had to lie to her on your behalf by telling her that red bandanna was in our house. I didn't like having to do that.

Anyway, I don't know why you got involved in such a mess and I really don't want to know. I guess you did it for the thrill. Thank goodness you didn't hurt anybody, at least as far as I know.

My lips are sealed because I love you.

Now let me address another issue.

I've accused you of having an affair. I shouldn't have done that without knowing for sure. In fact, if there's a silver lining to the Birmingham deal, it's the fact you weren't out of town with that bitch that weekend.

With that, I'll close with one more thought you should take to heart. I can forgive you for the criminal act, or at least put it aside and go on, but I could never forgive you for taking another woman into your arms.

Your secret is safe. My heart is open, only for you.

Take care of yourself while we're away.
I love you.

Midge —

Later that afternoon, *CNN* started airing news reports of disgruntled citizens who had been interviewed by the FBI, with the focus on James Lee McCurdy. At the dinner hour, Wilcox received a telephone call from Special Agent Mike Sullivan in Washington. He knew what to expect as he walked to his downstairs office.

"I thought I'd be hearing from you," Wilcox said.

"Jim, we're going to back away from this a little bit," Sullivan said. "It's getting messy again."

"I hope this isn't another pull the rug out from under me and take down the roadblocks routine," Wilcox said, shaking his head after thinking about his awkward phraseology.

"We're not packing it in. We just need to be quieter and treat people with more dignity."

"I can appreciate that," Wilcox said. "Some of those special agents have been crude."

"I'm glad you feel that way. Also, Jim, your guys in Birmingham are to be commended for showing restraint."

"Mike, I know you. This spiel is starting to sound like a sugarcoated bail out."

"We've just got to utilize our resources better," Sullivan said. "Those crooks got $530,000 in Birmingham. Somebody got $28 million on Long Island. We can't try to catch bream when there are sharks in the water."

"They aren't damn bream. At the worse they're trophy bass."

"Okay, my friend," Sullivan said. "But let me give it to you as straight as I can."

"Shoot," Wilcox said.

"If you don't get a break in a week, show some progress, well, it'll be you and you alone on this case."

"That's just fucking great," Wilcox said. "I'm about to become the only special agent in charge who couldn't solve a case before the damn FBI closed it."

"That's a little melodramatic," Sullivan said. "We've had others. Also, we've had some that were closed and then reopened when somebody came forward with good info."

"Mike, you know I love you like a brother," Wilcox said.

"I think so, yeah."

"But I've got to ask you a question."

"I'm listening," Sullivan said.

"If I couldn't get a nun with a heart of gold to help me, Monique Sanchez, where do you think I'm going to find a guardian angel at this stage of the game?"

"You need for one to swoop down quickly," Sullivan said.

CHAPTER THIRTY-EIGHT

Another month passed and the bank robberies in Birmingham, Alabama pretty much faded from memory, except among six men and one woman in Louisville, Kentucky. The men, Mark Cates, Carl McGraw, Ed Bass, Sam Mills, Fred Long and Ben Bobo, watched the calendar almost daily and anxiously waited for their payoff from a daring deed. The woman, Midge Cates, still refreshed by a pleasurable cruise, went about her business as a wife and mother and attempted to rekindle a blissful relationship with her husband.

Midge was jealous in another way, too, because the women who remained in the dark, Diana McGraw, Cindy Bass, Mamie Mills, Barb Long and Frances Bobo, were fortunate because they would be able to see the fruits of evil without having to pay an emotional price.

A lone Federal Bureau of Investigation special agent in charge, Jim Wilcox, worked on the case much more sporadically than before. But the telephone calls he placed and the occasional interviews he conducted led him nowhere. He had dreams about the unsolved case and almost every one had something to do with roadblocks that had been lifted against his profound wishes.

News organizations had moved on to bigger stories, although many of the reporters who had covered the bank robberies thought none of them bore as much interest. There were many nights when these men and women would sit in bars and talk about what went down at Sector, First Columbus, Central, Patriot and American. They tried to get to the bottom of the mystery for the FBI, coming up with a multitude of theories, but most of the gatherings resulted in them drinking too much and dreading headaches the following day.

The six bank robbers, the snowmen, had stories to tell, only they had to keep them confined to their small circle. Two of the more humorous involved Bobo and Mills.

Bobo admitted Cates had whipped him to a pulp as they sat inside a Pathfinder parked in the parking lot at SportPlex. Also, he told the group he had kicked his addiction to sedatives, but remained a fan of vodka on the rocks.

Mills talked about how he got a Pathfinder through a treeline and underbrush at Patriot Bank. He said he secured traction by stripping to his underwear on a frigid night and placing his clothes under the rear tires. They forgave him for taking a few slugs of whiskey as he labored.

In Madrid, Spain, Ferdinand Ballesteros was reaping enormous financial benefits at Guatemala Bay, where patrons continued to eat and drink until almost daylight. He entertained them with embellished stories about his congenial brush with the FBI and Central Intelligence Agency. He told them he was a bank robbery suspect who found answers to all of the questions presented him.

Sister Monique Sanchez was not as brazen. She went about her business of helping people and, in late hours when she was alone in her study, she looked at a map of the United States and attempted to come up with anything that would help the FBI.

Several individuals who owned oversized red bandannas made by Senora Constantina Calusso of Calusso Woven Goods International attempted to make profits by selling them. There were few buyers, but one collector paid $1,000 so he could spin yarns about the unusual item.

At locations worldwide, all unknown, the money taken from the five bank branches changed hands and was used for seedy purposes. Not even Sid Winestein or Edgar Swartz knew the pattern the cash was taking, only that it had multiplied by more than the three times estimated.

In a small town in Tennessee, Sleepy Hollow, two police officers poured through a Louisville Telephone Directory almost daily in an effort to come up with two names that rang a bell. They made weekly inquiries at the local Waffle House to see if anybody remembered the pair that escaped their grasps.

The seamstress who fashioned coats of many colors for Pathfinders never did see a connection between her labor and the bank robberies. But she realized she had accomplished something special and hired an agent to market replaceable covers for sports utility vehicles.

Pointless lawsuits were filed against the FBI by individuals who thought they had been mistreated. But all of the legal action was thrown out of court upon first review or dropped before it got that far.

The Snowmen Project had experienced quite a run in front of an international audience. But it had vanished from memory with the coming of a serial killer in Chicago, a terrorist attack in Ireland, a mad bomber from North Carolina, a volcano in Mexico, an airplane crash in Florida and, by all means, an unsolved diamonds heist in New York.

Then on a late summer afternoon the telephone rang at Midge and Mark Cates' house.

"Hello."

"Is this Midge Cates?"

"Yes, it is. Hello, Ike."

"It's time to move," said Ike Alexander of Imperial Surveillance Services.

Midge thought she would throw up.

"Midge?"

"Yes, Ike."

"I'm in the Galt House lobby. I've got pictures of them going inside."

Midge breathed deeply.

"I'm on my way."

"Bring a bunch of money, at least a grand."

Immediately, Midge called a dear friend and asked her to meet her at the hotel beside the river. When pressed for an explanation, she said it was an urgent issue, but nothing to be all that upset about.

Midge walked upstairs to a small safe in the master bedroom closet. She opened it and grabbed a handful of cash. She felt foolish using an emergency fund for what could become a nasty deed, but holding the money made her more determined.

When Midge arrived at the hotel, she saw Diana standing in the lobby not more than thirty feet from a stranger she knew well. Alexander, a short and thin 48-year-old man, was wearing plaid pants and a blue blazer. He had shiny patent leather loafers on his feet and a cabby hat on his almost totally bald head.

"What's going on?" Diana said after rushing toward her friend.

"Mark and his bitchy lawyer friend are having a little fun upstairs," Midge said.

"Dear God, no," Diana said.

"I'm afraid Midge is correct," Alexander said as he walked up to the women talking. "They're in Room 332."

Midge had been crying, but at that moment she was as solid as a rock. There was fury in her eyes.

"I'm sorry, Midge," Diana said.

"Sit on it, Diana," Midge said.

"Are you sure you want to take this step," Alexander said.

"Absolutely."

"Then let's go to the kitchen."

Midge did not know what he meant.

"I'll stay here," Diana said.

"No, you're going with me," Midge said. "I want you to see it and I need you there."

The trio was greeted outside the kitchen by the room service captain, Tim Perez. Already, Alexander had talked with him.

The trap was set.

"Like I said, sir, this is totally against hotel policy," Perez said. "It's not right for me to do this."

"What he's saying is it's time to pay — eight hundred," Alexander said.

Midge did not hesitate. She reached into her purse, counted the money and gave it to the room service captain.

"Ladies, let's go upstairs," Alexander said, now sounding more like a wolf than a gentleman.

Inside Room 332, Cates and Sandra Brewer were sipping wine while reclining nude in bed. They were old pros at the game by that point and they knew the longer they stayed the better the romance would seem.

Outside Room 332, in the hallway, Midge, Diana, Alexander and the room service captain stood and waited to spring into action. All eyes were focused on the emotionally wounded wife. She nodded, with lips tight, and pointed toward the door.

Perez knocked on the door, three quick pops, and said, "Room service, sir. I have your order."

There was not an answer. Inside Room 332, Cates looked at his lover and shrugged his shoulders.

"Sir, I have your room service order."

Confident after several such meetings had come off without a hitch, Cates reacted. In a loud voice he said, "I haven't ordered room service. You've got the wrong room."

Midge almost dropped to the floor when she heard his voice. Diana covered her face with both hands.

"I'm sorry to disturb you, Mr. Awtrey, but the order is for Room 332."

"Just leave it beside the door."

"Sir, hotel policy won't allow that," Perez said. "I'll have to get you to sign for the delivery."

"I didn't order a damn lunch," Cates said, now more agitated.

Midge clutched her stomach. Diana moved beside her and put an arm around her shoulders. At that moment, the tears reappeared, now much larger than before.

"Mr. Awtrey, I've got to get you to sign for this food," Perez said. "Health regulations will not allow me to leave it in the hallway."

Cates did not respond. He considered telling the room service captain to take the food back to the kitchen. But, he reasoned, it could not be a trap because anybody wanting to see him with his lover only had to remain patient and stay in the hallway until they emerged.

Brewer looked for a way out and did not find one.

"Okay, damn it, I'll take the food," Cates said as he got out of bed and started putting on his pants.

Cates opened the door a few inches and saw the room service captain through the crack. He felt relieved. He loosened the security latch and started opening the door far enough to sign for the food.

Midge bulled through the door, in a huff, opening it all of the way and knocking her husband backwards. She ran inside and saw the sultry redhead nude on the bed and scrambling to get under the covers. The camera flashed, first recording a picture of Cates, then flashed several times in rapid succession as the private investigator took shots of the bed, the discarded clothes, the wine bottle and anything else he could capture on such short notice.

"Damn," Cates said. Then, mysteriously, he turned his attention toward Diana, not his wife, and said, "What in hell is going on here?"

"I think we know the answer to that," Diana said.

"I'm suing this damn hotel," Cates said, still struggling to find the proper words.

Midge had seen and heard enough. She ran from the room. Diana chased after her. The private detective and the room service captain were not far behind.

Midge did not stop until she reached a bank of pay telephones in the lobby. The tears were gone. The fury had returned. Methodically, without the slightest hint of shaking hands, she reached into a pouch in her purse and pulled out a severely wrinkled small piece of paper. She deposited a quarter and a dime and dialed the number:

1-800-FBI-BANK.

Diana heard the conversations Midge had with FBI special agents, first with one in Washington, D.C. and then with Wilcox in Birmingham. Now she was alarmed, thinking her life was going to come unraveled at the same time her dear friend faced such a tragedy.

But before she could talk to Midge about what she was feeling, Cates appeared in the lobby and walked toward the two women. He attempted an explanation, but his wife cut him off.

In a stern voice, Midge said, "You've got a lot of problems, Mark, but you won't have to search hard for a lawyer to help you through them."

EPILOGUE

Mark Cates, a man with an unquestionable weakness for a pretty woman, was a rock when dealing with the Federal Bureau of Investigation after his arrest. While he confessed his involvement in the bank robberies, he refused to implicate Carl McGraw, Ed Bass, Sam Mills, Fred Long and Ben Bobo.

The interrogations went on for five weeks, at times heatedly, with Jim Wilcox on the point. Cates refused to point fingers. The news media coverage was complex. However, not even a plea bargain agreement that would reduce his prison sentence could alter his stance.

Cates contended he acted alone, which everybody knew was an impossibility. For obvious reasons, McGraw was the most logical accomplice because they were business partners, good friends and had been seen together numerous times.

The seamstress who constructed covers for the Pathfinders came forward and told her story.

The U.S. Justice Department deemed the testimony circumstantial and instructed the FBI to come up with more.

The Tennessee State Trooper who stopped the men for speeding in a truck loaded with concrete told his story.

The U.S. Justice Department said the FBI should produce more evidence than the mere thought of cash stashed under a tarp.

Circumstantial.

Circumstantial.

Circumstantial.

Circumstantial — and Wilcox started thinking implied meant something less than a smoking gun in the hand of a criminal.

McGraw was questioned extensively. He provided little information, on advice from his lawyer, to the extent he chose not to offer an alibi as to his whereabouts on the weekend of the bank robberies. Privately, he expressed gratitude that only a small sum of money from the Atlantic Shore Diamonds Exchange caper had been deposited into his bank account, that he had turned it over to the brotherhood to let it grow.

Cates refused to tell anybody how the bank branches were ransacked and where he went after the fact. He said he had no part in the diamonds heist on Long Island.

Months that seemed like years to some parties passed and, ultimately, Cates was sentenced to thirty years in the federal penitentiary in Lexington, Kentucky.

Wilcox continued to work on the case, more frustrated than ever. He ran into a familiar roadblock.

Circumstantial.

Circumstantial.

Circumstantial.

Midge Cates, who never divorced her husband, citing keeping their family together as the reason, assumed the position of managing partner at C&M Construction Company and, by a dear friend, was assured she and her children would someday realize financial gain from The Snowman Project and the diamonds heist.

Diana and Carl McGraw counted their blessings and, on a daily basis, said their prayers.

— THE END —

Al Browning